One look at Clay Heller, and Nia went weak in the knees.

Then she was introduced to him and their eyes met, His were a blue so bright they were practically neon, and were fringed with lashes long enough to make most women envious. In a word, mesmerizing.

His smile gave off a warmth she thought she could feel, and he extended his hand. "Nia," he said in a deep, rich voice that made a moment experienced by the whole group in the room seem as if it was just between the two of them.

She accepted Clay's hand and, despite her best efforts, Nia was very aware of the way his hand felt around hers—of the strengh, the heat of it. This man's handshake felt better than any she'd ever had before.

And even once her sister spoke up, Clay Heller still refused to release her hand, or take his ultra-bright blue eyes off her...until he was good and ready.

Once he did, Nia felt a chill that could only mean one thing: being around Clay would break her heart.

SAGA

VICTORIA PADE

Her sister's *keeper*

Published by Silhouette Books

America's Publisher of Contemporary Romance

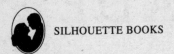 **SILHOUETTE BOOKS**

ISBN 0-373-28518-3

HER SISTER'S KEEPER

Dear Reader,

I'm so happy for the opportunity to return to Elk Creek and to explore not only the extended Heller family, but also the Molners. After so many mentions of the Molner mansion that houses the small town's medical facility, I thought it would be fun to finally get to know just who the Molners are, and the historic role they played—along with the Heller predecessors—in founding Elk Creek.

This time around there's also a little taste of the small town in recipes from Margie Wilson's Café. I hope you'll try them—even the elk meat recipe that I promise you is worth the trouble!

As I said, I'm thrilled to revisit Elk Creek, to catch up with characters that feel like old friends, and to meet some new ones (including more hot, hot, hot Heller men). I hope you enjoy it as much as I did.

All the best,

Victoria Pade

Dear Reader,

The editors at Harlequin and Silhouette are thrilled to be able to bring you a brand-new featured author program beginning in 2005! Signature Select aims to single out outstanding stories, contemporary themes and oft-requested classics by some of your favorite series authors and present them to you in a variety of formats bound by truly striking covers.

You may notice a number of different colored bands on the spine of this book. Each color corresponds to a different type of reading experience in the new Signature Select program. The Spotlight books will offer a single "big read" by a talented series author, the Collections will present three novellas on a selected theme in one volume, the Sagas will contain sprawling, sometimes multi-generational family tales (often related to a favorite family first introduced in series) and the Miniseries will feature requested, previously published books, with two or, occasionally, three complete stories in one volume. The Signature Select program will offer one book in each of these categories per month, and fans of limited continuity series will also find these continuing stories under the Signature Select umbrella.

In addition, these volumes will bring you bonus features...different in every single book! You may learn more about the author in an extended interview, more about the setting or inspiration for the book, more about subjects related to the theme and, often, a bonus short read will be included.

Watch for new stories from Vicki Lewis Thompson, Lori Foster, Donna Kauffman, Marie Ferrarella, Merline Lovelace, Roberta Gellis, Suzanne Forster, Stephanie Bond and scores more of the brightest talents in romance fiction!

We have an exciting year ahead!

Warm wishes for happy reading,

Marsha Zinberg

Marsha Zinberg
Executive Editor
The Signature Select Program

Chapter 1

"Pull over! Pull over!"

Nia Molner took her eyes off the road and glanced at her twin sister in the passenger seat.

Trina was white as a sheet, her brown eyes were deer-caught-in-headlights wide-open, and she was obviously having difficulty breathing.

Thinking fast, Nia reached into the back seat of their rental car for the bag their fast-food lunch had come in. When she'd located it, she upturned it to dump the remnants and wrappers on the floor and handed it to Trina.

"Breathe into this," Nia ordered, even as she eased the luxury sedan to the side of the road.

Trina did as Nia had instructed.

Only after Nia had come to a stop did she realize

what had probably brought on the anxiety attack. Up ahead, only a few yards from where she'd parked, was a hand-painted sign announcing that they were about to reach Elk Creek, Wyoming, Population 1804.

"Breathe slowly, it'll pass," Nia advised her twin in her most comforting voice.

Trina nodded her head even as her nose and mouth were buried in the paper bag.

"You're okay," Nia continued to croon soothingly. "It'll pass. You know it'll pass...."

While Nia waited for the attack to subside she glanced again at the sign and the banner that was stretched just beneath it between the side posts. The banner was a cheery proclamation of this, Elk Creek's centennial year, and gave the dates for the Founder's Day festivities that would celebrate it at the end of the coming week.

It was information Nia already had, and one of the reasons she and Trina were on their way to the small western town that their great-grandfather, Horatio Molner, had cofounded with Hyram Heller.

But it was the *other* reason they were headed for Elk Creek that was causing Trina's stress, and when Nia heard the rustling of the lunch sack, she looked over at her sister again, glad to find that Trina could breathe normally once more and had taken the bag away from her face.

"I don't know what's worse," Trina complained weakly, "not being able to breathe or hyperventilating into a bag that's had greasy hamburgers and french fries in it."

Nia smiled. "I told you we should bring a sack with us just in case."

"I was hoping I wouldn't do this," Trina said. "I thought if you were with me I could handle it."

"It'll be okay. You'll handle it fine," Nia assured her.

Trina didn't respond. Nor did she look convinced.

"Are you all right now?" Nia asked then.

"I don't think anything has been all right for the last three years, do you?"

It was Nia's turn not to respond. Certainly what had happened three years ago had had its own negative effects on her.

"I know I don't have any right to say that," Trina continued, apparently under the impression that she was reading Nia's thoughts. "Three years ago I caused everything to be *not* all right for you, and now I deserve anything I get—I have it coming. Only it keeps coming and coming…."

"This part now might work out, T," Nia reminded her, using the affectionate single-initial nickname she'd always used for Trina when she was consoling or comforting or soothing her sister.

"Or it might not work out," Trina countered ominously. "Because maybe it isn't meant to work out. Maybe I'm meant to suffer for the things I've done."

"This isn't a punishment. It could be something great."

Trina didn't look convinced of that, either. "What a mess I've made of things."

"It'll be okay," Nia repeated, because she couldn't

really dispute that her sister was in somewhat of a predicament.

But Trina merely stared out at that sign and shook her head. Nia was sorry to see how morose she was. Morose and pale.

An early health condition had left Trina with a hint more pallor than Nia had in her own finely textured skin, but the current circumstances and stresses certainly hadn't combined to add a rosy blush to her sister's face. The face that favored her own without being a mirror image of it.

They were fraternal twins, not identical, and so they had no more similarities than any two sisters might have. But even so, there was a strong resemblance between them.

They were both about four inches over five feet tall, with petite proportions—although Trina had a slightly larger bust size and had lorded it over Nia during puberty.

Trina's hair was a lighter shade of brown than Nia's deep auburn hue, and while Nia's was wavy and worn fairly long, slightly below her shoulders, Trina's shiny sable locks were cut into a sleek chin-length bob.

Their eye color was different, as well; Trina's were doe-brown, while Nia's were hazel, a mix of brown, green and flecks of gold. They both had the same high cheekbones and the same delicacy of features. Plus, when they smiled, identical dimples formed in their cheeks—an attribute that spurred people to ask if they were twins.

Trina turned to glance at Nia. "I don't know how I'd get through this if it weren't for you."

Nia chuckled and attempted to lighten the tone. "You make it sound like we're going to a funeral or something. It isn't *that* bad."

"It's bad enough. I feel like Candy Cochran from high school. First Drew. Now this—"

"Come on," Nia cajoled with a grimace at her sister's self-deprecation. "Candy Cochran slept with the whole football team in numerical order. You're a long way from that."

"A long way or a short way, I can't say I'm proud of myself," Trina insisted. "Not for what I did three years ago or now. I'm just grateful that you and I patched up things between us and you're here. I don't take that lightly. It's a very big deal to me."

"We're putting what happened three years ago behind us, remember?" Nia said. "Like when we were kids and you spilled ink on my favorite cashmere sweater—no grudges."

"That was an accident, though," Trina said with a hint of a smile at the mention of the old incident. "And while I didn't set out to do what I did three years ago, it could hardly be considered accidental."

"But you weren't alone in doing it, either," Nia countered. "And after the way things turned out for you… Well, what happened to me three years ago would obviously have happened eventually, anyway. So basically I just got things over with early."

"And handled them better. You didn't turn around and do something as stupid as I did."

"Who knows what I would have done if I had gotten as far in as you did?" Nia murmured.

"Probably not what I did," Trina persisted, gazing back at the Elk Creek sign again.

Then, after another moment, she said, "We could not go, you know."

"To Elk Creek?"

"We could turn around and go back to Denver," Trina clarified.

"We're expected now," Nia reminded her. "Dad promised I'd dig out Aunt Phoebe's journals for the newspaper to use. And we're representing the family at all the events."

Trina just went on staring at the sign.

"Plus you didn't want to do anything—anything *else*—rash, remember?" Nia reminded her. "You want this decision to be well thought out. You want it to have a good foundation. You don't want to make a mistake or do anything you'll end up regretting later."

"Since behaving rashly—three years ago and again six weeks ago—has done nothing but get me into trouble," Trina said, repeating the conclusion she'd come to as if it hadn't been her own. She leaned to one side and braced her head dejectedly against the passenger window.

"It'll be okay," Nia felt inclined to repeat.

"And if worse comes to worse," Trina said, again as if by rote, repeating what had come of extended discussions between them, "I won't tell him, we'll go back to Denver after Founder's Day, I'll explore the other option and just go on."

Nia hoped it didn't come to that, but she put some effort into keeping her own tone objective so as not to influence a decision she knew had to be Trina's.

"And all that will have happened," she stated firmly, "will be that another week has passed."

"And no one will be the wiser," Trina finished, raising a clenched hand to her mouth so she could bite her thumbnail.

"It'll stay our secret," Nia agreed.

Still, she could see that her sister was on the verge of telling her to turn the car around and take her back to the Cheyenne airport so she could skip the coming week. So that maybe she could choose the other option Nia didn't want her to choose, honestly believing that her sister would eventually be sorry if she did.

So yet again, Nia said, "It'll be okay. Seriously. Everything is jumbled right now and I know that the anticipation of facing him again, of telling him, of not knowing how he might react, seems like a big, scary thing—"

"A big, scary, embarrassing thing," Trina amended.

"But we're here to take this one step at a time. We're here so you can get to know him a little, so you can explore your own feelings—about him and about everything else. We're here so you can make just this first leg of the decision—whether or not to tell him, to involve him. Whether or not you even *want* to consider things going any further with him—"

"Or if he would want things to go any further with me."

"And once you've figured that out," Nia continued, "we'll go from there."

"And if I don't want to go from there with him—"

"Then we'll move on to step two—the other decision."

"Not such a nice decision."

"One step at a time," Nia repeated like a negotiator easing a jumper off a ledge.

The forlorn expression on Trina's face made it clear that she didn't find much solace in the platitude no matter how often Nia said it. But when her sister sat up straight again and stopped chewing her thumbnail, Nia took it as an indication that Trina was ready to go on.

"Elk Creek?" Nia asked to make sure.

"I guess so," Trina said feebly.

Nia put the car into Drive.

They were on a stretch of highway that ran through farm and ranch country, so there was no traffic to merge into, and she merely pulled off the shoulder of the road, heading in the direction they'd been going before.

As she drove past the sign, Trina's eyes stuck to it, dragging her head around to keep it in sight until it was behind them.

Nia half expected her sister to change her mind. But a mile later they reached the turnoff from the highway and minutes later the town of Elk Creek itself. All without Trina uttering a sound.

"I haven't been in Elk Creek since junior high," Nia said, for no reason other than to fill the silence and distract her sister.

It was true, though. Through the sisters' growing up years they'd been sent innumerable times by their parents from Colorado to Wyoming to see their grandparents. But during high school they'd been involved in so many activities they hadn't wanted to leave Denver and their friends behind. To accommodate that, their grandparents had visited them instead, even spending holidays in the city.

There was only one exception—for Trina, not for Nia. The summer before their senior year, Trina had come to stay in Elk Creek for the full three months, while Nia stayed at home to volunteer at the Denver Art Museum.

Not long after that their grandparents had been killed in a car accident, and though the twins' parents had inherited the Elk Creek house, Nia had never found the time to get back here since.

"I'll bet nothing has changed, has it?" she said as she neared the south end of town, where the train station stood.

The train depot certainly hadn't changed. It still reminded her of something out of an old western movie with its pale yellow station house complete with white-gingerbread-trimmed gables and a wooden platform. But there had been a change in the building across from it; what had formerly been a holding barn for cattle was now a honky-tonk called the Buckin' Bronco.

Still, as she headed down Center Street, the rest looked the same. The main thoroughfare remained wide enough for two lanes of traffic, plus nose-first parking in front of the businesses, boardwalks and Victorian streetlights that lined it.

Well-tended shops, including a genuine general store, occupied quaint, historic buildings with their own unique characteristics: carved cornices, decorative eaves and overhangs, shutters and awnings and big plate-glass windows decorated with homey displays. Some of the structures were wood, others brick, but none stood taller than three stories high, and most were one or two.

Nia knew that if she went far enough down Center Street the shops and stores ended and the street split to wrap the circular park in the heart of town. Everyone referred to it as the "park square," because that had been its original shape. Decades ago it had been altered to a circle to accommodate traffic, but the name had remained the same. Facing the lush patch of grass and trees was the church, the government building and the original house her family had built here and donated to the town as a medical facility when her grandparents had decided to build a new place.

But she didn't go that far, because just shy of the park stood the bank that had launched both the town and her family's fortunes. The bank her family still owned.

Retaining its own old-fashioned charm in tall, thin windows and a door that recessed into the corner itself, the bank stood on the juncture of Center Street and Molner Circle, and it was onto Molner Circle that Nia turned.

Molner Circle was just that—a road leading to and around the newer Molner estate. Two enormous oak trees stood sentry where the road forked around the property. Beyond the trees and the sprawling front lawn was the house.

It was a stately white, two-story Cape Cod, with an arched double door entrance and fanlight windows framed by black shutters.

"I still love this house," Nia said as she followed the curve of the road around to the garages in the rear.

But once they arrived at the garages there was already a vehicle parked outside one of the five bays. A white pickup truck that didn't belong to the older couple the family employed to take care of the place, which Nia and Trina's parents used for vacations or retreating from the world. And the sight of that truck instantly alarmed Trina.

"Oh, no," she groaned. "He's here!"

Up went the lunch sack to cover her nose and mouth again.

Nia pulled into the spot beside the truck Trina had apparently recognized and turned off the engine. "Cole Heller's truck," she guessed.

Trina nodded her head and the bag, confirming Nia's assumption.

"Well, he *is* still working on the remodel," Nia reasoned. "You knew there was a chance he'd be here."

Trina just stared at the truck.

"He also probably knew we were coming today," Nia added. "Simon and Fran knew and they would have told him. He might be here because he wants to say hello."

That didn't elicit anything from Trina. But she was beginning to breathe more normally.

"He's probably glad you decided to come back," Nia stated, because that line of reasoning seemed to have a positive effect. "Maybe he can't wait to see you again."

Trina's breathing was under control again so she took the lunch sack away. "I just thought I'd have some time before I had to face him," she said when she could.

"But that's all you have to do—just see him, say hello, no big deal."

Trina nodded, but once again she had that deer-caught-in-headlights look to her.

"I just can't believe it," she muttered. "It's bad enough that I got divorced. What was I thinking to come to Elk Creek with the idea of seeing an old boyfriend—as if that would make me feel better? And then, when Clay wasn't in town, how could I have ended up with his brother?"

"You're human. It just happened," Nia said.

"But it shouldn't have happened. I'm twenty-nine years old!"

"Me, too," Nia responded jokingly, to ease the tension.

It didn't help.

Trina finally tore her eyes away from the truck to level them on Nia. "But you aren't stupid enough to have unprotected sex with someone you don't even really know, and get pregnant." Then, in a bare whisper, she added, "Pregnant, Nia. I'm *pregnant*...."

"It'll all work out," Nia said, because she simply didn't know what else to say.

And having said it yet again, she could only hope she was right....

"There's our girls!"

The greeting Nia and Trina were met with made Nia smile as Fran and her husband, Simon, rushed out the back door at the same time the sisters approached.

Besides this house, the Molner family had residences in Denver, Boston and New York, all with staff to keep them running and maintained whether anyone was in residence or not. But only in Elk Creek did the people employed to look after the house and grounds treat the Molners like family. It was nice. And something Nia hadn't realized she missed until now.

"Look at you, little Nia! It's been so long since we've seen you—you were just a girl. And now you're a grown-up woman and you're so beautiful! Just like little Trina."

Nia laughed in the midst of being enfolded in a bear hug by Fran. "We're not so little anymore," she said, returning the hug just as firmly.

"To us you'll always be our little girls," Fran assured her. "Won't they, Simon?"

"Uh-yep," the grizzled old groundsman confirmed.

Not prone to waste words—or gestures, since his hands were hidden behind the bib of the overalls that covered the white undershirt he wore—he stood to one side and behind his wife. The late afternoon spring sunshine made his round bald head shine, and his chubby cheeks were ruddy evidence that he'd been outside most of the day.

On the other hand, Fran was prone to many words, and once she'd released Nia her pale blue eyes settled on Trina. "'Course, we did just get to see our little Trina a few weeks ago. But look at you, honey— where's the color in your cheeks? By the time you left I had you all rosy and bloomin' again and now here you are, lookin' as droopy and sad as you did when you came before. Doesn't she look all droopy 'n sad, Simon?"

"Uh-yep."

"We got up early this morning to travel. She just needs some rest," Nia interjected, to spare Trina explanations Nia knew her sister wasn't inclined to make.

The cool April air must have chilled the elderly woman suddenly because she crossed her arms over the crisp white apron that covered her shapeless yellow checkered dress, and shivered enough to make her jowls jiggle and the snow-white bun at the nape of her neck bounce. "What am I doin' keepin' us all out on the patio!" she said. "You know how spring can be here—warm one day, a blizzard the next. The weatherman says there's a storm comin' and he must be right because this mornin' it was short-sleeve hot and now that breeze'll chill you to the bone. You girls come on inside. Simon'll get your suitcases out of the car."

On command, Simon headed for the garage, while Nia and Trina followed the older woman through the back door.

One step across the threshold allowed Nia her first look at the remodeling that had been going on for several months. The walls of the large kitchen had been freshly painted in bright yellow, the countertops were tiled in cobalt-blue, and with the splashes of red here and there, it had a country French feel to it now.

"The kitchen looks good," she informed Fran.

"But the gadgets!" the older woman exclaimed. "The blender comes right out of the counter now, and there's the regular oven and the microwave and another one called a convection oven that I don't know what to do with. And a grill right on top of the stove and even a wood oven just for making pizzas! Your mama says it'll get used when they come, but otherwise? I don't think I'll be cookin' in that thing."

"I can't wait to see the rest," Nia said, with a laugh at the deluge of words that kept coming from the housekeeper.

"Go on and look," Fran urged. "I'll make some nice tea while Simon gets your bags put in your rooms. Trina can keep me company and tell me what I can cook for her to perk her up."

Trina had already taken a chair at the oblong pedestal table and looked as if she wanted to blend into the flowered paper on the wall behind her. That served to remind Nia of the truck outside. And the owner of it inside.

"We aren't the only ones here, are we?" she asked Fran.

"Well sure. Who else would be here? What with the passin' of your grandparents and your mama and daddy in Europe—that is where your mama and daddy are, isn't it?"

"Yes. But I saw the truck in the driveway—"

"Oh, that's just Cole. Still workin', even late on a Saturday afternoon. He's the one who's done all these marvels with the remodel. Trina met him when she was here before. He's in the den. Ask him would he like some tea, too, when you get there."

Nia shot a glance at her sister, unsure what to do in regards to Trina and the man with whom she had had a brief fling. The man who was apparently not there because he'd known Trina was returning today, after all.

"Do you want to come with me?" Nia asked her twin. "I'm sure there's been more work done since you were here last."

"There has," Fran confirmed. "That Cole is a workin' fool. The place is comin' up on bein' done by next month, he says. And all the rooms you really need are finished."

Fran's commentary went unremarked upon as the twins focused on each other.

"I'll just stay here," Trina finally answered.

Nia knew her sister was postponing seeing Cole Heller as long as she could, but she didn't push it.

Instead she said, "Will you be okay if I have a look around?"

"'Course she'll be okay, she's with me—isn't she?" Fran answered for Trina, waving a hand in the air to shoo Nia away. "Just go on."

Nia cast Trina another glance to make sure it was all right to leave her. Trina barely shrugged one shoulder and nodded her head once, so Nia said, "I'll only be a minute."

"Take your time," Fran said, even though Nia had aimed her promise at her sister.

Then the older woman began to occupy Trina with conversation, so Nia slipped out of the kitchen into the butler's pantry.

From there she went into the dining room. A new coat of peach paint was the only change there. The antique claw-footed dining table and twelve chairs, and the matching china cabinet and sideboard, were exactly the same.

From the dining room she went into the formal living room, where she could see the hand of her mother's favorite decorator in the white baseboards and ceiling moldings that bordered the deep Chinese-red walls. Walls that were a backdrop to the lighter-hued French provincial furniture her mother had purchased in France and had shipped here.

From the living room Nia entered the expansive

foyer, where hardwood floors had replaced the tiles
that had been original to the house. The staircase that
ran from there to the second floor had always been
Nia's favorite part of the place. The banister and posts
had been hand-carved, and it rose in a magnificence
all its own from very wide steps at the bottom, grace-
fully decreasing in size to the top.

The staircase made Nia think of the train of a wedding dress, and she and Trina had often played dress-
up and made grand entrances into imaginary galas
down those steps. She was glad to see that care and
special attention had been paid in refinishing it.

She didn't go up the steps to have a look at the bed-
rooms, though. She saved that for later, and instead
crossed the foyer to peek into the library at the new
shelves and desk, then into the recreation room, where
paneling on the walls, a refurbished fireplace and an
overstuffed leather sofa and chairs accommodated a
complete home theater system that replaced her grandparents' old console television and raggedy loungers.

Then she moved down the hallway that ran alongside the staircase to the den.

Where Fran had said Cole Heller was working.

During their childhood and early adolescent visits
to their grandparents, Nia and Trina had gotten to
know the branch of the Heller family that had remained in Elk Creek when the other branch had moved
on. Cole Heller and his brother Clay were among the
latter. And although Nia had heard about the Heller
cousins, they'd never visited Elk Creek at the same

time she had. So, unlike Trina—who had had an innocent teenage romance with Clay during that summer-long visit before their senior year in high school, and had now had a tryst with Cole—Nia had never met either brother.

She admitted that she was curious about them, though, these cousins of the family that *her* family had been associated with, friends with, for generations. The cousins who according to Trina had taken up permanent residence in the small town.

The cousins who had caught her sister's interest, and now would be connected to their own family through the child Trina carried…

The door was missing from the entrance to the den. It was inside the room, lying across two saw-horses. And because the man there was using a power sander on it, Nia's knock on the doorjamb went unheard.

Hoping that he would catch sight of her and stop the machine, or finish his task and turn it off, she stood there and waited, taking in the sight of him as she did.

He was in profile to her, bent over his work. But even so Nia could tell Trina hadn't been exaggerating when she'd described him.

She'd said that he wasn't her type. She'd always been attracted to sophisticated men—men in executive positions or from families with business or social ties to the Molners. Cole Heller wasn't like that. He was a died-in-the-wool cowboy who owned a small ranch and worked construction to supplement his income. It

was just that he was too much man *not* to take notice
of—that's the way Trina had put it and, as far as Nia
could see, it was true.

Nia herself didn't feel any stirrings of attraction
but she could appreciate the way he looked as she
might a Cellini sculpture.

Cole Heller was a big man—so big that even though
he was folded in, half leaning over the door, she could
still tell he was tall. Tall and powerfully built—something the no-room-to-spare flannel western shirt and
dusty blue jeans showed off to good effect. His arms
and legs were long and dense with muscles, his shoulders wide, his neck thick.

But it wasn't only his body that obviously accounted for Trina taking notice of him. His hair, while
a bit longer and shaggier than Nia liked, was a golden
blond mane. He had a face of strong bones and sun-
kissed tan skin that looked robustly healthy and out-
doorsy. His nose was slightly hawkish, his jaw and
chin pronounced, and put all together, Nia had to concede that if a woman needed a distraction from
heartache, this was the man to distract her.

But she couldn't very well stand there staring at him
forever, she decided. So she shuffled her feet and tried
knocking on the doorjamb again rather than risk being
caught gawking at him.

This time her movements garnered his attention. He
glanced up at her with intensely blue eyes, adding another element to the package.

Off went the sander, leaving a sudden silence as

eyebrows that were as sun-bleached as his hair arched in question.

"Hi," he said simply, before she'd adjusted to the quiet.

"I'm sorry to interrupt you," she apologized. "I'm—"

"Nia. You have to be Nia. Trina's twin."

"That's me," she said, her tone echoing with surprise that he'd guessed correctly.

"Fran said you and Trina were coming in today. Trina talked about you, and you look enough like her that I knew that's who you had to be," he explained.

Trina hadn't told Nia about him until she'd realized she was pregnant. But that certainly didn't seem like anything Nia should reveal, so instead she said, "And you must be Cole Heller."

"Right. Nice to meet you."

"You, too," she said.

They seemed to stall then, and Nia recalled that Trina had said he was a man of few words. Nia thought that left it to her to make conversation, and to that end she said, "I've admired what I've seen of your work between the kitchen and here."

"Thanks."

"Especially the staircase. I know over the years it had gotten scratched and nicked, and I heard that a few posts had actually been broken when some furniture was moved. But now it's beautiful again. I couldn't even tell which parts were new and which were original. You're very talented."

He merely raised his chin to acknowledge the praise, which seemed to embarrass him.

Definitely a man of few words.

And since Nia was running out of them herself, she got to the point. "Well, anyhow, Fran is making tea and we wondered if you wanted a cup."

"We? You and Fran and Trina?"

Was he wondering why, if Trina was here, she hadn't come to find him herself? Or did he care one way or another? It was difficult to tell.

But in case he *did* care, Nia was quick to make excuses for her sister's absence. She didn't want these two to get off on the wrong foot now that there was so much at stake. "Yes, Trina is here. But we just got in. Not ten minutes ago. She's in the kitchen with Fran. She's a little wrung out from the trip. Trina is, not Fran, of course."

Cole Heller merely nodded again, still showing no signs of emotion.

He took a cell phone out of the back pocket of his jeans then and held it up. "My brother left me with orders to call him as soon as you got here. He's hopin' you'll see him, set up a time to get started on whatever you'll be doin' for the newspaper. Do you mind?"

"No, I don't mind."

"Then maybe I'll see about the tea when he gets here."

"Okay," Nia said, although she wasn't completely convinced that Cole Heller actually would come and have tea with them even when his brother arrived. He didn't sound all that committed to the idea.

Still, his tone gave the impression that he was finished saying everything he had to say, and when his gaze went from her to his cell phone again, Nia assumed their exchange was at an end.

All she could do at that point was say, "I hope you'll join us," before she turned on her heel and left him to his phone call.

She decided to make a stop in the bathroom on the way back to the kitchen, and along the way wondered about Trina and the very serious Cole Heller.

She didn't feel too encouraged now that she'd met him. Cole wasn't a sophisticated business executive or a society swain, true. More than that, he was an entirely different temperament than the men Trina was ordinarily attracted to. Personable, outgoing, full-of-themselves, arrogant rogues were more what her sister tended toward. And no matter how handsome Cole Heller was, he certainly didn't seem to be any of those other things. It was a cause for concern for Nia.

Because while Trina had already decided she didn't want to have an abortion, if things didn't work out between her and Cole Heller on this trip, Nia knew it was very likely that her sister would opt for giving the baby up for adoption.

Nia was only in the bathroom for about five minutes, but as she approached the kitchen she knew Trina wasn't there with just Fran and possibly Simon. Nia knew it because she heard her sister laugh—not just any laugh, but her flirtatious one.

Nia hadn't heard it from her twin in a long time, and she assumed that Cole Heller must have made his phone call, left the den and proceeded to the kitchen to have tea, after all.

And if he could make Trina laugh like that, then maybe there was hope for them.

Only, when Nia retraced her steps through the butler's pantry to the kitchen again, she didn't find Cole Heller with Trina, Fran and Simon.

It was someone else entirely. Someone who had the other people all studying Trina so intently that none of them noticed Nia where she stopped, just inside the swinging door connecting the pantry to the kitchen.

"Twelve years! It's been twelve years since I saw you last, and you still look as good as you did then," he was saying to Trina, who was so pleased with the compliment she nearly glowed.

Clay Heller.

Nia realized instantly that the man had to be Cole's brother, because the two looked more alike than she and Trina did.

Clay Heller, the man Trina referred to as her first love.

The man she'd come to Elk Creek six weeks ago to see, in hopes of having her spirits boosted.

Which, had he not been out of town, he obviously would have done, since he'd already accomplished that just in the few minutes since Nia had left the kitchen.

It was easy to see how he could be a spirit booster. As difficult as it was to believe, Clay Heller was even better looking than his brother, and for a moment those good looks—or at least something about him—enthralled Nia, too.

She knew Clay Heller had made a small fortune owning newspapers, television and radio stations, and that he'd settled in Elk Creek after buying the small local paper. But to look at him she would never have guessed that he sat behind a desk to make his living. There was as much cowboy to him as there was to his brother. And he definitely didn't have the body of a desk jockey.

He was standing at the table, towering above the seated Trina, Fran and Simon, and he was very tall—at least two inches over six feet even without the cowboy boots he had on. He was also every bit as well-muscled and honed as his brother, so much so that the thickness of his thighs was evident in the blue jeans he wore. And his broad shoulders and back, his powerfully built chest, and what appeared to be some pretty amazing biceps filled out a chambray shirt like no media executive could be expected to do.

But for all his size, there didn't appear to be an ounce of excess fat anywhere on him. Certainly not in the narrow waist or the hips that tied the muscles together in a perfect physique.

And then there was the face and hair to go with the body-made-in-heaven.

His hair was very light brown—golden brown, ac-

tually, with a few even lighter, sun-kissed streaks. He
didn't wear his hair as long as Cole did, but cut short
on the sides and in back, with the slightly longer top
just mussed enough to make it interesting. And much
more to Nia's liking.

His face had the same strong bones and robustly
healthy appearance as his brother's. His nose was sim-
ilarly hawkish and just irregular enough to keep him
from being a pretty boy. And although his jaw and chin
were not quite as pronounced as Cole's, Nia liked the
sharp, chiseled lines there better, too.

All in all, what she decided she was seeing were his
brother's features refined, without taking away any of
the ruggedness. And while she'd appreciated Cole
Heller the way she could appreciate a great work of
art, something else happened with that first glimpse of
Clay. More than appreciating the sight of him, if he had
been a Greek statue on the auction block she might
have been compelled to put in a bid….

"Nia! You're back," Fran said, when she noticed her
standing there.

Looking at Clay Heller had actually weakened
Nia's knees, and even after she glanced away from him
it required conscious effort to put the starch back into
them. When she had, she crossed to the table to join
the group.

"Where's Cole?" Fran asked.

"I told him you were making tea, but he didn't say
whether he would come have a cup or not. He was
working," Nia answered.

"It's all right. Nia needs to meet Clay, anyway," Trina interjected, sounding so chipper Nia almost didn't recognize her sister's voice. Chipper and somewhat possessive when she said Clay's name.

"Nia, this is Clay Heller," Trina continued. "Clay, this is Nia."

For the first time since attention had been drawn to her, Nia let her gaze return to Clay Heller. Only this time her eyes met his, allowing her to see that he had his brother beat in that department, too. Because while Cole's eyes were an intense blue, Clay's were so bright a blue they were almost neon. And fringed with lashes long enough to make most women envious.

He smiled with a warmth she thought she could feel, and extended his hand to her. "Nia," he said in a deep, rich voice that managed to make even a moment shared by the whole group seem just between the two of them.

No wonder Trina had brightened, Nia thought, assuming he'd provided her sister with a helping of his understated charisma, too.

Still, Nia accepted his hand, working hard not to be quite as tuned in to his touch as she seemed to be to everything else about him. But despite her best efforts, she was aware of the way his hand felt around hers, of the strength, of the heat of it. Of it feeling better than any handshake she'd ever had before.

"I just left your brother in the process of calling you on his cell phone. How did you get here so quick?" she asked.

"I was at my office and saw a rental car go down Center Street. It isn't often that happens, and since the Molner sisters were expected, I thought I'd take a shot and come over without waiting for Cole's call."

"And Clay was right, it was us," Trina said.

Nia knew that tone of her sister's voice, too. It meant Trina was reminding everyone she was still in the room. But it didn't spur Clay to either release Nia's hand or to take those ultrabright blue eyes off her until a few moments later, when he was apparently good and ready.

And even then his focus didn't revert to Trina. It remained on Nia as he said, "I'm sorry to barge in like this before you've had a chance to even catch your breath. But I'm in such a rush for your aunt's journals that I couldn't put it off. My paper comes out once a week, but I want to do a couple of supplements in anticipation of Founder's Day, dealing with the early days of Elk Creek, the people who first settled here and what their lives were like—that sort of thing."

Before Nia could tell him that she had no intention of blithely handing over her aunt's journals, his brother came into the kitchen, announced by the sound of his boot heels.

"Cole…"

It was Trina who greeted him before anyone else had a chance, and although Nia heard the note of uncertainty in her sister's voice, she heard something else, too. Something softer, breathier. Something different from the girlish, superficial note that came into her tone when she was flirting. The one that had been in her tone when she'd spoken to Clay.

"Trina," Cole answered, his eyes fixed on her with such concentration that Nia sensed he wasn't aware of anyone else in the room.

Fran didn't seem to notice, though. The older woman got to her feet and began to order Cole around. "Come and take a load off. After workin' since sunup, you've earned it. I'll get you a cup of tea."

Cole merely gave one of those nods Nia had seen in the den, keeping his gaze on Trina as he sat across from her. "How've you been?" he asked.

Nia was surprised to see the suddenly relaxed smile that came over her sister's face, as if the man's presence had some kind of power to put her at ease in spite of why she'd come to Elk Creek and the secret she carried.

But Nia didn't have long to watch what was going on because Clay Heller moved to her side, leaned close to her ear and said, "Can I tear you away from teatime long enough to show me the journals?"

Obviously he was serious about being in a rush. Nia knew she needed to clear the air about the journals, anyway, so she agreed, leading the way to the basement once Fran had informed her that that was where they were to be found.

"I don't mean to be pushy," Clay said as they reached the basement and Nia turned on the light. "I have town records, some old letters a few families around here have given me and what stories I could glean from the older folks themselves. But I'm hoping to round it all out with excerpts from these journals."

"How did you find out about them, anyway?" Nia asked, spotting the box on top of the clothes dryer and crossing to it with him in tow.

"Cole had to install a new water heater down here. When he moved things around to work he came across the box. He didn't go through it or anything—he just saw the writing on the side of it." Clay pointed to where someone had written "Phoebe's Journals."

"Cole mentioned them when I told him I was looking for material for the Founder's Day supplements," he added.

"And that was when you called my dad."

"Right. For permission. He said you'd take care of that."

"About that…"

"Your dad said he didn't see any problem with my using the journals."

"I know. But we talked about it, and while we're still willing to let you see them, we decided there should be some stipulations."

"Stipulations," Clay Heller repeated.

"My great-aunt Phoebe was a very private person. She loved Elk Creek, and while we know she would have liked being a part of this celebration, we thought it would be best if I went through the journals with you. To make sure anything that might be too private or might embarrass her wouldn't be printed."

Clay's expression sobered and his eyebrows arched. "Ah."

"You don't like the idea of me going through the journals with you?" Nia asked.

"I don't like the idea of being censored—that *is* the point in the joint effort, isn't it? If there's something in the excerpts I want to publish that you think your aunt wouldn't have wanted aired, we could have a problem, couldn't we?"

"I don't think it's so much being censored as selective. Consider it this way—the people who shared stories with you probably didn't tell you things they wouldn't want to see in print. We just want Great-aunt Phoebe to have that same protection. And if what you're really looking for is just information on the early days of Elk Creek and what life was like…"

He smiled again, this time wryly. "Turned that around on me, didn't you? No wonder your father sent you as the family watchdog."

"Watchdog?" she repeated, making a face.

"I don't mean that in a bad way," he assured her. "I can just see that you're not going to be a pushover."

"I'm definitely not a pushover. When it comes to anything."

"Duly warned," he said. But he didn't seem daunted by her stipulation, now that he knew it. "You should know going in, though, that it isn't only information on the early days and what life was like back then that I'm looking for. A little human interest is always a good thing, too—what your aunt was feeling, what she was interested in, what her views and opinions were. I'm printing a newspaper, not a textbook. That's why I thought the journals would be perfect—we'd have an inside look into a founding father's own daughter."

"I don't anticipate that there will be any deep, dark secrets," Nia said. "If we come across what she thought of hemlines or the streetlights when they were put in or that she thought the mayor had a big nose, there's no reason you couldn't use it. But if she confesses that she stole penny candy from the general store when she was eight, I don't want you saying she was a kleptomaniac."

"Fair enough. No sensationalizing. I don't publish that kind of paper, anyway."

"Or even just saying that when she was eight she stole from the store, as a statement of fact. We wouldn't want that to be public knowledge, either."

"I get the point—nothing that would make Aunt Phoebe look bad," he said, as if that last warning had been unnecessary.

"And you're okay with my reading along at the same time?"

"It'll slow things down a little, but if you're willing to spend the time with me, I'm fine spending the time with you."

There was that charisma again. It was potent.

"I think I can handle it," Nia said with more certainty than she felt.

"Then all we need to do is figure out how we can actually get to work on them."

Nia took a closer look at the leather-bound diaries,

which were tossed haphazardly into the cardboard box, and said, "I think the first thing we're going to have to do is put them in order."

"Okay. When?"

"Tomorrow is Sunday, and your cousins have invited Trina and I to dinner—"

"Right. Cole and I will be there, too. But that isn't until the evening. How about if I come over here during the day and we get started?"

"You're willing to work on a Sunday?"

"I am if you are," he confirmed.

"Okay, sure," Nia agreed.

"Great. Then why don't we get these books out of the basement, put them upstairs somewhere, and they'll be ready to go when I get here?"

Nia motioned toward the dryer, giving him free access—at least in terms of carrying what looked to be a heavy box.

But as he hoisted it and retraced their path to the stairs, it finally struck Nia that there were a lot of journals there for them to go through, and that meant she would be spending a large amount of time with Clay Heller in order to read them all.

A large amount of time with a man who was very long on looks and charm.

But he was also a man who her sister had once had a romance with. A man who had been attracted to Trina. Who might still be attracted to her if there was more to the exchange Nia had walked in on in the kitchen than mere pleasantries.

And in spite of her sister's pregnancy and Nia's hope that Trina might have some sort of future with the father of her baby—with Cole Heller—any man with any connection to Trina went securely in the category of men Nia wouldn't touch with a ten-foot pole.

Chapter 2

"This is great—you want to come over every morning and make my coffee before I get up?" Clay said to his brother when he went into his kitchen Sunday morning and found Cole sitting at his table drinking a steaming cup of the brew himself.

"'Mornin'," Cole answered, as if it wasn't unusual for him to have let himself into Clay's house before his brother was even awake.

Hearing sounds coming from downstairs and then smelling the coffee, Clay had gotten out of bed and conceded to decency only by pulling on the jeans he'd left on the floor the night before. No socks, no shoes, no shirt, no shower, no shave. And even though he'd zipped his zipper, he hadn't bothered with the waistband button. Unlike Cole, who was clean-shaven and fully clothed in jeans, a plaid shirt and cowboy boots.

"Somethin' up?" Clay asked as he poured himself a cup of coffee and took it to the round, bleached-wood table to sit across from his brother, propping his feet on a third chair.

"Wanted to talk to you about somethin'," Cole said soberly, and with the scarcity of words that made him more like their cousin Jackson than like Clay.

"Sounds serious."

"Nah. Doesn't have to be. I just want to clear something with you."

"Okay," Clay said through the steam rising from his cup as he lifted it to his mouth and took a drink.

"It's about Trina Molner."

"Trina."

"Right." Cole drank some of his own coffee, molding both hands around the mug and staring into it after he had. "I told you I'd run into her when she was here a while back."

"You did," Clay confirmed. He didn't have any idea what was going on with his brother, but his curiosity was piqued enough to watch him closely.

"Yeah, well, I did a little more than just run into her," Cole confessed.

"Really?"

"I was workin' at the house, she hardly ever went out of it, we spent some time together."

"Okay," Clay repeated, still unsure what Cole was getting at.

"Then she left," Cole continued. "She didn't even tell me she was goin'. I just got there one day and Fran said Trina'd gone back to Denver. She didn't leave a note, didn't even tell Fran to say goodbye. She just hightailed it out. And when I didn't hear from her, I just figured, hey, we had a few laughs, no big deal—which is why I didn't make it a big deal when I told you before."

"But now it is a big deal?" Clay asked.

Cole took another drink of coffee and went back to looking at it rather than at Clay. "Not a big deal, no."

"But not nothin', either?"

Cole shrugged one shoulder and inclined his head. "Maybe not nothin'," he conceded. "Been havin' some trouble not thinkin' about her since she left."

That came out as quite a confession from the hold-his-cards-close-to-his-vest Heller brother.

"And now here she is, back again," Clay added.

"Yeah."

"And here you are on my doorstep, bright and early this morning. What for?"

"It was you she came thinkin' to see last time," Cole said flatly.

"But it was you she found."

"Still, you have the history with her," Cole said.

Clay laughed briefly. "Not much of a history, and it's pretty ancient—one summer when we were barely more than kids. She was seventeen, I was nineteen. That was twelve years ago."

"So what're you sayin'?"

"What're *you* sayin'?" Clay countered.

"Do you want her?"

That was Cole—blunt and to the point.

"Is that what this is about?" Clay asked. "Since I have a *history* with Trina Molner I get first right of refusal? But if I do refuse, you want her?"

"Didn't say I wanted her," Cole hedged. "Just that I'd like to know if you do. Or is the field open?"

"So the field was open when I was in Chicago and she was here lookin' me up, but not if I'm in town?" Clay said, giving his brother a hard time just to amuse himself.

But Cole was unruffled. "If you want her, just tell me and I'll bow out of the picture—that's all I'm sayin'."

Clay took another drink of his coffee and mulled over the situation out loud.

"We did have a lot of fun that summer, Trina and I," he said. "She was kind of on the wild side. Free-spirited, impulsive, you know? She had hair nearly down to her waist, wore these skimpy little bikinis and shorts sooo short…." Clay paused, as if he were enjoying the mental image. "I have some good memories of that summer."

"Does that mean you want to try for more of what you had before?"

"I didn't *have* anything but a few make-out sessions before. During a nice, carefree summer," Clay said, not wanting to let his brother believe more had gone on with Trina Molner than actually had. "But now…

Hmm." He went on pondering. "She grew up well, there's no denyin' that. Shiny hair. Those big brown eyes. Good body…"

But even as Clay cataloged Trina's assets, it was actually Nia who popped into his mind's eye. Nia Molner's long, wavy, burnished hair that looked like fine mahogany. Nia Molner's high cheekbones and porcelain skin so pure looking it had made him want to reach out and touch it. Nia Molner's eyes with all those colors—brown and green and even gold— bright and sparkling and alive. Nia Molner's rosy lips and those dimples that sprouted in her cheeks when she smiled, making him feel as if he'd ac- complished something special to make them appear. Even Nia Molner's slightly less well endowed body had given him a familiar itch that her sister hadn't inspired….

"I don't know," Clay said after that extended amount of mind wandering. "Seeing Trina yesterday was kind of like watching a repeat on television—it's okay, but it's still a repeat."

"And repeats aren't what you want to see," Cole agreed, encouraging that train of thought.

"Guess that makes Trina Molner not what I want, then."

"Who do you want?" Cole asked. "Nia Molner?"

"Nia?" Clay said, making it sound as if she'd never crossed his mind, when that was surprisingly not the case. Not by a long shot. "Did you see the way she was waitin' on Trina? Takin' care of her? Mothering her?

Even when Trina could have done for herself. Bad sign," he added, giving the reason why she *shouldn't* have crossed his mind.

"I thought she was just bein' nice," Cole countered.

"Reminded me of Shayna. No thanks."

Clay set his nearly empty coffee mug on the table and leveled his gaze on Cole. "But just because I'll take a pass on Nia doesn't mean that leaves me wanting Trina by default. They aren't the only two women in the world, you know. You can still have Trina." Clay laughed wryly then. "'Course, if either of them knew we were divvying them up like marbles they'd probably have us hog-tied and rolled into the river. I don't think this is too politically correct."

Cole stood and took his cup to the sink, rinsing it and putting it in the dishwasher. "Just makin' sure I wouldn't be trespassin'."

"Any more than you already have," Clay reminded him.

Cole didn't respond to that and there was something in his silence that caused Clay to think his brother had already trespassed further than he was letting on.

Instead Cole turned, leaned back against the counter's edge and said, "So you don't care if I see some of Trina Molner while she's here?"

"Have at it," Clay said.

Cole nodded, but stayed where he was even though Clay thought he'd given his brother what he'd come for, and half expected him to leave.

"Not good enough?" Clay asked then.

"Nah, sure, it's good enough. I was just wonderin' if I should do it, anyway."

"See Trina Molner while she's here? You'll probably have a hard time avoiding it, since you're still workin' on her house most days."

"Yeah, but I was wonderin' should I stick to only seein' her in passing."

Clay was more confused by Cole's words than he'd been by finding his brother in his kitchen bright and early on a Sunday morning, wanting to talk about Trina Molner.

"You came over here and made me coffee to make sure I'm okay with you going after Trina Molner, and now that I say it is, you aren't sure you want to?"

"You're her type, not me."

"How so?"

Cole shrugged. "You're on her level when it comes to money, to travelin' the world, to hobnobbin'. After the last time and the way she left and not hearin' from her… I don't know, could be she was just havin' a little thing with the hired help."

"Does that mean the two of you *had* a little thing?"

"Not the point," Cole said with a frown, making it clear this was more serious to him than Clay was taking it.

So Clay got more serious, too. "I can't say if Trina Molner was just having a little thing with the hired help when she was here a while back. I only spent a couple of months with her when we were kids and I haven't seen or heard from her since. I just plain don't know the woman."

Cole nodded. "Guess I'll have to make up my own mind."

"Guess you will. But maybe the fact that she's back again means something," Clay said.

"Could mean she came back when she knew you'd be here, so she could see you, after all."

Clay didn't tell his brother that there had been some flirtatiousness from Trina Molner when he'd first spoken to her the day before. Nothing had come of it and he didn't see any reason to blow it out of proportion.

Instead he said, "Seemed to me she was pretty happy to see you."

"You think?"

"It was you she talked to even after Nia and I got back upstairs with that box of journals."

Cole nodded again, as if he'd thought that might have been the case, but was happy to have it confirmed.

Then he shoved off the counter's edge and headed for the back door.

But before he left he paused to glance over his shoulder at Clay. "'Course, you were pretty busy talkin' to her sister after the two of you came up from the basement."

"Still, I didn't have the impression Trina *wanted* to talk to me."

"And it looked like you wanted to talk to Nia," Cole persisted. "Maybe you should think again about *that*."

"About Nia?"

"Mmm."

"Huh-uh. I know better," Clay said, as if he didn't have a single doubt.

But the truth was he'd had some trouble thinking about anything *but* Nia since the minute he'd laid eyes on her. And not just about the way she looked, either. About how she'd stood her ground with him when it came to the journals, and how much he liked a little challenge in a woman. About how much he was looking forward to reading those journals with her…

It just wasn't something he wanted to be true.

"Huh-uh," he repeated. "As far as I'm concerned you can go for it with Trina Molner. But when it comes to Nia Molner—she's strictly business for me."

Business and some fantasies he was trying like hell to put the kibosh on…

The sun on Nia's face felt wonderful. Warm, tropical sun that warmed her entire body where she lay on the white sandy beach, listening to the ocean's waves washing the shore just beyond her toes, as a light breeze rustled the palm fronds high over her head.

Now this is paradise….

Every inch of her body was so relaxed she was weak. And weighted. And she wasn't sure she could move even if she had to. Certainly she didn't want to.

Except that she was thirsty.

Sangria. Where was her sangria? She thought she'd

ordered it. She hoped she had. Sangria would be good. Frigid and fruity and good. She just hoped it came with a straw. Did they serve sangria with a straw? They should. Then she wouldn't have to lift her head from her pillow to drink it.

Sangria… It's time for my sangria….

There he was—the boy with the sangria.

Only he wasn't a boy. He was a man. A full-grown man.

And he wasn't carrying anything.

But suddenly Nia didn't care so much about the sangria anymore. She was just curious about the man. Coming toward her, with the sun at his back so she couldn't see anything but his silhouette.

It was a great silhouette, though. Wow, what a body! Did he have even a bathing suit on?

She couldn't tell. She could only tell that he had long legs that were bulky with muscles. That he had a narrow waist and hips that were the point in the V that his torso made as it widened to shoulders broad enough to take all that sunshine and bounce it back into the sky.

Nia tried to see into the shadow of his face but she couldn't. Not that it mattered. She knew he was there just for her. And she was glad. Really glad. Because everything inside her was warm now, too, now that he was there. Warm and excited and eager for him…

She wriggled just a bit—well, maybe she was writhing. But that's how eager she was. Eager for what she somehow also knew he was going to do to her.

Hurry... I can't wait...

He dropped to his knees beside her then and she should have been able to see him. But she still couldn't. He was only a dark shape surrounded by the glow of the sun.

But it was all right. Seeing him wasn't as important as feeling him.

She thought about raising her hand to press to his chest, only she was just too comfortable, too relaxed, to do it. No, it was all up to him. She would just lie here and let him do the work. Lie here and enjoy it. She was definitely going to enjoy it....

She did tilt her chin, just enough to let him know she was ready. And willing. Inviting him to lean over her. To come to her.

And he did.

He came closer. And closer. But so slowly.

Too slowly, when she wanted him as badly as she did. Badly enough that she yearned for him. Ached for him. Badly enough that she thought if he didn't kiss her she wouldn't be able to stand it.

Come on....

A moan of pure, wanton desire rumbled from her throat, for she knew this kiss would be astonishing. That was why she wanted it so much. So much she just had to have it.

Now...

Really...right now...

The kiss would be mind-boggling. A kiss to put all other kisses to shame. The ultimate kiss...

His mouth would be smooth and silky and hot—but not too hot. His lips would be parted, soft—as relaxed as her whole body was, but still in control. He'd possess her with that kiss. He'd own her with it. And she'd be glad of it. She'd feel the heat of his breath on her face just before those lips would open lazily and draw hers open, too. He'd nibble. He'd caress her with his mouth. He'd send his velvet tongue to savor hers. To arouse her…

Now! Now! I can't wait any longer. Kiss me now!

But he didn't kiss her.

And suddenly the sun was gone and she could see him. See who he was.

Clay Heller!

It was Clay Heller!

And Nia woke up.

She wasn't on a white sandy beach in the tropics. The sun that was on her face was just morning sunshine coming through the window near her bed.

And Clay Heller certainly wasn't kneeling beside her, on the verge of kissing her or doing anything else.

Nia actually did groan this time, suffering very real longings that lingered in spite of the fact that she'd only been dreaming.

Clay Heller? she thought. What was she doing dreaming about Clay Heller, of all people? And especially like *that!*

It didn't mean anything, she assured herself. Dreams were just dreams. Figments of the imagination released when the conscious mind had its guard down.

But did that mean that her *sub*conscious was fixated on Clay Heller?

Of course not, she reasoned. A dream wasn't a fixation. Dreams were just dreams, she repeated to herself.

And certainly *this* dream didn't mean anything. Except maybe that Clay Heller was someone she'd just met. A novelty to her psyche. Nothing more than that. Someone who wasn't yet commonplace to her.

But she'd just met his brother, too, and she hadn't dreamed about him.

Who knew why the mind did what it did, though? she continued rationalizing. She could just as easily have dreamed about kissing Cole Heller. It wouldn't have had any more importance than dreaming about Clay did. It was nothing. Only a dream.

A dream that had seemed so real.

And she'd wanted him so much....

But now she was awake and she didn't want him.

Well, maybe her body still wanted him a little. But *she* didn't want him. She knew better than to want him. Or anyone who had ever looked twice at Trina. And that was it. The bottom line. The be-all and end-all. Dream or no dream.

Yes, the man was hot, hot, hot. But he was also taboo. And she needed to remember that—when she was awake and when she was asleep. In paintings, in works of art, she was good at recognizing forgeries, fakes and frauds. She wasn't good at seeing signs of those same things in men. But she'd learned—the hard way—that the first clue of potential trouble was someone who showed an interest—or had ever shown an interest—in her sister.

Nia sat up in bed and swung her legs over the side of the mattress.

"Stupid dream," she muttered, disgusted with herself.

But even as she sat there with her feet firmly planted on the floor and her eyes wide open, some of the dream was still with her. She could still see Clay Heller the way she had at the very end of the dream—too handsome for his own good. Too handsome for *her* own good. His sharply angled features so finely honed it was as if they'd been created by an old master. Those blue eyes that were too brilliant a blue to believe. Those broad, broad shoulders and biceps that were so awe-inspiring they spoke of an eloquent masculine beauty even as they shouted strength and power.

And worse than remembering how he'd looked in her dream, she was also remembering how she'd somehow just known that when he kissed her it would be an earth-shaking, feel-it-to-her-toes remarkable kiss. A kiss that would only make her want more than a kiss from him….

"Stop!" she commanded out loud.

She did need to stop the things that were going through her head. She had to organize the journals with this man today, and have dinner with him and the extended Heller family tonight. And the last thing she needed was to be having thoughts like these about

Clay. *Yearnings* like these, for a man she'd just met. A man who was severely out of bounds for her, by her own immutable, implacable, unalterable decree.

Nia got to her feet and headed for the bathroom so she could shower and get going and leave behind what had begun in that bed.

"No more Clay Heller," she swore out loud as she did. No more thoughts of him. No more dreams of him. No more of anything but a passing acquaintance with him.

And she was firmly rooted—*cemented*—in that goal. For all the right reasons.

It was just that she took with her to the shower some strong physical urges that, for all the wrong reasons, were difficult to ignore....

Nia got through the afternoon of organizing her aunt's journals by steadfastly keeping her focus on the books and glancing as little as possible at Clay Heller.

Of course, it didn't help that the simple sound of his voice could severely tug at that focus, but she resisted with such force that by the time he left her to dress for dinner, she was exhausted and in need of a revitalizing shower.

She followed the shower and shampoo by the donning of a pair of black slacks, a tailored white blouse and what she considered her power shoes—a pair of handcrafted Italian sling-backs that made her feel as if she could take on the world when she wore them.

She twisted her hair into a French knot, leaving an artful spray of curly ends at her crown, paid special attention to her blush and mascara, and then took one last assessment of herself in the cheval mirror that stood in one corner of her room.

She looked more together than she felt, she decided, as tiny butterflies took flight in her stomach at the thought of the evening to come and the presence of the man she'd dreamed so vividly of that morning and then spent the afternoon trying not to really notice.

There was some comfort in the knowledge that no one else would know about the butterflies—or the dream.

But it wasn't much.

Because the Molner house was on his way, Clay had insisted he pick up Nia and Trina and drive them out to the ranch where the dinner was being held.

Nia purposely left the front passenger seat of his sedan to Trina and slipped into the back seat.

But despite the fact that her own maneuverings had provoked the seating arrangement—and despite the fact that it served part of the purpose she'd intended by allowing her to sit quietly in the rear while conversation-making duties fell to her sister—Nia still had to fight a contrary streak of jealousy when she was left to witness the front seat occupants chatting and laughing together.

It made the short drive seem long. And it *was* a short drive.

The dinner was being held at the Heller ranch just outside of town, past the Heller-owned lumber mill. The main house, a sprawling H-shaped, two-story log structure, now belonged to Shag Heller's son Jackson and his wife, Ally. Jackson's sister, Beth, and her husband, Ash Blackwolf, had remodeled the old bunkhouse behind it into an equally large home of their own, while the eldest of Shag Heller's three children, Linc, lived in town with his wife, Kansas, who ran the general store.

There were more guests than Nia expected when she, Trina and Clay arrived. The Heller clan had multiplied considerably since Nia's visits to her grandparents. With the exception of Cole and Clay, the Hellers had all married and either had children of their own or adopted them. And while most of the kids were in Beth Heller's house with a nanny, there was still quite a crowd of adults for dinner. Particularly since the other set of Heller cousins from across the road— Ivey and Savannah and their respective spouses, Cully and Clint Culhane, and the third Culhane brother, Yance, and his wife, Della—had been invited, too.

Catching up with everyone kept conversation going smoothly and consistently throughout the evening. Nia enjoyed hearing about the thriving ranches and business concerns of the Hellers and the Culhanes, and the recent expansion of Kansas's general store. She also liked seeing all the pictures that were passed around of the numerous Heller and Culhane children, but she understood when Trina showed little interest in that.

She knew it struck too close to home for her sister, so Nia went overboard in her own enthusiasm and praise to cover up for Trina's apathy and eventual wandering out of the room.

Besides, Nia still had one aim for the evening—trying not to be aware of Clay Heller's every movement, every nuance, every word. Trying harder not to remember that dream about him. And diving into baby pictures offered aid in that cause.

But then the evening came to a close and Trina pulled Nia aside to tell her that Cole had offered her a ride home.

"Is that okay with you? Are you all right with Clay driving just you?" Trina asked.

What could she say? Nia wanted to encourage any time her twin might spend with the man who had fathered her baby. And she certainly couldn't tell Trina that she felt awkward because she might be susceptible to Clay's attributes, or that she was uncomfortable being with him at all because he'd been the star attraction in a steamy dream she'd had that morning.

So she merely smiled and said, "That's fine," hiding just how not fine it really was.

And then, before she knew it, good-nights had been said, she'd left behind every bit of distraction and there she was—alone with Clay in the front seat of his SUV.

"Cold?" he asked with a quick glance at her as he headed down the drive, away from what had amounted to her safety net for the evening.

"A little," Nia answered, realizing that she must appear more chilled than the spring air had actually left her because she was sitting with her hands clenched between her knees like a parochial schoolgirl waiting for a reprimand from the Mother Superior.

She pulled her hands out of hiding and tried for a more relaxed pose while Clay turned on the heat.

"Your dad said something about you working at a museum?" Clay said as warm air began to waft around them.

"He did?"

"When we talked about my using the journals. I was surprised that you weren't in the family business."

"Banking is more Trina's bailiwick—she's on the board of directors in Denver. But I've always leaned more toward the arts. Not that I have any talent at anything," she was quick to add. "I just love being around it all."

"What museum do you work at and what do you do there?"

"I'm in acquisitions for the Denver Art Museum."

She was putting effort into not looking at him, because the sight of him had such a potent effect on her. But when his handsome head pivoted in her direction again she could see him from the corner of her eye.

"That's the big leagues," he marveled, his eyebrows arched slightly.

"I started there as a volunteer the summer before my senior year in high school, to get my foot in the door, and worked my way up," she said. It was a sore spot with her that, as a rule, anyone learning what she did for a living assumed it was a token position available to her because of the family name and social status.

"Did you stop to go to college, or work while you were in school, too?"

He got points for asking the question in a tone that sounded merely curious, not as if it was impossible to believe that the little rich girl might really have worked and gone to school.

"I worked the whole time. In fact, I made sure to go to DU—Denver University—because it's in the city and that meant I could do both."

"So you were dedicated."

"I was," Nia admitted, letting go of the defensiveness this subject had a tendency to bring out in her. "What about you?" she said then. "How did you get to be a media mogul?"

That made him laugh, and it was such a nice sound in the shared quiet of the SUV that it warmed her more than the heater.

"Media mogul?" he repeated. "I don't know about that."

"I understand you own newspapers, radio and television stations—doesn't that make you a mogul?"

"It makes me an owner of newspapers, radio and television stations—but not that many of them and they're all pretty modest."

Nia thought it was Clay Heller who was modest. But she liked that humility. "How did you become a media *entrepreneur*—do you like that better than mogul?" she teased, venturing a glance at him and discovering his profile was as chiseled and sexy as his face was from the front.

He shot her a smile. "I think entrepreneur is a little better, yeah," he said, still not taking himself too seriously. "I lucked into it, to tell you the truth."

"How so?"

"I went to work at the local radio station in the small town in Texas where I grew up. I had visions of being a DJ because it seemed like a good way to get girls—"

"Was it? A good way to get girls?"

"Pretty good," he conceded with an intriguing tilt to his head. "But I didn't start at the mike. My job at first was to get the station owner coffee, dust and sweep the studio, answer the phone—grunt work."

"But you went from grunt work to owning the place?"

"Inheriting it. The station owner was an old guy. He and his wife had never had any kids, his wife had died, and when he passed on he surprised the hell out of everybody by leaving the station to me—a nineteen-year-old kid."

"You owned your first radio station at age nineteen?"

"Not so hard to do when someone wills it to you," he reminded her, maintaining his humility.

"And how did you go from inheriting that one station to owning other radio stations and TV stations and newspapers?"

He shrugged. "I was too young and dumb to know better," he joked. "I took risks an older, wiser man probably wouldn't have taken, and they paid off. Then I reinvested the payoffs and things just grew from there."

"How many stations and papers do you own?"

He shrugged again and didn't look altogether comfortable. "Half a dozen radio and four television stations—three radio in major markets and two TV—and six newspapers. But before long I'll be down to just one newspaper—the *Elk Creek Gazette*."

Nia couldn't conceal her shock at that announcement. "You're getting rid of everything?"

"Everything but the *Elk Creek Gazette*," he confirmed.

"Why?"

Another shrug. "It's just time. I can make enough money from the sales to never have to worry about money again, and the life I've been living just isn't the way I want to go on."

"You want out of the rat race?" Nia guessed, intrigued by the man in spite of herself.

"Basically. I'm tired of traveling, of keeping on top of a million different things at once—most of it numbers and rules and regulations and a whole lot of stuff that bores me to tears. I'm tired of not even knowing most of the people who work for me. I actually sat next to a guy at a bar in Houston six months ago, had a whole conversation with him—heard about the lousy politics he was dealing with in his job, how unhappy he was, how miserable conditions were with his family because of unreasonable demands his boss was making. There I was, commiserating with him, and then I found out he actually worked for me—"

"You were his unreasonable boss?"

"No, someone else down the ladder was, and I dealt with the person and the situation. But the point is, that conversation in a bar brought to light just how far I've come from where I began. And that it wasn't a place I wanted to be."

"You wanted to be in Elk Creek?" Nia said teasingly. It seemed so farfetched.

But Clay didn't take it as a joke. "As a matter of fact, yes," he admitted. "I wanted to be somewhere where I know most all of the faces and most everyone knows mine, too. I want to get up in the morning to do something that's stimulating but fun, something I actually enjoy and look forward to doing. I want to get back to my roots. Well, in the sense that I'm in the same kind of small town I grew up in in Texas, that I'm near to my brother and cousins—to family—and that I'm back to working hands-on."

"Typesetting? Rolling ink over letter blocks?"

This time her joke did make him laugh. "Computers have taken us a little beyond hand-setting type and rolling ink over letters. But I'm doing part of the writing—I'll be doing all of it for the supplements this week. I oversee everything. Not a word goes into print that I haven't read first. I get to hash out and investigate stories, do interviews, keep my finger on the pulse.

I'm in on the whole process, start to finish, and that's how I like it."

He seemed to mean that, because there was a vigor to his voice, an energy in his attitude when he talked about it all that made it obvious he genuinely was happy to be doing what he was doing.

They'd arrived at the Molner house by then, and with a nod in that direction he gave her a self-deprecating half grin and said, "Count your blessings that you're home before I go on any more about my change of life."

Nia returned his smile. "I did ask," she pointed out, realizing that not only hadn't she minded hearing about his so-called change of life, but somewhere during that conversation and the ride home she'd begun to have a good time with him.

Clay turned off the SUV's engine and reached for the door handle to get out.

When it registered with Nia that he was probably going to walk her to her door, she said, "No, don't bother—I can get in by myself."

"Oh no, you don't," he said, as if she'd suggested something unheard of. "My daddy'd roll over in his grave if he ever thought I sent a lady up to her door alone." There was just enough humor in his tone to leave Nia wondering if he was serious or simply using his father as an excuse because he wanted to do it.

Regardless of why—although it did please her a bit to think he might just *want* to walk her to the door— he got out from behind the wheel.

Nia left the vehicle, too, not waiting for him to come around to open the door for her, because she didn't want to give the impression that there was any kind of man-woman thing going on between them.

Even if she was feeling very much a woman in the presence of the big, broad-shouldered cowboy.

"So, can we get down to business tomorrow?" Clay asked when they'd reached the front door.

Nia tested the door handle to find it unlocked, opened it but remained standing there on the landing in the glow of the two carriage lights that welcomed her home and bathed Clay Heller's striking features and artfully disarrayed hair in a golden glow.

"Down to business reading the journals?" she asked for clarification, as her contrary brain chose that moment to remind her of her dream of him.

"Right. Can I come over here in the morning?"

"Nine o'clock?"

"Nine is good for me," he confirmed. "Any chance I can have the whole day? Maybe into the evening so I can get things rolling by Tuesday, have the first supplement out on Wednesday?"

"I'm at your disposal," Nia said, not intending the slightly breathy quality that somehow entered her voice. It was just that suddenly her dream was very vivid in her mind, and she was almost reliving the anticipation she'd felt as she'd watched the man—Clay Heller—walking toward her, his naked torso backlit by the sun. The anticipation of knowing he was going to kiss her. Of wanting him to.

And worse than reliving the dream and the desires she'd felt in the midst of it, as she gazed up into his starkly handsome face, into his nearly neon blue eyes— and as those eyes peered down at her—she became aware of a new desire to have him kiss her. For real, right then…

"At my disposal, huh?" he repeated, his own voice an octave lower, deeper, and somehow more sensuous than it had been before.

"To go through the journals," she clarified.

"Sure. What else?" he said with a dangerously, deliciously devilish undertone that made her wonder if he somehow knew what was going through her mind.

"So tomorrow morning at nine," she said again, ignoring whatever was passing between them.

"I'll be here," he promised.

"Me, too."

"Good, because it wouldn't be the same without you."

For a moment Nia just stood there, wishing she had a comeback, when all she could do was wonder if kissing him for real would be anything at all like she'd been so certain it would be in her dream.

Then she gained some control over her own thoughts and said, "See you in the morning."

"Yes, you will," he said, stepping off the landing.

She stole one last glimpse of him and then went inside, closing the door between them and reminding herself as she did that he was not a man she would even consider pursuing any kind of personal relationship with.

But reminder or no reminder, she still stood there for a moment wondering if an actual kiss from him would have been anywhere near as fantastic as the one she'd been having fantasies of since waking up that morning.

Wondering if an actual kiss from him might be even better...

Chapter 3

When Nia came downstairs for breakfast on Monday morning there was a message waiting for her from Clay. He had computer problems at the newspaper and one of his employees had been called out of town on a family emergency, so he couldn't begin reading the journals with her at nine o'clock. He would be there as soon as he could.

Nia had already showered, shampooed, tied her hair back in an at-the-nape ponytail, and dressed in a pair of jeans and a dual-layered, black-over-white boatneck T-shirt when she got the message, so she was left with time on her hands until Clay either arrived or let her know when he would. Since she'd heard stirrings in her sister's room as she'd passed the door on her way downstairs to breakfast—and knowing that Trina generally didn't feel too well in the mornings lately—Nia decided to use the spare time to bring tea and toast to her in bed. And to get the scoop on how the rest of last evening had gone for her and Cole.

"It's just me," Nia announced, after knocking on her sister's door.

"Come in," Trina called.

Nia balanced the tray she was carrying on her hip so she could have a free hand to turn the knob. Then she slipped into the room and closed the door behind her.

Trina was sitting up in bed, looking the way she had every morning for the past two weeks or so—pale and drawn.

"Morning sickness again?" Nia asked, crossing to the canopy bed that was a holdover from Trina's childhood.

"Ugh." Trina's only answer was a groan.

"I brought some tea and dry toast."

Trina closed her eyes and made a face. "Thanks. Maybe in a few minutes."

Nia set the tray on the nightstand and perched on the edge of her sister's bed, facing her. "Are you too sick to talk?"

"No, company helps. Then I don't think so much about how I feel." Trina opened her eyes again but left her head resting against the pillows that were arranged behind her. "What do you want to talk about? Anything in particular?"

"I just wanted to know how things went with Cole after the two of you left the Hellers' last night."

Trina's well-shaped eyebrows arched and she shrugged weakly. "Good," she said, as if she wasn't sure about it. "He took me on a drive, we stopped for a while and looked at the stars, talked…."

"That sounds nice," Nia said, her inflection inviting her sister to say more.

"It was nice," Trina agreed, but she didn't sound certain of that, either.

"Was there something *not* nice about it?"

"No, it was all nice. He's a really easy person to be with. Well, it wasn't so easy to explain that I was kind of freaked out about our getting carried away and sleeping together when I was here six weeks ago, and that that's why I left in such a hurry, without even saying goodbye to him. But he didn't seem to hold it against me once we talked about it, and from then on… It was just like it was when I was here before. He made me laugh, we never seemed to run out of things to say. It *was* nice."

"Okay. Good. So why do you still sound sort of on-the-fence about it?"

"I just came home wondering even more if we're right for each other," Trina said quietly. "I mean, part of what he talked about was his farm or ranch or whatever it is. About how much he loves the place, about what a kick he gets out of being up before sunrise to milk cows and feed chickens. About the peace of being out in the open mending fences. Even the construction that he does… He likes working with his hands, fixing things. I don't know, I just kept thinking that I couldn't even begin to see the appeal in any of that."

"Was he asking you to do any of it?"

"No. But what if this whole thing does go somewhere? I mean, he's…I don't know. He's a *farm boy,* Nia."

"You know you always feel down and depressed on these mornings when you're sick. In a few hours, when your stomach settles, everything will look better to you."

"But Cole will still be a *farm boy.* He'll still be someone who lives a whole different life than I do. Than I want to…"

"He also seems like a good guy, a decent man, and he's definitely not hard to look at," Nia said, wanting to bring the positives to light, too.

Trina managed a feeble smile. "He is gorgeous, isn't he? That body, that hair, those big rough hands—they're soo sexy."

"Big rough hands come from hard work," Nia pointed out. "And you just said he makes you laugh, he's easy to be with, easy to talk to. Easy to look at…"

"But what if his being easy to look at is the main thing? What if there's only a physical attraction between us? Like there was with Drew—because let's face it, with Drew there wasn't much more than a physical attraction, and look what happened."

"Cole doesn't seem anything at all like Drew," Nia stated.

"No, Drew and I had a whole lot more in common than Cole and I do," Trina said, being contrary. "Probably the way Clay and I would have."

That comment bothered Nia. Like fingernails run across a chalkboard.

She knew it shouldn't have. That it was Trina's business—and Trina's business alone—if her sister had any thoughts whatsoever about Clay.

But still, it definitely bothered Nia.

Only not because she'd ended up having such a good time with Clay the night before, she tried to tell herself. Not because she'd dreamed of kissing him and even wondered what it might have been like to actually do it. If she was bothered by Trina bringing Clay into this again it was only due to the fact that Trina was carrying Cole's baby, that Nia was pulling for Trina and Cole to get together so her sister would keep that baby and maybe be able to make a family with the baby's father.

But regardless of the kind of spin Nia put on it, she was still bothered.

"Just give Cole a chance," Nia advised her twin. "Remember, you're here to take things one step at a time, to see what happens between the two of you, if there's a chance it could work out. Try to judge Cole on his own merits—the man himself, separate from what he does for a living. In the end that's what's really important. And for now, you like being with him, so just think about that and see where it goes from there."

"I know you're right," Trina conceded. "I mean, if I wasn't pregnant, maybe I could just write him off because he's a farm boy—"

"How about trying not to think of him like that, for starters?" Nia suggested, with a flinch at her sister's use of the term again.

"Country boy—is that better?"

"Why not just think of him as Cole—nice, great-looking, easy-to-be-with guy, who makes you laugh, who you have a good time with—without labeling him as anything else?"

"Okay, I'll try. But it would be so much easier if Cole was the big-deal businessman and Clay was the…country guy."

"I hate to burst your bubble, but there's a whole lot of country guy in Clay, too. He's selling off everything he owns except the local newspaper so he can get back to his roots."

Trina wrinkled her nose. "What is it with these Hellers? They must have hayseeds in their blood or something."

"They must," Nia agreed with a laugh.

"And I just need to focus on the one who got me into trouble," Trina concluded.

"Seems like the best idea," Nia confirmed.

But as she told her sister she'd let her rest and left Trina's room, Nia was a little disgusted with herself.

Because Trina's conclusion that she should focus on Cole rather than on Clay just shouldn't have caused Nia to feel quite as elated as it did….

September 13, 1940

Today is a happy, happy day for me and for the Molner family. Arlen Fitzwilliam has asked me to marry him! Of course I accepted his proposal. I loved him almost from the moment I met him, but was afraid to even imagine that he might become mine. After one joyous month together this last spring when Father took me with him to Boston on his business trip and introduced me to Arlen, the entire Fitzwilliam family returned our visit this week. Although I had hoped against hope that Arlen and I would once again find that same rapport and affection we'd discovered in Boston, never did I expect a proposal of marriage so soon. But this evening, while we sat in the new park square, Arlen went down on one knee and did indeed ask me to be his wife. I was so overjoyed I could hardly keep from blubbering like a baby and embarrassing myself.

Father will be so thrilled when I tell him tomorrow! Maude's betrothal to Jacob Heller was a dream come true for Father and for Hyram, who have always wanted their deep and abiding friendship sealed with a union of our families. And now this, the joining of not only the Molners and the Fitzwilliams, but the invaluable connection Father was eager for between all the Fitzwilliam banks and the Molner Savings and Loan.

Oh, how I wish Maude was still awake! I can't wait to tell her, too! She was certain she would find Arlen stuffy and has not. In fact, on several occasions dur-

ing his time here, my Arlen has gone out of his way to engage my sister in the kind of stimulating conversation and debate she so loves. I'm quite sure he's won her over and that she's now as fond of him as I am of Jacob. How wonderful it will be for Maude and Jacob and Arlen and me to usher in a new generation for Elk Creek as the closest of friends and family!

"I didn't know your great-aunt Maude was engaged to my great-uncle Jacob," Clay said when Nia had read that portion of the journal and passed it to Clay because she knew it would be useful to him.

"It's news to me, too," she admitted, glancing at the entry a second time when he gave back the journal she'd been working on while he plowed through another one.

It was late Monday evening when they reached that portion of the diaries, and they were alone in the offices of the *Elk Creek Gazette* by then. Clay's computer crash had made it impossible for him to leave while technicians sorted through the problem, so after several updates on the status of the crises of his virus-infected system, Nia had offered to take the journals to him so they could continue going through them.

Due to the fact that there were so many diaries and so little time, it was impossible for Nia to read them all first and then hand over anything pertinent to Clay—the way she'd envisioned this process. Instead she'd had to concede to each of them reading separate journals at the same time and sharing whatever they came across that might be of interest in the Founder's Day supplements.

"That's what it says, though," she confirmed after her second look at what her great-aunt had written. "Phoebe and Arlen Fitzwilliam, and Maude and Jacob Heller."

"I know Phoebe did end up married to Arlen—he ran the bank here until he died in '76. And they had a son who was killed in a horseback riding accident here, too, that same year."

"Curtis." Nia supplied the name. "That was the year Aunt Phoebe left Elk Creek. After that my grandparents were the only Molners in town because my aunt Maude had moved on years before. But Maude never married at all."

"This is great, though," Clay said. "This is just the kind of human interest thing that'll add to the supplements—a romance between a Molner and a Heller. It's better than I'd hoped for. Everybody will want to find out what happened, why they didn't get married."

"But what if the reason they didn't get married makes my aunt Maude look bad? That's exactly the reason I'm playing watchdog, as you put it, over these journals."

"I know—so nothing besmirches the Molner name. But a broken romance isn't a character flaw—like shoplifting," he said, referring back to Nia's initial hypothetical scenario. "Besides, I'm taking the same risk," he pointed out. "It could just as easily be something my great-uncle did that made things go sour."

Nia considered that. But before she'd come to any conclusions, Clay said, "My great-uncle *did* end up married—to my aunt Julie. And if Maude never married, it seems to me the odds are in your favor. Jacob probably did something that left a bad taste in her mouth when it came to the whole idea of marriage, and turned her into a lifelong bachelorette."

"'Spinster' was actually what poor Maude was referred to behind her back—my spinster great-aunt."

"So maybe Jacob was such a jerk he turned her off men for the rest of her life."

No one had ever said why Maude had never married, so that was a possibility. But it wasn't a guarantee that Maude wouldn't come out looking bad.

"I don't know…" Nia hedged. "I think we should just stick with the town stuff. You're getting plenty of information about the early growth of Elk Creek—"

"But it's all pretty dry. What would you be more likely to read—a plain old chronology of which buildings were built when and why, or that while the town was developing there was a budding romance between the son and daughter of the town's two founding fathers? A romance that didn't end up joining the families, after all? A romance that, to this point, no one has mentioned, which tells me it probably isn't widely known about? A romance that's a revelation?"

"Of course I'd be wanting to pick up the next installment to find out why Maude and Jacob didn't make it to the altar. I'm curious about it now. But this is still my aunt—"

"And my uncle," Clay said again.

"That notwithstanding—"

"Look at the possibilities here," Clay said, interrupting her. "We know those old Hellers were cantankerous SOBs—Phoebe has already talked about my great-grandfather Hyram not even waiting a month between the death of his first wife and marrying his second, and basically telling the disapproving Elk Creek minister that he could stick it where the sun don't shine when the minister voiced his disapproval. We know that Savannah's and Ivey's father, Silas Heller, was as mean and ornery as they come. We know that Shag was not only mean and ornery but that he also had a long-term affair with Margie Wilson before dumping her for another woman in Denver. Those aren't stellar reputations when it comes to my forefathers and their history with women. And what do we know about Maude?"

"She apparently didn't expect to like Arlen Fitzwilliam because she thought he'd be stuffy, and she liked good conversation and debate," Nia said, supplying the information that had been in the journal.

"Yes, but we also know that both Maude and Phoebe were upstanding young women of their day. Churchgoers. Charity workers. Basically, that they were good girls. And what about later in life? What were your impressions of them as people?"

Nia thought about that. "They've both been dead over a dozen years, but I remember Phoebe better than Maude—we saw her more often at holidays and family functions. To me she was just a sweet old lady—a little prim and proper, but nice. She gave great birthday and Christmas gifts, and always took the time to talk to Trina and me, to find out what we were interested in, what we were doing. I liked her."

"And Maude?"

"Maude lived in London, England, from long before I was born. She had a quiet life that everyone said suited her. I thought she was nice, too, but I didn't really know her all that well. I think I only saw her three or four times before she died, and she didn't go out of her way to have much to do with Trina and me. She was always too busy catching up with the adults."

"But there wasn't anything about her that would lead you to think Jacob didn't marry her because she killed someone or held up the jewelry store or kicked dogs."

Nia laughed. "No. She just seemed like less fun than Phoebe. She was more straitlaced—more no-elbows-on-the-table. But I definitely never saw her kick a dog."

"So doesn't that tip the odds in your favor? Isn't it more likely that Maude didn't end up marrying Jacob because of something Jacob did rather than because of anything Maude did?"

He had a point.

"Come on," Clay urged once more, flashing a grin that could have tempted a saint to sin. "Let's both take the risk. Right here and now, let's agree to print whatever it is we find out about this romance. We're not talking kleptomania or serial killer or child abuser or anything that would be a big deal. We're talking a romance that happened over sixty years ago between people who have all passed on now, and even if they hadn't, probably wouldn't care if the whole world learned what broke them up when they were—how old? Pretty young. Everybody has a soft spot for affairs of the heart. It's just love and romance and relationships—what's the harm in letting the story unfold?"

Those were all good points, too.

"Maude *was* young," Nia said, thinking out loud as she calculated her aunt's age in 1940. "She would only have been eighteen."

Clay seemed to be doing a little math himself before he said, "Now that I think about it, that's what Jacob would have been, too. Two eighteen-year-olds. We'll probably get through the journals and find out that they only got engaged in the first place because Hyram and Horatio wanted their friendship sealed, and pressured them into it. Or arranged it, and Maude and Jacob couldn't go through with it. But however it plays out, it's still more of a story than we had before. So what do you say? Can we agree to run with it? No matter where it leads?"

Nia wasn't overly enthusiastic about the no-matter-where-it-leads part, but she had to admit that Clay was right. This was the most engaging thing they'd come across in her great-aunt's journals. And it did have human interest value. And applied to the occasion of Founder's Day.

Plus, when she thought about the fact that Maude and Jacob had been so young, about the kind of person she believed Maude to have been, about the fact that both Maude and Jacob seemed to have gone on and lived lives they were satisfied with, it really didn't seem as if Nia were taking that great a gamble to agree to allow Clay to print whatever they came across about the early romance between the founding fathers' children.

"Okay," she said somewhat tentatively.

The smile Clay gave in response almost caused her to reconsider; it was the smile she imagined the devil bestowing when he'd just persuaded someone to give up his or her soul. Although she had to admit that on that handsome Heller face, it still looked good.

"But with the proviso," she felt obliged to add, "that if for some reason Maude and Jacob *did* break up because of something embarrassing—"

"Ah, and you were so close to living dangerously," Clay joked with a mock-pained expression. "Don't wimp out on me now. Remember these were two eighteen-year-old kids in 1940—one of them probably caught the other yawning in public. Live on the edge! Say yes and let go of the provisos and censors and stipulations."

Sitting across from each other at a small table that he'd said acted as the lunch and conference table for himself and his four-person staff, Nia and Clay weren't far apart. And although she had spent the hours they'd been together trying not to look at him any more than necessary, even through the sandwich dinner they'd barely taken time out to eat, at that moment Nia had no choice but to meet his gaze. No choice but to take in the full impact of the man's knee-and-will-weakening masculine beauty.

There he was—his hair partly spiked on top, the sharp lines and angles of his face accentuating wickedly sensual features, his electric blue eyes full of mischief and invitation for her to be mischievous, too. And between the way he looked and the pure power of his personality, she was a goner. She just couldn't bring herself to say no. To go on being as rigid as he seemed to think she was.

"Okay, okay," she conceded.

"I'm trusting you, you know," he warned, but with a broad, pleased grin this time that said he was also enjoying this back and forth. "If I start the story of Maude Molner and Jacob Heller's romance, I'm going to want to finish it."

"I'm trusting you, too—to report the facts without embellishments or exaggerations. And with kindness, if Maude broke off with Jacob because she couldn't stand the sight of his cowlick. You won't turn her into some kind of control freak or obsessive-compulsive nut-job to make it better copy."

"Just the facts, ma'am. I'm committed to just the facts."

Nia had to laugh at his overly serious tone. "Don't make me sorry," she warned in return.

"Never," he promised with a voice full of innuendo that made her skin tingle.

Nia tried to ignore the feeling but it wasn't easy. Especially when he leaned far back in his chair and reached both arms high over his head to stretch that long, muscular body.

"And with that," he said, "I think we can quit for the day, safe in the knowledge that we have the lead for the first supplement."

Nia barely heard him. She was too lost in watching him stretch. And in the fact that watching him made the tingling go deeper than just her skin.

"I've been in this office, sitting down, for too long today. How about a walk?" he suggested.

Those words penetrated. Maybe because they carried an allure all their own.

It had been a warm spring day when Nia left home that afternoon, and from the look of it through the plate-glass window at the front of the office, the evening was equally nice. It made his idea all the more appealing—and it was appealing enough just to think of prolonging this time with him.

But caution prevailed, and she glanced at the big schoolhouse clock on the wall. "It's already nine o'clock. I should get back. I don't like to leave Trina alone too long."

Her words made his brow crease slightly. "Why not? She's a big girl, isn't she?"

"Yes. But she's also not good at entertaining herself and—"

"Call her," he said. "Maybe she's lost in a book or

watching a movie or something, and you can stay out until ten."

It did sound ridiculous when he put it like that—as if Nia were a teenager needing permission to stay out past nine o'clock. Coupled with the growing urge to take that walk with him, she conceded.

"All right, I'll call. But if Trina is just sitting around bored, I'll have to get home."

Clay nodded, but with confusion remaining on his handsome face as Nia made her phone call, only to discover that after his day's work on the house, Cole had stayed to have dinner with Trina and that they were playing gin rummy.

"Well, I guess I'm not needed at home," Nia announced when she'd hung up, going on to explain the reason.

Something about the explanation made Clay grin again. "Dinner and gin rummy, huh?"

"Apparently your brother and my sister have made an evening of it."

"Good. That's nice."

Nia studied his expression and weighed the tone of his voice, trying to judge whether he genuinely meant what he said or if there might be any signs of jealousy lurking around the edges.

If there were any, she didn't see or hear them. But rather than relaxing her guard, she reminded herself that signs or no signs, Clay could still be *feeling* jealous that his brother was with Trina.

Not relaxing her guard didn't dampen Nia's desire

to take that walk with Clay, though, so when he pushed his chair away from the table and said, "Looks like you'll have to keep me company now because if you go home too soon you'll be interrupting them," she had to admit that no, that didn't sound like the sentiments of a jealous man. Still, Nia held the possibility in reserve, anyway. Even as she agreed.

"I wouldn't mind a little exercise and some fresh air."

"Great! Let's go."

Clay held the light jacket she'd brought with her so she could slip into it, and even though there was never any actual contact between them, the mere heat of his body so close behind her warmed Nia more than she wished it did.

Luckily, there was distance between them again the moment her coat was on and he headed for the door. But the memory of that earlier tingling of her skin, of that warmth, left her aware of the effect the man could have on her, and the need to keep her resolution in mind as she stepped through the door he held open for her, and into the crisp evening air.

"Think you can make the whole mile of Center Street?" Clay asked once they were out on the boardwalk in front of his office.

"I think so," Nia said, as if she were accepting a challenge.

The office was on the east side of the street and Clay swept one arm to the north, in the direction of the park square. "Just in case you can't, let's do the longest leg first."

They settled in to stroll side by side, passing the general store next door to the newspaper office. Of course, it was closed for the night—not many things stayed open late in the small town. And because nothing much was open, Nia and Clay had the boardwalk beneath the tall wrought-iron Victorian streetlights to themselves.

"Elk Creek has a boutique now?" Nia observed as they passed the general store and came to a quaint and charming stone facade.

"A few things *do* change around here," Clay said. "For instance, the bakery up ahead is now in the hands of Shawna Jersey's son and daughter-in-law, and Shawna has retired. And the Lodge, beyond that, has new owners as of a year or so ago. Our former mayor bought it when his nephew beat him out of the job last election. It was a huge scandal that family member ran against family member," Clay confided.

The Lodge was the only local motel, a semicircular grouping of ten tiny log cabins built around the matching main office.

There was slightly more activity as they reached the section of Center Street that circled the park square. But not much. Two firemen were sitting outside the station and greeted Clay before he introduced them to Nia. After moving beyond the firehouse, Nia saw a young couple on the sidewalk that surrounded the park, holding hands and kissing.

"I always thought the park *square* should have been called the park circle, when that's what it was changed into," Nia observed as they rounded the grassy area with its towering oak trees.

"Good point," Clay agreed. "Maybe I'll start a petition to have it changed now."

Nia chuckled. "It'll never catch on."

The courthouse was dark except for the lights in the sheriff's office to one side of it, and the church they passed next showed no signs of life. But as they approached Nia's family's old house—the current medical facility—there were a group of people standing outside.

"The childbirth class must have just ended for the night," Clay said. "Tallie McDermot—"

"McDermot? I thought that was Tallie Shanahan," Nia said of the only woman in the gathering who wasn't obviously pregnant.

"You're right. At least she was Tallie Shanahan before she moved away. When she came back to Elk Creek she hooked up with Ry McDermot."

"That name still isn't familiar to me."

"Oh, that's right, you probably wouldn't know the McDermots. I didn't know them from my summers here as a kid, either, because they weren't around then. Remember old Buzz Martindale?"

"He owns one of the ranches out past your family's place?"

"Right. Well, a while back he turned his ranch over to his grandchildren, the McDermots. Those are the kids his daughter had after she eloped against Buzz's wishes when she was just a teenager. What I understand is that Buzz and his daughter mended fences after years and years of not speaking to each other, and what came of those mended fences was that the McDermot offspring took over for him. They're all here now. There's Ry, Matt, Kate and Bax—Bax is our doctor. Anyway, Tallie married Ry. And that lady in the red sweater, with her arm hooked through Brady Brown's—"

"Brady Brown?"

"He's the local crop duster. He and Kate McDermot are married. This is their second baby. Their first was what got them together."

Nia nodded. "I do recognize the Brimley brothers, though," she said of the other two men in the group. "Isn't that Jace and Josh?"

"It is. And their wives, both havin' first babies."

"It helps to get shown around by a newspaperman—you know all the details," Nia said with another laugh, just before they reached the group.

Conversation stopped for greetings to Clay and Nia before Nia was introduced to the members she didn't already know. Besides Brady and Kate Brown, she met Jace Brimley's wife, Clair, and Josh's wife, Megan, who suffered some teasing about her profession as an acupuncturist and the question she'd apparently asked in class about pain medication during delivery.

At the first opportunity Clay informed the group that he and Nia were just taking a walk, and they moved on. It wasn't until they had passed the bank, crossed Molner Circle, and strolled in front of the lawyer's office to reach Margie Wilson's Café that they had another indication that they weren't the only people out and about. And even though the lights were still on inside the diner and they could see Margie's daughter Maya closing out the cash register, the place was closed.

"Don't tell me—Maya Wilson is married, too," Nia guessed as she waved but kept on going.

"Maya married another one of the McDermots— Shane."

"Is *everybody* around here married?"

"I'm not," Clay pointed out. "But there has seemed to be a rash of weddings and babies in the last few years."

They'd made it far enough around the loop of Center Street to be across from the newspaper office and Nia's car parked in front of it. That prompted Clay to nod in that direction. "Can you keep on going or have you had enough?"

"I think there's a little more walk left in me," she said.

"Good," he said with a one-sided smile that made him look rakish and just a touch dangerous.

He kept up the commentary as they made their way to the southern end of Center Street, glancing west to the old holding barn that was now the Buckin' Bronco Nia had heard about the previous night at the Hellers' dinner. But they didn't go far enough off their path to actually get to it. Instead Clay kept to a straight course, crossing to the sleeping train station that bordered the town on the south side.

"I like to sit in the shadows up there sometimes and look down Center Street at the whole town," he informed her. "Are you interested or in a hurry to get home?"

"Interested," she heard herself say before she'd thought it through.

It wasn't bad enough that saying so made it sound as if she were interested in more than whiling away some time at the train station, but she'd said it with what could have been interpreted as an almost flirtatious tone.

But there was nothing she could do for damage control and simply followed Clay when he climbed the wooden steps to the station platform, hoping he hadn't taken her "interested" answer the way she was afraid he might have.

The platform was protected from the elements by a gingerbread-trimmed overhang. Beneath the overhang were two rows of whitewashed benches providing seating for travelers waiting for their trains. The benches were back-to-back, one row facing the tracks, the other facing Elk Creek. It was to the benches facing town that Clay motioned, waiting for Nia to sit before he joined her. When he did, he rested one cowboy-booted foot over the opposite knee and stretched both his arms along the back rail, making himself comfortable. Nia sat a bit primly beside him, keeping several inches separating them, and yet still ultra-aware of his massive thigh nearby. And of just how potently male he was…

"Were your aunts close?" he asked then, out of the blue.

It took Nia a moment to drag her thoughts from his thigh and actually process his question.

The journals…he's talking about the journals….

"Phoebe and Maude?" she said. "It sounded as though they were in Phoebe's writings, didn't it?"

"But were they close when you knew them?"

Nia thought about that. "It's hard to say," she concluded. "I saw Maude so rarely, and while Phoebe was always there when Maude was, so was the rest of my family. You can't always tell who might be close when they're in a group. Plus I was a child. I wasn't paying any attention to the relationships between any of my family members. I guess it doesn't seem like Phoebe and Maude would have been *really* close, since they lived on different continents. And I don't remember ever hearing that Phoebe went to England to visit Maude, although she may have and I just didn't know it."

Clay nodded, accepting the answer that wasn't really an answer at all. "What about you and Trina?" he asked then. "You must be really close if you'll rush home to entertain her when she's bored."

Apparently he hadn't let that go.

"I suppose it's that twin thing," he added before she'd had a chance to respond.

"We're close, yes. But I don't think it's only the twin

thing. It isn't as if we can't survive without each other. In fact, there was a gap when we weren't close at all…." She wasn't ready to explain what had happened, so she merely went on trying to make him understand why she would have gone home tonight had Trina not been with Cole.

"Trina has always just been the baby of the family. Everyone, including me, looks out for her and, I suppose, pampers her."

"Why? Was she born five minutes later than you were?" he joked.

"Nine minutes, actually."

"And that was enough to cast her in the role of baby of the family?"

"It probably wouldn't have been enough, no, had we been the same at birth. But we weren't."

"Because you're fraternal twins?"

"No, there was more to it than that. When we were born Trina was a pound smaller than I was and she wasn't well—she had a heart valve problem and a very weak immune system. She was frail and sickly—"

That seemed to surprise him. "She's always seemed fine."

"She *is* fine now. The valve was repaired when she was thirteen and she's been in perfect health ever since."

"But there were still thirteen years when you were the strong, healthy sister and Trina wasn't."

"When my activities didn't have to be limited and hers did. When a cold or a trip to the dentist wasn't life threatening to me, but might have been to Trina. When it was impressed upon me that I needed to take care of her…"

That wasn't something Nia had ever confided to anyone, and she didn't know why she'd just told Clay Heller.

"So you were trained early to mother her," he said.

"I guess. In a way. I was just the stronger of the two of us."

"And the one expected to sacrifice for the weaker twin?"

"I don't know if I would say *sacrifice.*"

"Isn't that what you were willing to do tonight? All Trina would have had to do was say she wanted you there and you'd have bypassed our walk to do it."

"A walk isn't such a big deal that I'd consider it a sacrifice," she said, even though she definitely would have regretted it, regretted not being with him at that moment, sitting in the shadows of the train station, in the clear night air. And yes, even though she might not want to admit it, she would have regretted leaving him behind.

But she didn't say any of that. What she said was, "For the most part I haven't minded the roles Trina and I play. I certainly wouldn't have wanted to have her health problems or the surgery to fix her heart valve. And given the choice, I'd rather be the stronger one, the caretaker, than the one in need of caretaking."

"So you like being needed."

Nia didn't know why, but he made her role sound

more like a detriment than an attribute. "I don't know about that. I only know that I never wanted to trade places with Trina." Well, except for a while three years ago, but she wasn't about to get into that with Clay right then. "I don't consider it a sacrifice, or even that she *needs* me. It's just the way things started out, and the way they've stayed, to some degree. It's the pattern that Trina is the delicate flower and I'm the worker bee."

"An heiress who's a worker bee?" he said with yet another smile that made it appear that that notion amused him.

"Heiress?" she repeated. "I've never thought of myself as an heiress."

"You're in line to inherit the Molner banking fortune one day, aren't you?"

"Trina and I are," she amended. "But still—"

"Doesn't that make you heiresses?"

"That sounds so…vacuous."

"I take it back then. You don't strike me as vacuous, that's for sure."

"Thank you. I think."

He laughed once more, and it was an even better sound than the slight breeze whistling through the rafters of the train station's overhang.

Despite the fact that the Buckin' Bronco honky-tonk was a distance away, when the bright neon sign over its front door went out, the darkness on the platform deepened somewhat. Both Nia and Clay glanced in that direction.

"Monday night in Elk Creek," Clay observed. "It must be ten-thirty."

"I should get home before they roll up the sidewalks," Nia joked.

This time Clay didn't argue with her. He just stood and so did she.

"This was nice, though," he said as they descended the wooden steps and headed back down Center Street.

"It was," Nia agreed, trying not to think about just *how* nice it had been.

"I'm glad we could do it."

Nia wasn't sure if he was just voicing the sentiment or if it was another comment on the fact that she might not have taken the walk with him had Trina not been otherwise occupied, so she didn't say anything.

When they reached the newspaper office again they went inside to gather up the journals that had yet to be read and those that had already been gone through and discarded, leaving those Clay would take excerpts from. Then he carried the box out to Nia's car.

"Are you going home, too? And where *is* home for you, now that I think of it?" she asked as he set the box on her passenger seat and walked with her around to the driver's side to open the door for her.

Clay pointed his chiseled chin over the car's roof in the direction of the corner on which the newspaper building took up space. "I have a house on the cross street behind the office—it makes for an easy job commute. But I'm not going there now, no. I have to get back to work. I want to write up what we found today and go to press tomorrow so that it'll be out on Wednesday."

"We shouldn't have wasted time taking a walk, then. I didn't know you still had work to do."

"I didn't consider it a waste of time," he said, his voice an octave deeper than it had been before as he watched her intently with those vibrant blue eyes.

She remained standing in the lee of her car door, facing him. "Still, you could be finished by now."

"It was worth it," he assured her.

Those eyes of his were locked on her, and for a moment everything but the sight of him seemed to blank out of Nia's mind. She didn't move. It didn't occur to her to actually get in her car. She merely stood there, looking up at him. Waiting, almost.

But for what? For him to kiss her good-night?

No, that was silly.

Or was it?

The previous night she'd convinced herself that the idea of a kiss good-night was only in her own mind, a remnant of the dream she'd had about him. But tonight she wasn't so sure it was just a figment of her imagination.

Tonight the air around them was different. It was charged and vibrant. It seemed to suggest that there was a kiss in the wind.

Plus he wasn't moving, either. He was staying put. Studying her.

Maybe even leaning forward a little...

He was going to kiss her.

She really thought he was.

Until he reared back and the moment passed.

"Tomorrow," he said then, as if refocusing himself. "Even though my computers are disinfected I'm short-handed now that I've lost one of my staff. His mother didn't survive the car accident she was in and he'll be in Cheyenne for a while now."

"Do you want me to come here again?" Nia offered.

"Actually, I'll come to you if there's any chance you could work in the evenings. I'm going to have to do John's work while he's away so I'll be more swamped than usual during the day. But if you'll give me your nights, I'll make it worth your while…."

"Really…" she said, sounding intrigued even though she hadn't intended to. "How would you do that?"

He grinned. "I don't know. But I'll come up with something."

There was even more innuendo in his voice. Innuendo she almost answered with more of the flirting she'd just engaged in. But even if he *had* pulled back from the kiss she still thought he might have been on the verge of, it seemed better not to leave on the horizon his offer to make anything worth her while. It just left too much temptation.

With that in mind, she amended her own tone to sound completely casual and said, "That's okay. Evenings are fine and you don't have to make it up to me."

Clay raised his chin in such a way that she wasn't

sure if he was happy to get what he wanted without being left on the hook to reward it, or if he might be disappointed.

But she'd never know, because he replied, "Whatever you say. Thanks for today and for being flexible."

That last word had held another hint of insinuation, a sexy undertone that she didn't think he'd put there on purpose, because his expression suggested it had just slipped out. Then he added, "Flexible about coming to the office to work, and about letting me use the romance between Maude and Jacob, and about working evenings from here on."

"Sure," she repeated, as if nothing else had ever crossed her mind. Then she decided she'd better get in her car before whatever it was that was in the wind made her more confused. "I'll see you tomorrow," she said as she finally got behind the wheel.

He didn't close her door immediately, and there was a split second when Nia wondered if he might come around, lean in and kiss her, after all.

Or maybe that was just what she was hoping he would do.

Instead, he finally pushed the door shut. With both big hands against the glass of the window.

And while it might have still been silly, Nia had the sense that he wasn't only pushing on that door, he was also pushing against what could have happened between them. Or his own inclination for it to.

No, that really was silly, she told herself as she

started the car and backed away from the curb under his watchful gaze.

She must have only imagined that he might have been about to kiss her. It was probably a holdover from that dream and the previous night's replay of it when they'd said goodbye. Some kind of flashback.

Of course that was what it was—just some kind of flashback, she tried to convince herself as she turned onto Molner Circle.

And yet despite all her attempts to believe it, something told her that tonight their attraction hadn't been only her imagination.

Chapter 4

In order to report on the goings-on of the local Cattleman's Association, Clay attended the meeting Tuesday morning. His brother and his cousin Jackson had offered to pick him up on their way, but since the meeting hall was only two blocks from Clay's house, he walked over.

There was a breakfast at the hall afterward, and because the Hellers were at the same table with the Culhane brothers, Shane, Ry and Matt McDermot, and Jace Brimley, Clay waited until the non-Hellers had left to bring up the subject he wanted to quiz Cole and Jackson on.

"Did either of you ever hear about old Jacob being engaged to a Molner once upon a time?"

"My grandfather?" Jackson asked. "He was engaged to a Molner? Which one?"

"Maude," Clay said, figuring he had his answer in the shocked tone of his cousin's voice.

"It's news to me," Jackson declared.

"Me, too," Cole added. "Who, exactly, was Maude?"

Jackson fielded that question. "You two probably weren't around enough to have contact with those older Molners—"

"We didn't," Cole confirmed. "But we know it's Phoebe Molner who wrote the journals I found in the Molners' basement. The writings Clay's usin' for the Founder's Day supplements."

"Well," Jackson continued, "Maude was Phoebe's sister."

"Ah," Cole said as light dawned. "So Maude was Trina's and Nia's great-aunt, too."

"Right," Jackson confirmed. "But Maude moved out of Elk Creek before I was even born, I think. I only recall meetin' her once—she came here on a visit when I was a kid. The Molners had hired me to pick weeds out of their yard and I was there the day she showed up. But that's about the extent of what I know about her. I sure never heard she might have married into the family. Why didn't she?"

"That's what I'm wondering," Clay said. "I'm sure it'll come up in the journals. I was just curious if it was common knowledge around here or not that there was something between old Jacob and Maude Molner."

"It's not common knowledge to me," Jackson said.

"But you could ask your grandfather, couldn't you? He ought to know what went on with his brother's love life."

"Yeah, I thought about that, too," Clay said. "But I'd have to call him at the care center and hope I hit a lucid moment. He's not what you'd call sharp as a tack anymore. You know he's eighty-three, and dementia has really set in."

"He does better remembering the old stuff, though," Cole stated. "Last time I talked to him I asked him what he'd had for breakfast two hours earlier and he couldn't say. But he told me every detail about some French-woman he met when he was on furlough during the war."

They all laughed before Clay said, "I know he has more of a grasp of the distant past than of the present. I was in to see him last week and he told me all about a woman he spent some time with in Dallas in 1953. He called her 'a little filly with big bazooms.' But as far as using him as a source, he's my last resort. I don't think I can consider him too reliable."

"Unless Maude Molner had big bazooms," Jackson said.

"But since there's no way for me to know that," Clay pointed out with another laugh, "I don't think that I can trust him. I was just hoping one of you had heard something somewhere along the line."

"Not me," Cole said.

"Sorry," Jackson added. "And old Jacob is the last of that generation in our family, so there's no one else to talk to."

"I guess I'll just have to be patient and keep sifting through the diaries," Clay concluded.

After a moment of musing, Jackson said, "So Maude Molner could have been my grandmother?"

"It appears to have been a possibility," Clay said.

"That would have made Trina and Nia our cousins," Cole murmured, putting two and two together.

"Right."

"Huh…" Jackson shook his head. "Funny how things happen. And how they *could* have happened."

He got up from the table then, nodding toward the president of the Cattleman's Association. "I better catch Garland before he leaves. I need to get him to put that feed issue on the agenda again for the next meeting. We have to talk more about it."

Once Jackson had left them, Clay turned to Cole and used the subject of the Molner and Heller connection as a segue. "I'm thinkin' you wouldn't have been too happy if Trina Molner had ended up our cousin."

Cole merely cocked one eyebrow, revealing nothing.

But in ornery brotherly fashion, Clay persisted. "Dinner and gin rummy last night, as I understand," he said, letting his brother know he was aware of how Cole had spent the previous evening. And with whom.

A small smile took its time appearing on Cole's mouth. "I was still there when Nia got home from bein' with you."

Clay laughed at the counterattack. "I was working with Nia. Dinner and gin rummy aren't work."

"Workin'? Takin' her for a walk around town in the moonlight? Was that workin'?"

"That was purely therapeutic—legs needed to be stretched."

"And now you're tryin' to pull mine."

Clay laughed again and Cole grinned at his own success in turning the tables.

But still Clay didn't give up. He just omitted the teasing tone when he said, "I take it you made up your mind to pursue things with Trina and not worry anymore about her just having a fling with the hired help?"

Cole wasn't so quick to answer that, and his expression sobered considerably before he did. "Can't say I'm not worried about it, no. I *am* worried about it. But…" He shrugged. "I don't know. I guess I'm just hopin' that isn't the case."

"Because you couldn't make yourself steer clear?" Clay asked.

Cole shrugged a second time. "There's just somethin' about her. Somethin' that happens the minute I set eyes on her. I guess it makes me take the risk. I know it doesn't make me run the other way even when I tell myself I should."

"But you do tell yourself you should?"

"Hell, about a dozen times between when she invited me to stay for dinner and when I said yes."

"It's a good sign that she invited you to dinner. I wondered if Fran had insisted on feeding you and things had just gone from there."

"No, it was Trina who asked me."

"And what was your take on it? Fling or more than a fling?"

Cole shook his head. "Can't say. Seems to go pretty well when we're together. There's no problem talkin'…"

"And more than talkin'?"

Okay, so maybe there was a slight return of the goading note in that. But Cole didn't seem to catch it because he answered honestly.

"I kissed her good-night, but that's tonin' it down from what went on last time she was here. And I didn't do anything *but* kiss her good-night—once, that's all."

"And you got away with it?"

"She didn't slap me, if that's what you're askin'."

"But did she kiss you back? Or invite you to bring your tool belt upstairs to play handier handyman?"

"She kissed me back but, no, she didn't invite me to bring my tool belt upstairs."

"That could be another good sign. If she just wanted to fool around with the help wouldn't she have gone for more than dinner and gin rummy when you kissed her?"

"Yeah, I thought the same thing."

"So maybe she's come to town now thinkin' to start over with you. Only slower this time."

"Maybe," Cole conceded, but he clearly had continuing reservations. "Why're you so interested, anyway?" he asked then. "Did you change your mind since Sunday morning? Are you thinkin' maybe you want to check Trina out yourself, after all?"

"I'm just curious," Clay answered. "I'd like to see somethin' good come of this for you. I know that last

deal with Marilou burned you bad. You deserve somebody better than that."

"And you think Trina is it?"

Clay took a turn at shrugging. "Like I said before,
I don't really know the woman. But if you want her,
I'm pullin' for her wantin' you, too."

"Thanks," Cole said. "And I'm still thinkin' maybe
you ought to give some consideration to Nia. There
hasn't been anyone else you've taken for a moonlight
stroll since you got to town."

"Purely therapeutic leg stretching," Clay repeated.
But not without a half grin he couldn't seem to suppress.

Maybe because it was such a flat-out lie.

And maybe, too, because when all was said and
done, he was damn glad Nia *wasn't* his cousin.

January 5, 1941

*Winter has set in with a vengeance to welcome Arlen
and I back from our honeymoon to New York. After such
a lovely Christmas wedding and a wonderful wedding
trip that took Arlen away only once to meet with the
board of directors of the Fitzwilliams' Manhattan
branch bank, we returned home to Elk Creek and a rag-
ing blizzard. Arlen went directly to work managing
Molner Savings and Loan so that Father could have a
well-earned break. But I have been indoors for what
seems like forever. The storm finally passed yesterday
and today the sun broke through. What a glorious sight!*

Maude and I spent the entire morning planning for

her wedding to Jacob on February 14. I wish my heart were lighter when I think of that day's fast approach. But I'm beginning to worry what might be happening between them. In the past Maude has affectionately referred to Jacob as an intense man. But it seems that intensity is showing some unappealing temper. The day before yesterday he was very stern with her—right in front of me—because she asked that the ceremony be held in the church rather than at home. And just this morning I accidentally overheard him berating poor Maude horribly because she inquired about his preference in table linens for their wedding dinner. He didn't want to be bothered with what he called 'such nonsense.'

Of course, I didn't let Maude know that I'd been privy to this morning's exchange. She was so terribly embarrassed by my being witness to yesterday's altercation. Had I known when I heard their voices in the kitchen that it would end the way it did, I would have made my presence in the sunroom known. But at first I could only tell that Jacob had arrived, and since I couldn't make out what they were saying, I continued reading the Elk Creek Gazette *and minding my own business. And when voices were raised and I couldn't help but hear them, it seemed too late. So I just sat there, forced to listen to Jacob being very ugly to my sister. Afterward Maude ran sobbing to her room and Jacob stormed out, and when my sister did join me for our scheduled wedding preparations, she was* down in the dumps and very distracted. I felt so awful for her!

I felt even more awful for her when, out of the blue over lunch, she told me how lucky I am that Arlen is mild-mannered and patient, that he never raises his voice to me. Shortly after our midday meal Jacob telephoned Maude. She motioned for me to stay in the room while she took the call so I could continue to address the wedding invitations we'd been working on. Apparently Jacob attempted to atone for his bad behavior by inviting my sister to ice skate on his pond. I also did not think that it boded well for them when Maude insisted that Arlen and I be included. It made me wonder if she was wary of being alone with Jacob after their morning's blowup. I don't believe he's a violent man or that he would strike Maude, but she should not feel uncomfortable being alone with the person she's about to marry.

Jacob allowed for her to invite us and, of course, out of concern for Maude, I accepted and persuaded Arlen to leave work early to join us.

Because the roads are impassable by any motor vehicle, Jacob hitched horses to his sleigh and came into town to pick us all up. That was fun and festive, and I hoped the morning's incident would prove to be water under the bridge by the time we reached the pond. But despite Jacob's efforts to make amends, Maude remained withdrawn.

I think I had the best time of the four of us. I was so enjoying the fresh air and the beauty of the snow-

kissed trees and the icy pond! But Arlen isn't fond of the cold and it wasn't long before he made it known that he would prefer being inside again. In an attempt, I believe, to shun Jacob, Maude claimed that the cold was bothering her as well and insisted Jacob and I go on skating while she and Arlen return to the Heller ranch house and have a hired hand bring the sleigh back out for us. It was an awkward situation, but I felt Maude should have her way.

While I was alone with Jacob I weighed the idea of pointing out to him that Maude is a very sensitive person and that harshness of any kind wounds her deeply. But I decided it was best not to interfere.

Arlen had raised Maude's spirits by the time Jacob and I grew chilled ourselves and returned to the house, and Maude was more receptive to Jacob's overtures as we drank hot chocolate. So maybe what I was witness to today and tonight was merely prewedding nerves. I will keep my fingers crossed that that is the case, but I can't help recalling all the times Father has commented on the heat of Hyram Heller's temper. I guess I'll carry my concerns silently inside and only hope and pray that this is not an indication that Jacob follows in his father's footsteps.

"Uh-oh. Things are looking a little iffy for my team," Clay said after reading that passage in the journals.

"Yes, they are," Nia agreed as she closed the diary that that entry finished.

It was late Tuesday evening and they'd already decided that that journal would be the last they went through for the day, not knowing it would end with an indictment of sorts against Jacob Heller.

"But now that you've gotten this started—"

"I know," Clay said, cutting her off. "It's my own fault. You were the one who thought I should be careful about publishing the private side of things in these journals in case we discovered something unflattering. And now here it is, only it's about *my* family instead of yours."

Nia merely raised her eyebrows in confirmation.

"But if you'll recall, I told you the odds were in favor of a Heller being the one to throw a wrench into the works, so there's no reason for you to be smug," Clay joked.

"*Smug* is not a nice word. Let's just remember that it was you who was determined to do this even if it meant exposing the skeleton in someone's closet. So I'm not unhappy that it's your own skeletons coming to light."

"Smug," he repeated, and Nia couldn't suppress a small smile.

"Are you going to print this?" she asked then.

"It's still good stuff," he said, sitting back in his chair at the Molners' kitchen table, where they'd been working since he'd arrived just after dinner tonight. "But like I said before, it's no secret that the Hellers have a history of contrary dispositions, so yeah, I think it goes in the next installment."

"Brave man," Nia teased. "But how do you stack up when it comes to the Hellers' contrary dispositions?"

That made Clay laugh. "The present-day Hellers are a much more mellow lot," he assured her. "The take-no-prisoners Hellers got away with it when they were building empires with their bare hands or being rough-and-tumble ranchers. But these days? We're a kinder, gentler bunch."

"I think I'll reserve judgment," Nia decreed, even as she basked in the roguish grin he cast her.

There wasn't anything remarkable about the way he was dressed tonight; he had on a pair of aged jeans and a navy blue Henley T-shirt behind which a white crew-necked T-shirt showed through the unfastened top button. But he still managed to look remarkable, and she had been trying for hours not to notice.

Just the way she'd tried not to put too much prior thought into her own appearance in anticipation of his arrival tonight and ended up in a simple pair of denim trousers and a tan turtleneck sweater, with her hair twisted at the back of her head and the ends left to sprout like a fountain at her crown.

Their encounters should be completely casual, and to Nia that meant no special attention to her appearance and no special notice of his. It was just that that was a particularly difficult trick to pull off.

And even worse than how great looking he was and how hard it was not to be aware of it, she found it just as difficult to ignore how charismatic he could be. How funny and charming and interesting. When she wasn't working at fighting her attraction to him, he was just so easy to be with. And she was enjoying herself. A whole lot.

"What pond do you think Phoebe was talking about?" Nia asked then, for no reason other than to keep herself from thinking about how much she liked being there with Clay.

"There are a couple of choices, but since she said there were trees nearby, I'd bet it's the one that's on the property Cole bought from Jackson."

"Then Trina probably got to see it today during the tour of the ranch."

Cole had picked Trina up late in the afternoon for that purpose and he hadn't brought her home yet.

"Sometimes when I'm reading the journals," Nia said then, "it seems kind of strange to think I'm here, in the same place, seeing the same things through my perspective. I feel like I want to go out and take a look around through Phoebe's eyes, just for the heck of it."

"We can," Clay said. "We can go out to the pond right now."

"Oh, no, I wasn't fishing for that," Nia was quick to say, afraid that he had misconstrued what had genuinely only been thinking out loud.

"Actually, I've had the same thought here and there. I'll be walking past a building or something I hardly pay any attention to myself, and it'll strike me that we've just read about how exciting or momentous it was when it came into being. I like to stop and imagine what it must have been like all those years ago for your family and mine and everyone else around here. So I wouldn't mind a trip out to the pond myself. Although we'll have to go by car instead of by horse-drawn sleigh—I'm fresh out of those. Want to?"

There was that potent charm peeking out at her, enticing her. And before Nia found the wherewithal to resist it, she heard herself say, "You're sure?"

"Positive. It'll give me another dimension when I write the introduction to this part of the next supplement." He grinned and added, "Besides, I'm not ready to throw in the towel on tonight yet."

Nia wasn't sure what that last comment meant and it occurred to her that the hint of the devil in his grin should probably serve as a warning for her to beware. That she should probably make up an excuse and turn him down, after all.

But that wasn't what she did.

"Trina is still out and I didn't have plans for anything but to thumb through a few magazines," she said, thinking aloud once more.

"Trina again?" Clay said, teasingly chastising her. "She does her own things, and you should, too. Come on, let's just go."

Nia spent only another moment considering it before she said, "Okay. You gather up the journals you're using excerpts from while I grab a jacket."

"I'll take them out to the car and warm the engine—the weather was turning cold by the time I got here tonight. I heard we have a storm coming in."

"I'll only be a minute."

Nia hurried to her room, refusing to allow any more doubts or self-recriminations to intrude as she snatched the first blazer she located in her closet and rushed back down the stairs and out the front door to Clay and his waiting SUV.

He did have the engine running by then, but he got out from behind the wheel to open the passenger door for her as she reached it.

"So the pond is on land that belongs to Cole now?" Nia asked as they headed down Molner Circle once he was back behind the wheel.

"Right. But it's all still in the family. When Cole decided he wanted to put down roots in Elk Creek he called Jackson about scoping out a place to buy. I guess Jackson had been playing with the idea of selling off a few parcels on the south edge of his ranch because he just didn't need them anymore, and since what he was willing to part with ran alongside another small ranch that was up for sale, he gave Cole a reasonable enough price for Cole to afford both—as long as he does some construction and remodeling work on the side for a while."

"So Jackson and Cole are next-door neighbors."

"They are. And they join forces to help each other out whenever the need arises for either of them, so it's good for them both. Actually, since Beth and Linc co-own the main Heller ranch but leave Jackson basically alone to run it, Jackson is happy to have another family member share some of the load, even if means paying Cole back by working his place now and then, too."

"Cole and Jackson are close?"

"Yeah, they're kind of kindred spirits. They have similar temperaments. Interests. Paces."

Nia wondered if Cole was closer to Jackson than he was to Clay, but as they'd talked he had driven from Elk Creek proper out into the countryside and off the main road, so that the pond was coming into view up ahead. Complete with what looked to be a small bonfire burning on one of its banks and a truck backed up to it not far away.

"Is that Trina and Cole?" Nia asked, rather than questioning Clay about his relationship with his brother.

"Looks like it."

"Are we interrupting something?"

"I think the sound of us coming did the trick," Clay said, as the two people perched on the tailgate of the big white truck drew apart. Cole hopped down to the ground, while Trina stayed where she was.

"Add some ice to the pond and four pairs of skates and I guess we're Maude and Phoebe and Arlen and Jacob," Clay joked as he pulled the SUV to a stop beside the truck.

"Does that mean you want to take Trina home?" Nia said.

Clay glanced at her with a confused expression. "I don't think so," he responded, as if that had been a strange thing for her to ask.

Nia didn't want him exploring the concerns that had inspired the question, so the moment he'd turned off the engine she opened her own door and got out.

"Sorry if we're barging in," she said right away.

"We didn't know you'd be here," Clay added from behind her, once he'd left the vehicle, too.

"You're not barging in," Cole assured them, although both he and Trina had the air of teenagers caught doing something they shouldn't have been doing.

"I just told Cole about a night one summer when I was visiting Grandma and Grandpa," Trina explained. "A bunch of us came out here, built a fire and sat around talking. Cole and I thought it might be fun to relive it tonight."

"What're you two doin' out here?" Cole asked.

"Takin' a stroll down memory lane, too," Clay answered. "Only this one is down a memory lane that came from what we read in the journals a little while ago. We just wanted a visual to put with it."

"We were about ready to head in, though," Cole said then. "I was just going to put out the fire—"

"I'll bet," Clay muttered with a chuckle.

Cole ignored the innuendo-laden remark and continued with what he'd been about to say. "Shall I leave it or won't you be stayin?"

"I think you can leave it," Clay answered without consulting Nia. "Or you can stay, too—we don't want to run you off."

"No, really," Trina assured them. "I'm getting cold and we were about to go, anyway."

Nia wasn't convinced that was true and still had the sense that she and Clay were an unwelcome interruption. But there was nothing to be done about it so she didn't try. Instead she and Clay watched as Cole clasped his hands on either side of Trina's waist and lifted her down from the truckbed. When he had, he leaned back over the tailgate and pulled out a small shovel that he tossed to Clay. "You'll need this to bury the fire when you're through."

"Uh-huh," Clay said, amusement remaining just under the surface of his voice.

"See you at home later," Trina said to Nia as Cole ushered her to the passenger side of the truck.

"I shouldn't be long," Nia replied.

Cole merely raised a chin at both Clay and Nia once he'd rounded the truck and opened his own door.

Clay responded the same way just before his brother got in and the truck roared to life, leaving them in the dust.

"I don't know whether to feel guilty about that or not," Nia said as they both watched the retreat.

"So we cut short a little romantic interlude—it happens to the best of us. I don't think we did anything to feel guilty about," Clay said, with a laugh that made it clear he wasn't sorry.

"Did you really not know they'd be out here?"

"How would I have known? And why would I have busted in on them if I had?"

Good questions. "I'm not sure," she admitted. "But *did* you know, and would you have broken them up?"

"No. On both counts."

He moved nearer to the fire and tossed in a few

small chunks of the wood Cole had apparently gathered to keep it going.

"Do you think our old-timers had a fire that day?" Clay asked then, changing the subject.

But Nia wasn't entirely ready to let it go. For a moment she watched him, looking for any indication that he might have purposely suggested they come out here to interfere with time Cole was spending with Trina. But even to her leery mind it was too much of a coincidence that a passage in her great-aunt's journal had given him the opening. So she finally decided she was being unduly suspicious, and joined him at the bonfire, indulging his change of subject, as well.

"If there had been a fire that day, it seems like Maude and Arlen would have just stayed near it rather than going all the way back to the ranch."

"Good point," Clay conceded. "It's nice now, though."

"It is," Nia agreed.

He left her side to walk a few yards away and drag back a large log.

"Seating," he said, positioning it so that the fire was in front of it and they could peer beyond the flames at the pond.

He motioned for Nia to sit, and she did. Then he joined her. Not so near that they were touching in any way, but close enough for her to be very aware of the magnitude of the man there beside her, his legs spread wide and crossed sort of Indian fashion in front of the log.

She might have been imagining it, but to her it felt as if Clay was giving off about as much heat as the flames were. A more sensual, charged heat that, unlike the comfort of the fire, set off a rush of something more like sexual energy through her.

But while Trina might have come out to the pond for a romantic tryst with Cole, Nia reminded herself that was *not* why she was there with Clay, and concentrated hard on focusing on things other than him. Things like the pond itself. And picturing her great-aunts there sixty-five years in the past.

She wasn't sure what the difference was between a pond and a lake, but to her the body of water she steadfastly looked out at could have been called the latter. It was probably a full city block across, with a stand of huge fir trees clustered at the edge of the water on the opposite shore.

But whether it qualified as a pond or a lake, it was a beautiful spot. Calm and quiet and peaceful. She could understand how her great-aunt Phoebe had liked being there at any time, but particularly after being cooped up inside during a long snowstorm. The air would have been crisp and cold—colder than the spring chill that was seeping through Nia's wool blazer at that moment. Everything would have been blanketed in pure, crystalline white snow. The water that was a clear blue now would have been frozen over to an undisturbed glassy mirror. Phoebe, Maude, Arlen and Jacob would have been all bundled up in warm winter coats, hats, gloves, scarves and muffs, skates on their feet to glide along the pond's smooth surface as if they were flying. It all seemed so idyllic....

And such a shame that anger had invaded that day.

"I wonder how things were between Jacob and Arlen?" Nia said as the thought came into her head. "I wonder if they liked each other or were friendly at all? Phoebe hasn't said."

"The banker and the rancher? I don't know," Clay answered. "They might not have had too much in common."

"And without golf or raquetball to bond them, there might not have been anything to bring them together," Nia joked, pleased more than she should have been when she made Clay laugh, and feeling that laughter like sparkles skittering across the surface of her bare skin.

But again trying to avoid things like that, she forced her thoughts in a different direction, ending up recalling her earlier curiosity about whether or not Cole was closer to Jackson than he was to Clay. And this seemed like an opening for her to ask.

"What about you and Cole? He's a rancher and you're more the businessman. Does that mean you don't have much in common?"

"That's different. We're brothers. Family. We grew up together, played together, made mischief together, did the same chores, the same things to fill our time on the ranch our folks owned in Texas."

"You said Cole and Jackson are kindred spirits— would you say you and Cole are, too?"

"No, I wouldn't say that," Clay admitted. "Jackson and Cole understand each other without even talking about much of anything. They're cut from the same cloth. But Cole and me? Our mother used to say that Cole had his feet planted firmly on the ground and I had my head in the clouds. Which, I guess—since he ended up a rancher and a contractor, and I ended up trucking in written words and airwaves—seems pretty much the case."

"But you get along?" Nia continued to probe.

"Sure. We do now."

"You didn't in the past, though?"

"Well, as kids there was the kind of rivalry boys are good for—who could climb a rope fastest or hold their breath the longest. That held over into high school. Cole is only eleven months older than I am, so we were just a year apart, and when he was a senior and I was a junior there was a sophomore girl we vied for pretty seriously. And a couple of years after college, we had a falling out."

That spurred enough curiosity for Nia to glance at him. But only for a moment before she began to admire his profile too much and went back to looking out at the pond before she said, "A serious falling out?"

"Serious enough. The ranch had some hard times— they hit about three years after I'd inherited the radio station. I'd just risked everything to buy my second station and was doing my damnedest to keep them both going. Cole wanted me to chuck what I was doing and just work the place with him and Dad."

"And you didn't do it."

"I talked it over with Dad, who didn't agree that my giving up what I was doing and bailing hay would make enough of a difference for me to do it. I took him at his word and it turned out okay. But Cole was P.O.'d at me for a long time. Even after things got better. He thought I'd let everyone down."

"Family is important to him," Nia said, thinking about how that might translate for Trina should Cole discover she was pregnant.

"Family is no more important to Cole than it is to me. I just think that this particular situation went back to the feet-on-the-ground thing. To Cole, the ranch was tangible, and that made it more important than what I was doing with two radio stations. He said what I wanted was a pipe dream and I needed to grow up and realize it and forget about it. And I didn't feel that way."

"When did you make up?"

"Oh, I don't know. There wasn't one defining moment over a parent's sickbed or anything. As time went by Cole took over the running of the Texas ranch more and more, and I think he discovered that he liked doing it on his own. And I started to have some success myself, so he stopped seeing what I was doing as a pipe dream and accepted it. We just eased out of being mad at each other, I guess."

Nia nodded, understanding that more than he could know. But she certainly didn't want to bring up the topic of her own rocky patch with Trina, so she said,

"What happened to the ranch in Texas? Do your parents still own it?"

"Our folks died there. In a tornado four years ago. I was in Chicago, Cole was in the small town five miles from home when it hit. He thought the twister looked like it touched down near the ranch, but he had no idea until he got home that it had demolished the place—the barn and the house, too. The folks were in the barn—we'll never know why, since they'd always told us to get to the basement in the house whenever there were tornado warnings, and if they'd done that they would have been okay. But the barn was flattened and that's where they were. They didn't make it out."

Nia could hear how difficult it was for him to tell her this story, and when she looked at him this time she saw the sorrow etched in the lines of his handsome face.

"I'm so sorry," she said quietly.

He nodded and for a moment neither of them said anything. Then, maybe when he could talk without his voice being clouded with emotion, he continued. "Anyway, after that Cole could have stayed and rebuilt, but he didn't have the heart. I understood, and since I was long gone from the place and crazed with my own work by then, we sold the land and Cole used the money to stake him here."

"Where he could be with family," Nia said, still thinking how important that was to both brothers, apparently.

"Where he could be with family," Clay confirmed.

"And then you followed Cole to Elk Creek yourself. Partly for the same reason," Nia concluded, recalling what he'd told her when she'd asked what he was doing in the small town.

"Right."

That seemed to wrap up the subject of Clay and his brother, but there was still one more thing he'd said that lingered in her mind—his mention of him and Cole vying for a girl in high school.

"So who was the sophomore girl you both wanted?" she asked with another sidelong glance at him and a teasing tone to lighten the mood again.

It worked, because he gave a nostalgic-sounding chuckle. "Her name was Amanda."

"Amanda," Nia said, continuing to tease him by repeating the name as if it were an endearment.

He played along with a voice filled with mock longing. "She was just one of those girls every guy in the school wanted," he said with a sigh.

"So of course both the Heller boys went after her."

"Fiercely."

"Did you arm wrestle for her or what?"

"We were much more brutal—and underhanded—than that. At first if she called for one of us and the other one intercepted the call, we didn't pass along the message. But then we escalated to sabotage and some unflattering lies. It was all-out war."

"What kind of sabotage and unflattering lies?"

"There was a lot of showing up on the other guy's

date, secretly putting suspicious-looking stains on the seat of jeans, swiping the money out of wallets so when it came time to pay she had to—rotten stuff like that."

"And the unflattering lies?" Again Nia stole a glance at him, finding him smiling from ear to ear at the memories.

"The unflattering lies had to do with sexually transmitted diseases."

It was Nia's turn to laugh. "Who ended up getting the girl?"

"A guy named Artie. All Cole and I succeeded at was blowing each other out of the water. And ruining about four months of future dates with anyone else because the whole school thought we both had ugly social diseases."

"Served you right," Nia decreed with another laugh.

"We knew it. But we didn't like it."

"So you have a track record of being attracted to the same women," Nia surmised.

"Only that once."

"And Trina," Nia reminded him.

Clay had been primarily gazing out at the pond while they talked, too. But now Nia felt him look directly at her. "I don't know if that qualifies. Doesn't being attracted to the same woman imply at the same time? Not a dozen years apart?"

Nia merely shrugged, compelled for no reason she understood to pursue this, and yet annoyed with herself that she was.

Clay shook his head. "I guarantee that I did not put cooking oil on the seat of Cole's pants tonight to make it look like he had some kind of accident, and I haven't sent your sister a note saying he has an STD, either. And if you're still wondering, I really didn't know they'd be here when I suggested we check out the pond. If I had, I wouldn't have come. I'd be happy to see them hook up."

"Really? Why?"

"They seem to like each other," Clay answered simply, without having to think about it beforehand. "And I am not feeling any jealousy, if that's what you're thinking."

She was thinking a lot of things, and his denials didn't change much of it. She'd heard denials like that before, she'd *believed* denials like that before, and only ended up being misled. So she couldn't take it too seriously. Much as she might have wished she could.

A gust of particularly cold wind whipped around them just then, sparing her from responding to his proclamations when Clay went from looking at her to gazing up at the overcast night sky. "Looks like the weather forecast is right and we have a spring storm on the way. I should probably get this fire out so the wind doesn't blow embers into something we don't want burning."

Nia nodded in agreement.

"Want to wait in the car to get out of the wind while I do that?" he asked.

"No, I'm okay," she said, not wanting to appear

weak. And also not wanting to leave him behind and miss getting to watch him at work. Although she was reluctant to admit that to herself.

Clay took her at her word, though, and stood, grabbing the shovel his brother had given him and attacking the flames that were faltering in the wind, anyway.

He was blocking her view of the pond and that seemed to give Nia license to watch him instead. He had put on a jean jacket over his Henley T-shirt, but despite the layers she could still see a hint of the muscles of his broad back flexing beneath the fabric as he bent to jam the shovel's blade into the ground, then scoop up the dirt, tossing it onto the fire before moving to another spot for a second supply.

This time she took in the sight of his legs—knees bent, thick thighs bulging against the denim of his jeans, bearing the weight of the piled-high shovel without a problem.

And by the third shovelful, when he was forced to present his back to her to throw dirt onto the flames from a different angle, she got to see his rear end.

There just wasn't any view of him that wasn't worth staring at, and she couldn't help the deep breath her lungs drew in at the sight of that great derriere, so tight and barely rounded.

Nia had forgotten all about the cold when the fire was finally extinguished and buried, and Clay turned back to her.

"That should do it," he said.

She was slightly slow on the uptake, yanking her

gaze to his face a bit belatedly. Then she overcompensated by nearly jumping to her feet. "Looks like the fire's out to me," she said, pretending that she'd paid attention to the task rather than to the man performing it.

But if Clay had an inkling that she'd been ogling him, he didn't show it. He just said, "You're probably freezing. Come on, let's get you out of the cold."

The trouble with giving in to studying him while he'd buried the bonfire was that once they were back in his SUV Nia couldn't seem to stop. Only now, riding to her house in silence, it was his hands that caught and held her attention.

His *hands* of all things!

What was the big deal about his hands?

But for no explainable reason, she couldn't stop herself from surreptitiously drinking in the sight of them on the steering wheel.

She marveled at how they could seem so powerful even doing something mundane and commonplace. She mentally measured the length and thickness of his fingers against her own. She imagined what it might be like to have those hands holding hers, their fingers entwined.

Somewhere along the way she began to be almost able to feel those hands placed gently at the small of her spine. Or higher up, to guide her on the dance floor. She started to fantasize that he was caressing her face with them. Sliding them down the side of her neck. Cupping her breasts...

Stop, stop, stop! she ordered herself. But it wasn't

until they turned onto Molner Circle and the house came into view that she had any success returning to reality.

Maybe it was the cowboy thing, she thought, rationalizing what had just occupied—no, what had just obsessed her. Clay might not be the same dyed-in-the-wool kind of cowboy that his brother was, but the cowboy thing was still there in his clothes, his attitude, his body language, his body….

And it was potent. It was what Trina was finding in Cole, Nia realized suddenly—the heady appeal of that totally masculine, earthy, primal man. It apparently brought to life some kind of primitive response even when there might be other aspects that raised red flags. Like Cole not being the button-down-collar type. Or like Clay's connection to Trina.

Cowboy charisma—that's what it was. And it was difficult not to be swept away by it.

Still, Nia tried to gain some control as Clay pulled the vehicle to a halt right in front of the house and said, "Here we are."

"Here we are," she repeated feebly, grateful that thoughts weren't broadcast.

He got out from behind the wheel to come around to her side of the SUV. Again Nia didn't wait for him to get there before she climbed out, too.

"Tomorrow night to read the journals? Same time? Here?" he asked as he walked her to the door.

"I don't have any other plans," Nia said as she

turned to face him. "Tomorrow is when the first supplement comes out, isn't it?"

"Yep," he confirmed.

"I'll be anxious to see it."

"Just to warn you—there's a little piece on you," he said then.

That surprised her. "There is?"

"To say thanks for your help going through the journals. I called your museum in Denver for some background and found out that you're very respected in your field."

Nia could feel her face turning red, but before she could think of what to say, Clay continued. "I understand you're an accomplished art historian and that you've had a couple of coups spotting forgeries that have come on the block for sale."

"All in a day's work," she joked, downplaying the accolades. "I hope you didn't go into all that in the supplement. Talk about boring your readers..."

"I used the 'accomplished and well-respected art historian' part. But I'm beginning to think that I could do a whole article on you. Maybe after the Founder's Day stories."

"I don't know about that," Nia demurred. "It just sounds embarrassing."

He was looking down at her very intently, studying her face as she'd been studying him while he doused the fire and drove home. And it occurred to her that maybe he hadn't been as oblivious as she'd thought, that maybe he was paying her back for her scrutiny of him.

But even as she considered that, it didn't seem to fit. His expression just didn't support the theory. His eyes simply held hers, and he was smiling slightly.

"I'll tell you what I left out of the supplement," he said, his voice more quiet, more intimate, more intriguing than it had been.

"What?" she asked.

"I left out how good you always smell. Like…I don't know, bluegrass and a field of wildflowers. Fresh and sweet and good enough to make me wish I was breathing in that same scent at night when I close my eyes to go to sleep."

She *really* didn't know what to say to that, although it gave her a fluttery little thrill to hear it. And to know that he thought about her at night when he closed his eyes to go to sleep.

But then suddenly commenting didn't seem all that important because he leaned forward and kissed her.

A small, almost infinitesimal kiss. A kiss so quick she barely felt it. A kiss so quick she didn't even have time to kiss him back.

And yet it was enough to make that fluttery little thrill expand like the wings of a monarch butterfly.

When it was over he didn't move away, though. He angled to her right so his mouth was near her ear and said, "Nope. Not thinkin' about anything or *anyone* but you. Not since the minute I laid eyes on you."

Nia couldn't help the smile that came in answer to that as he finally did straighten up to grin down at her and say, "'Night, Nia."

"Good night," she responded, sounding as foggy as she felt as the fact that he'd actually kissed her wrapped her brain in cotton.

Then he spun around and left her there on the doorstep, watching him go.

And thinking how impossible it seemed that that tiny, quick kiss had had such an impact on her. Enough of an impact to leave her feeling weak-kneed. And so weak-willed that if he'd stayed around, she might have done just about anything for a second one.

But impossible or not, that was how it was.

Chapter 5

Six inches of snow fell overnight. Heavy, wet spring snow that looked like whipped cream coating every tree branch and frosting the ground and the rooftops in pristine white brilliance.

The storm had moved through by morning, leaving a clear blue sky and an abundance of sunshine to glitter like sequins sewn onto the milky blanket.

Nia woke early despite the fact that the kiss Clay had left her with the night before had kept her up into the wee hours thinking about it. And him.

But as she'd lain awake in her bed she'd left her curtains open so she could watch the snow that had begun to fall at about midnight. When the sun rose, the light reflecting into her room was too bright to sleep through.

Besides, she knew the first Founder's Day supplement to the *Elk Creek Gazette* would be coming out and she was eager to read it.

By 7:30 she was up, showered, shampooed and dressed. Since the Molners were not usually in residence and Fran and Simon received their own copies at home, the *Gazette* wasn't delivered to the house. Nia had to go out to get one. After checking to make sure Trina was still sleeping and not in need of help getting through her morning sickness yet, Nia left through the front door.

She was surprised by how many other people were on Center Street when she walked from Molner Circle onto the town's main drag. She'd forgotten that in farm and ranch country days began at dawn. Even in town, where business owners and clerks were shoveling the boardwalk outside their shops and storefronts, deliveries were being made, and shoppers and diners looking for a hearty breakfast from Margie Wilson's Café were starting to gather.

There was a different feel to it all, though, than she would have found on the streets of downtown Denver on her way into the museum. No one was in a hurry. No one complained about the slush on the road or grumbled about having to shovel snow in April. No one seemed frazzled or overwhelmed or inconvenienced or stressed out. Instead the citizens of Elk Creek seemed to feel the way Nia did—energized and invigorated by the last taste of winter, and enjoying the clean, crisp air and the camaraderie of a lot of other people being out and about.

There was one metal box in front of the bank where the *Elk Creek Gazette* could be purchased for fifty cents. But it was still empty when Nia reached it, letting her know that the paper hadn't come out yet.

The smell of hot, fresh cinnamon rolls was wafting her way from the bakery, directly across Center Street and even though she knew Fran would chastise her for not coming home to eat a more well-rounded breakfast, Nia couldn't resist. Why not have a cinnamon roll while she waited? Surely the paper would be out any minute.

There weren't any cars coming from either direction, so she made her way across the wide avenue, high-stepping over mounds of snow and dodging puddles to get to the other side. But it was worth it, because the closer she got to the bakery, the stronger the scent of cinnamon.

Still, that was nothing compared to when she went inside. The whole shop was redolent with the aroma, and as she waited for the man in line in front of her to pay, she breathed deeply and let the scent carry her away on a cloud of sweet yeast and cinnamon heaven.

When it was her turn at the counter she had to drag herself out of her aromatic reverie to place her order. She didn't recognize the woman who took it, and the woman didn't seem to know her, either, but in true small town fashion, they chatted like old friends.

Nia asked to have a dozen rolls boxed to go so she could share the treat at home, and one for herself to eat right there. Along with a cup of hot, strong hazelnut coffee complete with sugar and cream—real cream. But hey, if she was going to be bad and eat nothing but a fat-, calorie- and carbohydrate-laden sweet roll for breakfast, she might as well be thoroughly bad.

Then she took her boxed pastries, her coffee and her single roll on its doily-lined china plate to a tiny café table in the corner of the bakery, positioning herself so she could look out the window at Center Street and the newspaper box.

But before the metal box was filled, a teenage boy came into the bakery to pass a stack of papers across the counter to the woman who had filled Nia's order moments before.

Nia took one more bite of the exquisite confection she was savoring and returned to the counter to buy a newspaper to go with it.

"Oh, I know. I have to keep one for myself, too," her newfound friend said when Nia asked for one of the newspapers. "I can't wait to read the Founder's Day special supplements that start today."

"Me, neither," Nia said, handing over her two quarters.

Back at her table, she bypassed the regular sections and went straight for the supplement hidden inside. She skimmed headlines until she located the piece from her great-aunt's journals.

Clay hadn't included entire entries from the diaries, just interesting excerpts that mentioned the town itself and its development, along with the portions about

Phoebe, Maude, Arlen Fitzwilliam and Jacob Heller. But he'd been true to her aunt's writings, and Nia was glad to see that.

Then she found the four paragraphs he'd written about her.

He thanked her for sifting through the journals with him and then did a brief biography that included where she lived now, her marital status and her position in acquisitions for the Denver Art Museum. It was mainly simple facts until the last paragraph, where he not only included the accolades he'd garnered from speaking to whoever he had at the museum, but also reported that in working with her himself, he'd found her to be intelligent, discerning, astute, articulate, bright, beautiful, caring, loyal and a pleasure to be with.

Oh.

Nia read that again, as if she might have misread it the first time.

Then she read it once more.

"Intelligent, discerning, astute, articulate, bright, beautiful, caring, loyal and a pleasure to be with..."

She'd never had such a glowing review. And she wasn't too sure what to make of it.

Was Clay flattering her out of gratitude for her participation with the journals? Or was that what he genuinely thought of her? And what if it *was*?

Well, it was nice. Really nice. But a little unnerving, too.

She'd been trying to deny that what was going on with her was an attraction to Clay. Certainly she didn't *want* to be attracted to him. Or to any man who had ever been interested in Trina. Any man who had ever been involved with Trina. Any man who could ever be attracted to or involved with Trina again.

But if all the times Nia couldn't keep from looking at Clay, from studying him, from being bowled over by the sight of him, if all the times she couldn't keep from nearly hanging on his every word and wanting to prolong every minute she had with him, didn't qualify as an attraction to him, she didn't know what did.

And now she had to wonder if he was actually attracted to her, too.

Of course, the fact that he'd kissed her the night before was an indication all on its own. That kiss, coupled with the article, made him being attracted to her even more of a possibility. And more dangerous than her simple, secret, denied attraction to him. That kind was a whole lot easier to not take seriously. But a kiss and publicly revealing what he thought of her? That could carry some weight.

Or was she making more of both things than they warranted? she asked herself, wary of jumping to conclusions. Especially when it came to a man.

She read the short piece in the supplement a fourth time, forcing herself to look at it objectively.

Intelligent. Discerning. Astute. Articulate. Caring. Loyal.

Those were good adjectives, but they weren't romantic. Anyone could say them about anyone else and it wouldn't be construed as a declaration of affection.

She could say them about Fergus, her assistant at work; he had all those qualities, but she wasn't attracted to him.

Bright—that was another word that didn't necessarily make a proclamation of devotion.

Beautiful was more personal, but might have just been that cowboy charm coming out. It might be something he would write about any woman. An empty compliment to be kind.

And *a pleasure to be with*? Nia's two schnauzers at home were a pleasure to be with.

So, okay, maybe she'd blown this out of proportion. At best, she could say that Clay might consider her intellectually stimulating company and that he didn't find it too difficult to spend time with her. But that didn't scream attraction. It just said he didn't hate her or having to spend time with her.

On the other hand, he'd also said he liked the way she smelled, she recalled. Not in the article; just before he'd kissed her the previous evening. But she liked the way the bakery smelled. That didn't mean she was *attracted* to it.

And the kiss? That hadn't been a hot number, she reminded herself.

Yes, he had kissed her, and people didn't go around kissing people who repulsed them. But when she took another, more analytical look at that, too, Nia decided it could have been nothing but a friendly sort of peck. Maybe a little more than a kiss between friends, because it *had* been on the lips, but still, just a friendly sort of kiss. Nothing to write home about. Nothing to make a big deal about. In fact, the more she thought it over, the more she decided it might have been a test-the-water kiss. Maybe to see how she would react. Or simply to see if he felt any sparks himself when he did it.

And if he'd felt any sparks, wouldn't he have tried for more? For at least a *real* kiss?

Or worse yet, maybe it had been a *comparison* kiss. A kiss to see how she measured up against long-ago kisses with Trina...

That notion shed an entirely new light on everything for Nia.

A comparison kiss.

It had happened before. Once, in the eighth grade. It had been a twin thing. People were always curious about twins, particularly about just how much alike they were. And apparently the boys they'd gone to school with had wondered if they kissed alike. So one of them had finagled kisses from them both so he could report back.

A comparison kiss.

That seemed the most likely scenario, suddenly. Even if afterward Clay had said that he hadn't been thinking about Trina. Maybe just bringing it up in the first place had been an indication that Trina *had* been on his mind. And again, if he'd been comparing them and Nia had come out the winner, it seemed as if he would have come back for more. Which he hadn't.

So maybe she'd disappointed him.

And just the fact that she might be in competition with her sister was enough to change everything for Nia. Enough to warn her that she'd been right before—she needed *not* to be attracted to Clay Heller. And even if she couldn't always help it, she had to absolutely not let it get out of control, or act on it. Regardless of whether he was attracted to her or not.

She'd finished her cinnamon roll and coffee, refolded the supplement and newspaper and left them on the table with her used plate and cup, taking only the box of pastries with her as she stood to go.

And even though stepping out onto Center Street and into the beautiful snow-blanketed day still felt good, Nia's spirits weren't quite as high as they'd been before.

But that was the price she paid for messing around with any man who had any ties to Trina.

And why Nia redoubled her determination not to do so.

It was just that a tiny, tiny part of her couldn't help regretting that Clay Heller—especially Clay Heller—was one of those men.

The sound of Trina's laughter carried to Nia as she came out of the kitchen early that evening. Nia hoped it was Cole in the living room with her sister, causing that moment of lightheartedness. But it was Clay. Laughing, too.

"Oh, hi, Nia," Trina called when Nia joined them. "Clay was just reminding me of a dumb practical joke we played that summer I was here when we were teenagers."

Nia smiled, thinking that the fact that Clay could make her sister laugh like that, that he was willing to put the effort into it, and that the two of them were clearly enjoying their moment together, also helped remind her of her renewed vow to keep her own attraction to Clay under lock and key.

"Cole isn't here yet?" Nia asked.

Cole was taking Trina out to dinner.

"He's on his way," Trina said, and Nia was at least glad that she didn't detect so much as a hint of disappointment in her sister's tone that might indicate Trina was sorry to leave Clay behind. In fact, sounding delighted, Trina added, "He's taking me into Cheyenne to a little restaurant I like. So don't wait up."

The doorbell rang just then and Trina wasted no time getting to her feet from the chair near Clay, who had apparently been sitting on the sofa until he'd stood when Nia entered the room.

"That'll be Cole now, and we want to get on the road, so I'll just say good-night to you two."

"Have a good time," Nia called to her sister's retreating back as Clay returned Trina's good-night.

Then to Nia, he said, "Looks like she's feeling better."

Nia had come home from her cinnamon roll breakfast to find Trina sicker than usual. And because she'd remained ill well into the afternoon, Nia had begun to worry that it wasn't going to pass, and that she might not be able to go through more journals with Clay that evening. In order to give him fair warning, she'd called to say that might be a possibility. Then Trina had improved and decided both she and Nia should carry on with their original plans. .

"I guess it was a fast-moving flu or something," Nia said in response to Clay's comment. "One minute she was miserable, and an hour later she was fine," she said, adding the truth to make the lie more believable.

Then, not wanting to dwell on the subject, she nodded in the direction from which she'd come. "The journals are waiting for us in the kitchen and Fran left us food before she and Simon went home for the day."

To make up for the false alarm, when Nia had rescheduled with Clay she'd promised him some of Fran's cooking.

"I hope you like meat loaf," she said. "And parsley-buttered potatoes, homemade bread and Fran's secret vinaigrette dressing on salad."

"Fran won a cooking contest with that meat loaf—it's a treat," Clay said. But rather than heading for the kitchen, he held out a copy of the *Elk Creek Gazette*. "I promised I'd bring you one of these."

Nia accepted the paper, but set it on the coffee table. "Thanks, but I couldn't wait. I went out early this morning and got a copy."

"What did you think?"

"It's good. Interesting. Faithful to Phoebe's writings. The piece on me was nice, too. But you really didn't have to do that," she said, her voice none too forceful or enthusiastic when she got to the part about her own article.

"You're turning red," he said with a chuckle. "I embarrassed you."

Embarrassed and confused her. But she wasn't about to admit that, so instead repeated, "It was nice," before she changed the subject. "We'd better get busy and have that meat loaf before it dries out."

Clay grinned but conceded, motioning for her to lead the way.

Just as she'd said, the diaries were on the kitchen table, and two places had been set for them. As Nia began taking serving platters from the warming oven as Fran had instructed, she tried not to pay attention to how good Clay looked. He had on a pair of jeans that fitted him to perfection and a gray cashmere, mock turtleneck sweater that hugged his broad shoulders, back, chest and biceps. Once again what he wore was nothing special, but he still managed to look so terrific she could have wasted hours just memorizing every inch of that big, masculine body that didn't seem to have any flaws.

Nia had again not gone overboard in her own selection of what to wear tonight, opting for pinstriped brown slacks and a plain crew-necked, cream-colored T-shirt that Trina always said was a size too big for her.

Nia had conceded to vanity, though, in not leaving her hair in the plain ponytail she'd worn all day. Instead she'd brushed it out and then caught it up at her crown, helping the natural waves to curl a bit more by using a curing iron on them. Plus she'd applied mascara and blush, but she'd reasoned that she would have done that even if she'd been having dinner alone with Trina.

"Does your sister always require so much of your care and attention?" Clay asked as he pitched in to help bring the food to the table.

"She was sick," Nia reasoned, applying his question only to that day.

"When I get the flu I don't expect Cole to sit with me. He might give me a call, ask if I need anything, but he wouldn't play nursemaid."

"I didn't mind. I puttered around while Trina napped, looked in on her and kept her company when she woke up, brought her tea and toast. It wasn't any big chore."

"Sounds like you might have even liked it."

"I didn't hate it," she acknowledged. "I was happy to do what I could, since she was feeling so miserable. And everything worked out. Here we are, after all."

Clay just nodded and Nia couldn't tell what he was thinking, so she let the subject drop. Once their meal was on the table and iced tea had been poured, she suggested they get to work.

Clay responded with another nod, but for a long moment his blue eyes remained on her, as if he were trying to figure her out.

She had no idea if he'd come to any conclusions, but just as she was becoming uncomfortable with his scrutiny he turned his attention to the journals and dinner, and allowed her to do the same.

* * *

"Here it is," Clay announced. "Maude and Jacob's wedding is off."

After a dinner occupied with passing journals and food back and forth, Nia had suggested they move to the living room so they could read in front of the fire. Clay had agreed, and he transferred the stacks of books to that location while Nia stored the leftovers and did a cursory cleanup. Then they'd gotten right back to work, reading and sharing portions of the journals that seemed to meet Clay's needs for the supplements. They'd been at it for hours before he made the statement about the cancellation of their ancestors' wedding, and Nia looked up from what she was reading, happy for the break.

"Apparently they went right down to the wire," she said, referring to the fact that, while they'd come across more negative entries about Maude and Jacob's relationship, they'd yet to find that the wedding itself had actually been called off.

"It didn't happen until the night before the ceremony," Clay confirmed. "Maude and Jacob had a big blowup and she finally said she wasn't going to marry him. It's the last entry in this journal."

"Let me see," Nia said, reaching for the leather-bound diary and handing him the one she'd been going through. "There's some things in here about your family starting the lumber mill that you might want to see."

"Thanks," he said. But rather than looking at it, he set

it down and opened the journal next in line after the one he'd given Nia. "I need to see what happens," he explained.

"Nosy," Nia teased with a laugh before she settled in to read the portion of her great-aunt's journal that began on February 13.

Phoebe outlined the bitter argument Maude and Jacob had had when Jacob had suddenly announced that they wouldn't be taking a honeymoon, after all, because he wanted to spend their travel money on a new bull instead.

...the trip itself was not so important to Maude. This was simply the straw that broke the camel's back. Not only did Jacob dictate the turn of events without so much as consulting her or considering what the change of plans might mean to her, but he also made it very clear when Maude protested that she was of secondary importance to the ranch and his own desires and ambitions, that he viewed her position in his life as no more than someone to meet his needs, bear and raise his children, and serve his every whim. It was a very unappealing prospect for her future, and I believe she was right in canceling her nuptials even at such a late date.

Father was beside himself and Hyram was anything but gracious. The rift occurred over the meal we were all to share on this, the eve of the wedding, and with everyone there to witness it, sides were taken— the Hellers against the Molners. Terribly harsh words

were exchanged and for a time I thought fists might fly,
as well. I don't know that fences will ever be mended
between Father and Hyram, who believes, as his son
does, that a woman has less value in a man's life than
a head of cattle. It was an ugly, ugly scene and at the
center of it all was poor Maude, devastated by the out-
come....

"Okay, the wedding's off," Nia said when she'd finished the entry, marked it with one of the scraps of
paper they used to keep the place of noteworthy portions, and closed the journal.

But when she glanced at Clay again she found him
engrossed in the next book, a frown creasing his brow.

"You're not going to like this part," he said.

"It gets worse?"

They'd pushed aside the coffee table and were sitting on the floor, Nia with her back against the sofa,
her legs crossed, and Clay facing her, his back against
one of the two matching chairs. His long legs were
stretched out to one side of her and crossed at the ankles. Nia watched him flip back a few pages in the
journal he'd gone on to while she'd read about the
wedding eve fiasco. Then he leaned forward to hand
it to her.

"There," he said, pointing a long index finger at the
February 20 entry.

Nia read what her aunt had written on that day.
Then, much as she'd done with the article Clay had
written about her, she read it again to be certain she

hadn't misunderstood what she'd found on the pages in front of her.

"Phoebe saw Arlen kissing Maude?" she said, still surprised even after the second go-through.

"Apparently old Arlen was really understanding of the breakup and did a whole lot of comforting of his sister-in-law. But up to then Phoebe was happy that her husband was being so considerate of Maude."

"And Phoebe just backed out of the room without letting them know she'd seen them?"

"Yep."

"Oh, that's not good," Nia said ominously.

"Maybe it doesn't turn out *too* bad, though. You said Phoebe and Arlen were married until he died. That they had a son," Clay pointed out.

Nia knew what he was thinking—that she wasn't going to want this indiscretion printed for all of Elk Creek to read. And he was right.

"It's Jacob's fault," Clay said then, as if he'd read Nia's thoughts as easily as he'd read the written words on the page. "He was a jerk and treated Maude like dirt. Hyram and Horatio were at odds—their whole friendship was in jeopardy—and Maude had to feel responsible for that. One thing must have just led to another when Arlen was comforting her."

"Poor Phoebe," Nia said. "After all the time she supported Maude, Maude repaid her by getting it on with her husband?"

"Getting it *on*?" Clay repeated with a grin. "Was it called that back then?"

"You know what I mean."

"Actually, as far as we know, Maude and Arlen just kissed."

"Just kissed?" Nia couldn't keep her tone even.

"Okay, granted, that's a big enough deal. But we don't know that they went all the way to *getting it on.* Maybe it was a single lapse in judgment that rose out of the moment, and never happened again or went any further."

Or maybe not, Nia thought, knowing she could be projecting some of her own baggage onto this, but still not having a good feeling about it.

"Am I going to be able to use this?" Clay asked then, nodding toward the journal Nia still held open.

She closed it without marking the place and set it on the floor near her knee. "You already have a lot of material," she reasoned, without actually answering his question. "Enough to stretch out for the Friday supplement *and* for the last one on Founder's Day on Saturday, if you work it right. I don't know that you really need more. The breakup explains why the two founding families didn't end up united in marriage, and that seems like a logical place to end the Phoebe-Maude-Arlen-Jacob stuff."

Clay narrowed his eyes at her, but in a playfully ominous way. "I knew you'd say that. But we don't know what happened *after* this, which would make a better finish for the Founder's Day supplement. Especially when it comes to Hyram and Horatio—the *founding fathers.* We don't know if they patched things up in their own friendship or went on to have some kind of silent feud or maybe an all-out cold war. At this point I'd be leaving my readers wondering, and that doesn't seem fair."

"You only want to know what happened between Hyram and Horatio, then."

He had the good grace to grin sheepishly. "Well, I'd like to know where things went with Phoebe and Arlen and Maude, too," he admitted. "And if *I* want to know, my readers will."

"If they never know Phoebe saw Maude and Arlen kissing, your readers will be satisfied with a general summary—you know, like Phoebe and Arlen went on to have a son named Curtis, and Maude never married and moved to England."

"Which might be exactly what happened. But we won't know that unless we read on," Clay pointed out.

"But if we read on and it turns into something juicy, I won't have any guarantee that you won't publish it," Nia countered.

"Haven't we already had this argument?" Clay asked, smiling just enough to let her know he wasn't angry.

"I think we have," Nia answered, not smiling, but not angry, either.

"So the ball is just gonna be in your court again, huh?" Clay concluded.

"I'll definitely have to think it over."

"And read ahead without me so you know in advance if you want me to have the details," he guessed.

This time Nia did smile. But she didn't admit anything.

After a moment of a blue-eyes-to-hazel-eyes stare down, Clay conceded with a slight chuckle. "I know—this time nothing is going to make you budge. It's okay if my guy comes off bad, but there's a limit to how much you'll let your family's reputation be sullied."

"Sullied?"

"Sullied. Soiled. Tainted. Tarnished. Besmirched. Pick one. Whatever you want to call it, you don't want it happening."

"No, I don't."

"So I guess I just wait and see," he said, but with a question in his voice, as if he hoped he might be wrong.

He wasn't.

"I guess," Nia confirmed.

"You're a hard woman, Nia Molner."

She made a fist and flexed her arm like a weight lifter showing off her biceps.

What she didn't expect was for Clay to reach over and squeeze the puny muscle she made. And even that teasing touch through the sleeve of her T-shirt was enough to send little shock waves through her.

"Yep, hard as nails," Clay joked.

He had no way of knowing just how soft that physical contact made her. In fact, she was glad she was sitting, because she needed the support.

Luckily, the contact was brief before he sat back

again, not seeming to notice that he'd turned her insides to mush.

"Did you ever kiss one of Trina's beaus?" he challenged then.

"No," she said, after a split second delay to switch gears and register that he was changing the subject.

"How about Trina?" he asked. "Did she ever kiss one of yours?"

Nia didn't want to answer that, so she didn't. Instead she turned the tables on him. "We already know you and Cole shared one girl—what was her name? Amanda? Were there more that either of *you* trespassed on?"

"Amanda was just kid stuff. We'd never go near each other's wives."

"Do you both have wives hidden somewhere?" Nia teased.

"Well, I don't, but who knows what Cole might have stashed out at his ranch?"

"Cole *doesn't* have a wife stashed somewhere, does he?" she said.

Clay laughed. "No, he doesn't. Don't freak out— your sister isn't dating a married man. I was just kidding."

"Has he ever been married?" Nia asked.

"Going to bat for your sister again, huh? No, Cole has never been married. He wanted to be, but the woman shot him down. Trina is the first person he's shown any interest in since. And it ended with Marilou over a year and a half ago."

"Really? He must have been very hurt."

"Hurt, insulted, put down—Marilou just cut him off at the knees when he proposed. But then, that was her style," Clay added under his breath.

"It doesn't sound like you were too fond of her," Nia observed, wanting to keep him talking about this.

"I wasn't."

"Was she from Elk Creek?"

"No, she was from Cheyenne. Her father owns a car dealership there. She worked in sales and sold Cole his truck. That's how they met."

"What didn't you like about her?"

Clay made a face. "Cole called it her sense of humor. But it always took the form of snide remarks about him and it was never funny. He didn't take offense, but I did."

"What kind of remarks?"

"About him being a hick cowboy or a dumb rancher or a dimwitted construction worker—things like that. Things that were a long way from being true. Cole is quiet and he works with his hands. For her, apparently, that translated to a lack of intelligence. But she seemed to overlook the fact that while he was working the ranch in Texas, he still managed to get his master's degree in agriculture. I stopped after my bachelor's degree, so that's more education than I have. And no, he's not flashy but he's not uncultured, either, and he's sure as hell nobody's dummy."

"Was Cole okay with her remarks?"

"I saw him flinch once or twice, but then just laugh it off. He was willing to accept it because he loved her, I suppose."

"And then he proposed and she insulted him and put him down along with rejecting the proposal?"

Clay nodded. "She said it was one thing to date him, but she'd never settle for someone like him. That she wanted more out of life than he'd ever be able to provide."

"Ouch."

"It was a low blow," Clay agreed.

And not completely different from Trina's own misgivings when it came to Cole. But Nia certainly wasn't going to tell Clay that.

He bent one knee and braced his elbow on it, and even though it seemed completely insane, Nia was suddenly very aware of the casual, unselfconscious sensuality in the way he moved, in the drape of his arm over the arch of his leg, of his hand dangling there so nonchalantly—the hand that had touched her and aroused her more than he knew….

"What about Trina?" he asked then.

"Trina?" Nia repeated, yanked from her reverie by the fear that she'd somehow transmitted her earlier thoughts that her sister had concerns when it came to Cole's station in life.

But that wasn't what was on Clay's mind, because he said, "I know she's divorced. Cole said that was why she was here the last time—that she was recovering from the breakup of her marriage."

Ah, it was Trina's past he was interested in. Trina's marriage…

Trina's marriage was something Nia didn't even like to think about, and she still didn't want to air it all to Clay. But it also seemed unfair to completely avoid answering him when he'd been candid in response to her questions about Cole's past relationship.

So, carefully choosing her words, and only commenting on the end of Trina's marriage, she said, "Trina had a hard time, too. She and Drew had been together a little less than two years when she came home early from a board meeting at the bank and found him in bed with someone else."

"Oh, that's ugly. And a shock, I would imagine."

"Mmm."

"It *wasn't* a shock?"

Nia shrugged. "Sure. Yes. Of course it was. But, well, it wasn't altogether out of character for him."

"This guy must have been a gem."

"He was pretty slick."

"And you didn't like him any better than I liked Marilou," Clay guessed.

"Not by then."

Nia wasn't willing to get into any more details. But she was spared any awkwardness in avoiding it when the front door opened and Trina and Cole came in, talking and laughing much the way Trina had been laughing with Clay earlier in the evening.

Nia was glad to see—and hear—that the other Heller brother could inspire the same kind of amusement, and she wanted to encourage it to continue, so she said, "Since we're finished here maybe we should give the living room to them."

Clay didn't budge except to crane his head in the direction of the foyer and casually say, "Hey, guys," to let the other couple know they were there.

Trina and Cole came only as far as the archway to the living room to exchange greetings. Once they'd done that and talked about how icy the roads to Cheyenne had been, Trina held up the case of a DVD and said, "We're going to watch a movie in the den."

"Want to join us?" Cole added.

"I can't," Clay said before Nia had the chance. "It's late and I still have work to do at the office before I can get home tonight. But thanks, anyway."

"I'll pass, too," Nia added.

Neither Trina nor Cole persisted, and Nia had the impression they were both glad the offer hadn't been accepted, because they wasted no time bidding them good-night and making themselves scarce.

"Looks like they had a good time and it's still going on," Clay said when he and Nia were alone once more.

"It does," Nia agreed. "And I hope it's true."

"You're pulling for them to get together?"

"If it's what's best for them. Does that seem strange to you?" she asked.

"No, I guess not," Clay answered, as if he'd considered it and had come to only a tentative conclusion. "You just seem to be such a mother hen when it comes to Trina—"

The grandfather clock in the corner struck midnight then, cutting off what he was saying. And since Nia wasn't particularly eager to get into the subject of mothering her sister, she hoped to throw Clay off the track by using the interruption to begin sorting the journals, making a pile of those Clay would want to take with him, another pile of those they'd already gone through but didn't need, and those that hadn't yet been read.

"That must be my cue to get going," Clay commented.

Nia wasn't sure if he was referring to the midnight chimes or to her cleaning up until he added, "I really do have more work tonight, and it's late. I'll be glad when this week and putting out the supplements is over."

Nia was glad he didn't think she was hinting for him to leave, because she genuinely hadn't been. In fact, she wasn't ecstatic that that was what he'd decided to do. She tried not to let it show, but somehow couldn't keep herself from saying, "You don't have to go…."

"You mean you aren't champing at the bit to get rid of me so you can read ahead?" he joked, goading her just a little.

Nia gave him an enigmatic smile.

It made him laugh, but didn't do anything in the way of stalling his departure. He got to his feet, taking with him the journals with page markers in them.

Then he held out his free hand to help Nia up, too.

She knew how treacherous it was to take that hand

but it would have been odd for her not to. So she accepted it, trying to think of anything but how good it felt to slip her fingers into that warm, strong grasp.

Still, as long as his hand held hers, there wasn't anything else she *could* think about. Until he let go of her, and then she just thought about how much she wished he hadn't.

"Tomorrow night is the unveiling of the statue of Hyram and Horatio," Clay said as Nia walked him to the door. "Think we could have dinner afterward? Maybe talk about where I can go from here with the diaries for the third-and-last supplement?"

For a split second Nia thought he was simply asking her to have dinner with him. And even though it shouldn't have, it gave her a tiny thrill. But then he'd added the part about the journals, and she'd realized that was his motive. Which was exactly as it should have been. Nothing more. But the tiny thrill was replaced by disappointment.

"I'll have to check with Trina. We'll go to the unveiling together and I'll have to see what she wants to do afterward."

"She could come, too. Although if things go the way they have been since the two of you got to town, I'm betting she and Cole will have plans of their own. But either way, if I'm going to use anything out of the next few journals for the Founder's Day supplement, I'll need it by tomorrow night. If you won't have dinner with me, then maybe I can come by later?"

She didn't know why, but that had a less worklike

ring to it that managed to wash away her disappointment.

"Something can probably be worked out," Nia assured him. "I'll talk to Trina and let you know."

They were at the door by then and she offered to hold the journals while Clay put on his coat, a leather jacket that looked as if it had the smooth texture of butter, and made her want to reach out and test it.

She resisted, waiting until he was ready to take the diaries back and then handing them over.

But once she had, Clay didn't make any move to leave, and instead she discovered him looking first down the corridor that ran alongside the staircase, in the direction Trina and Cole had gone, then at her.

"That'd be nice," he mused. "You and I getting to just chill out and watch a late movie."

"You can stay," Nia offered, not having intended so much hopefulness to echo in her voice, as she, too, felt a sharp tug toward doing something with him that had no other purpose than for them to be together.

Clay seemed to be tempted, and as he apparently weighed the idea, she drank in the sight of that oh-so-fine bone structure that made him more handsome than any man should be.

But in the end he took a deep breath, shook his head and said, "I really can't." Then he lowered his warm blue gaze to her. "I'd like to, though."

"It would be nice. Sometime…" she admitted in a quiet voice.

He went on looking at her, studying her the way she'd been studying him moments before. "Some-time," he echoed. "I'm going to hold you to that."

She hoped he did. But she didn't say it.

"Thanks for this tonight," he said then, raising the journals slightly. "There are probably a lot of things you could be doing that would be more fun."

She couldn't think of any. Not when anything else she might be doing wouldn't involve him, so didn't seem like fun at all.

But she didn't say that, either. Instead she murmured, "I don't mind. I'm enjoying it."

"Good. Me, too."

He went on staring down into her eyes for a moment longer before he leaned forward and kissed her.

She should have seen it coming, but she didn't. And yet even without preparation, when his lips touched hers, hers responded instinctively, kissing him in return.

Plus tonight she had the chance. Because when he kissed her, it wasn't a quick hit-and-run kiss the way it had been the previous night. Instead he lingered.

He lingered long enough to let his lips part over hers. Long enough to give her time to part hers, too. Long enough to deepen what started as a very soft kiss into one that was more insistent, more commanding. A kiss that turned up the volume on all of her senses as the scent of his aftershave wafted around her. As her eyes closed to a dreamy mental image of his amazingly handsome face. As the barely audible sound of his breathing mingled with the sound of hers. As she indulged not only in the feel of his mouth against hers, the feel of his heated breath brushing her cheek, but also in the feel of the leather of his jacket beneath her palm when she raised her hand to his strong chest....

Then he ended the kiss, taking his time about it. Easing them both out of it and then kissing her once more, quickly, as if after the bond had been broken he'd regretted it and wanted just a bit more.

"I'll talk to you tomorrow. See you tomorrow night—hopefully for dinner," he said, his deep voice even deeper, huskier, and definitely for her ears alone.

But that was still better than Nia could manage, because she was speechless and only nodded in answer before he let himself out.

A comparison kiss—that was what she'd decided Tuesday night's kiss had been. A comparison between her and Trina.

But she wasn't so convinced of that now. Because try as she might, she couldn't find anything in the kiss they'd just shared to make her think Clay was comparison shopping. No, this one had been all her own. She felt sure of it.

Her own kiss...

And when she finally turned back to the living room and the waiting journals, she knew that the best she was going to be able to do was gather them up and read them tomorrow.

Because there was no way she would be able to concentrate on them anymore tonight.

Not with that kiss that had been all her own still warm on her lips.

From a man she knew she shouldn't let herself think of as hers.

Chapter 6

"Nia? Are you in a trance or what?"

It was late the next afternoon when Trina's voice drew Nia from her thoughts. And from the tone of her sister's voice, Nia had the impression that wasn't the first time Trina had tried to get her attention.

"I'm sorry, have you been standing there long?" Nia said, glancing up from the journals she'd been staring at as her mind whirled with what she'd read.

"That's the third time I've said your name. I was beginning to think maybe you were asleep with your eyes open or something," Trina said as she came to the kitchen table and took a chair across from her.

"What's up?" Nia asked. "Your morning sickness

didn't change its mind and decide to show up late today, did it?"

"No, I still feel fine for a change. I wanted to talk to you about tonight."

"The unveiling of the statue?"

"Right. I know we're going together, but what about afterward?"

"I needed to talk to you about that, too," Nia said. Trina had felt so well when she'd gotten up this morning that she'd gone out to do some shopping, so Nia hadn't had the opportunity to discuss post-ceremony activities with her. And now that Nia had read ahead in their great-aunt's diaries, it was more important than ever for her to see Clay.

But before she could launch into that, Trina blurted out, "I almost let Cole stay the night last night."

"Really," Nia said, feeling her eyebrows arch at that news. "Things are going that well?"

"Pretty well, I think," Trina confirmed with a hint of reservation lurking in the shadows of her expression. "Or at least things are going, anyway."

"What does that mean?" Nia asked with a laugh.

"It's all still kind of confusing. When I'm with him it's good. I'm happy. I have the best time. And I just want…" Trina smiled a bad-girl smile. "Well, I just want his hands on me every minute."

"Uh-huh," Nia said, trying not to think about herself and Clay in those same terms. "That definitely sounds like things are going well."

"When I'm with him," Trina reminded her.

"But when you're not with him, things are different." Like when Nia was with Clay and lost sight of her determination to keep him and her attraction to him at bay.

"When I'm *not* with him I start to think of all I'd be giving up to live on a small ranch in the middle of nowhere," Trina said.

"Except that you wouldn't be in the middle of nowhere. Cole's ranch is fifteen minutes outside of town."

"A town with less than two thousand people in it—none of them really my friends or family—and without a single shopping mall," Trina countered.

Nia couldn't dispute Trina's concerns, so instead she attempted to throw some light on the second hole she could see in her sister's reasoning. "And you know, you have your own money, your own trust fund. Maybe you wouldn't be living in this house itself—although I don't know why you couldn't do that if you wanted to. But you could afford to build whatever kind of house you wanted on Cole's land, assuming the two of you got married or whatever. It isn't as if you'd be abdicating the throne to have a future with him."

"But would he resent that the money came from me and not him?"

"That I can't tell you," Nia said. "Do you think it would injure Cole's pride somehow?"

Trina considered it. "I just don't know. There's that whole male ego thing. I know he absolutely wouldn't accept financial help from Clay when he wanted to buy his own place, even though Clay offered."

"So it would have to be handled sensitively."

"If even that would help."

"It might help that he cares about you and wants you to be happy. To have what you want."

"It might," Trina conceded, but clearly with continuing reservations.

"But what if all your concerns could be handled sensitively and worked out and you could have a beautiful home of your own out on Cole's ranch? *Then* would it be what you want?"

Nia could tell her sister remained conflicted.

"Just between you and me?" Trina confided. "I'm afraid I might still want Cole in an Italian suit behind a desk in Denver."

Nia couldn't help laughing slightly at that. "Sounded more to me a minute ago like you want Cole *out* of even his jeans and cowboy boots. And definitely not behind a desk anywhere."

Trina couldn't suppress a smile, it seemed. "But what if that's just the hormones?"

"Or what if that's because it's just Cole you want?"

"I know. It's hard to sort out. If only there was more time to do it."

Nia couldn't provide that, so simply nodded in commiseration.

Then Trina got back to what had begun the conversation in the first place. "Tonight," she said, to remind them both. "I think I'm going to leave after the ceremony and go out to Cole's place. And I may not be home until tomorrow sometime."

"Okay."

Trina must have heard the lack of enthusiasm in Nia's voice because she said, "I know, maybe it isn't smart to sleep with him again. But you just can't imagine how it is when I'm with him…."

Nia could not only imagine it, she was relatively sure she was experiencing the same thing with his brother. But she was trying to fight her own inclinations in that direction when it came to Clay, and she wasn't convinced her sister shouldn't be waging the same battle.

"I'm just worried," Nia said, "that if you don't come to the conclusion that you want to be with Cole for the long haul, sleeping with him again will only confuse things even more."

"I know. I've thought of that, too. But on the other hand," Trina countered, "not only do I *want* to sleep with him, I thought it was something I should experience again to factor into my decision. I mean, what if I'm remembering it better than it actually was? And then I tell him about the baby and we try to make things work out together and I realize sex with him wasn't so great, after all?"

"I guess there is that."

"Besides, he's been after me to spend some time at his ranch. I think it's sort of a test run for him, too, to see if I like it or hate it, because I know he doesn't want someone who hates it."

Nia weighed whether or not to tell her sister what she'd learned the night before about Cole's past relationship. But Clay hadn't told her any of it in confidence, so she said, "Do you know about Cole's past with a woman named Marilou?"

"He just told me yesterday," Trina said.

"And did he tell you why she wouldn't marry him?"

"That she thought she'd be settling for less than the best? He told me. I know—it's not much different from what I've been worrying about. I feel guilty for that. But it isn't as if I don't know Cole is a great guy. He is. It's me I'm worried about. Me in the long run. And if I can adjust to downsizing to Elk Creek. So I think it's good for me to try out the whole ranch thing a little. Maybe I'll love it. Maybe I'll like waking up to the sound of a rooster crowing instead of an alarm clock."

Nia thought she'd keep her fingers crossed that that proved to be the case. But the topic brought up another concern. "What about your morning sickness?"

"I'm hoping I'll get lucky the way I did today and I won't have it."

Clearly, Trina wasn't going to be talked out of this idea. And Nia wasn't altogether sure she should be. Especially when there was the chance that making love with Cole again and seeing what it was really like to live his life might sway her in his direction.

"I suppose you should have as much of the whole picture as you can before you make your decision," Nia said, hoping they both weren't just rationalizing.

"So you don't mind if I leave you right after the unveiling?" Trina asked.

"No. In fact, Clay wanted me to have dinner with him."

Something about that made Trina grin.

"To go over what's in the journals," Nia qualified, unable to keep a somewhat ominous note out of her voice.

But Trina continued grinning. "I saw you kiss him good-night yesterday."

"You did? How?"

"I went into the kitchen for movie goodies and there you were—at the door, in a clinch. Not a really hot clinch, but a clinch."

"It was just a good-night kiss. Nothing, really," Nia said, downplaying it.

"It's okay," Trina replied. "After I saw the two of you last night I thought about it, and I think I have to accept that my little teenage romance with Clay was not as monumental as I've been making it in my mind. I was grasping at straws when I came back here looking for him before."

But Trina *had* come back here looking for him, Nia thought, knowing that was something she couldn't forget. Any more than she could lose sight of the fact that had things been different, had Clay been in town, he might be the father of Trina's baby now rather than Cole….

Trina was still speaking, though, and Nia made herself concentrate on it.

"…with everything that's going on with Cole, it isn't as if I have any kind of claim on Clay or anything. He's free. You're free. Why shouldn't the two of you get together? It's great."

Nia wasn't too sure she believed those were her sister's honest sentiments.

"The two of us aren't getting together," she said. "That isn't what I want."

"Why not?"

"It just isn't."

"Well, if it turns out to be, it's all right with me. I just wanted you to know."

That sounded more genuine, but it still didn't change Nia's views when it came to Clay. And even if a relationship with him had half a chance, that half was reduced further when she glanced down at the journals and recalled what she'd just read in them.

"I think you should just concentrate on yourself and Cole and things between the two of you."

"I am," Trina assured her. "And you can concentrate on yourself and Clay—if that's what you want."

"It isn't," Nia insisted. Although knowing now that Trina and Cole had discussed Cole's past, Nia couldn't help wondering how much of Trina's past Cole knew. And could pass along to Clay.

"Did you tell Cole about Drew?" Nia asked her sister.

"I told him about Drew when I was here before."

"Everything?"

"Everything at the end. Not anything about our getting together. I was too embarrassed to admit that to him. I didn't want him to think badly of me." Trina paused as the source of Nia's question apparently sank in. "So there's no way Clay knows about—"

"I was just curious. It doesn't matter."

Trina again smiled knowingly. "I think Clay matters more to you than you want to admit. To me or to yourself." She got up from the table then, putting an end to their conversation. "I better pack a few things," she announced.

"If you wake up sick tomorrow morning and want me to come out to the ranch to get you, just call."

"Keep your fingers crossed that I feel as good tomorrow morning as I did today, okay?" Trina said, heading out of the kitchen and leaving Nia alone with the journals once more.

And that was enough to return her thoughts to what she'd discovered in them. What had been preoccupying her so intensely that she hadn't heard Trina's initial entrance into the kitchen.

The journals.

The journals that had revealed to Nia a secret her aunt had gone to great, great lengths to keep quiet.

Such lengths that Nia knew Phoebe would never want it revealed. Even now. A secret Phoebe had believed so strongly would bring shame and embarrassment to their family that she'd sacrificed more than anyone had ever known.

A secret Nia now felt she needed to keep. From Clay and from everyone else. For Phoebe's sake.

But Nia knew keeping that secret wasn't going to make Clay happy.

Not one bit.

"I hear you're all mine tonight." The words were only half-teasing, delivered in a deep, quiet voice from behind Nia.

Moments before, Elk Creek's mayor had expressed to her his hope that she approved of the statue unveiled at the ceremony that had ended an hour ago. Nia had smiled and chatted appropriately, thanking him and the community for the fine tribute to her family.

The man who spoke now was so close to her ear that his breath heated her skin and her entire back absorbed a whole other kind of warmth. A sensual warmth emanating from a big, masculine body.

And Nia couldn't refrain from smiling even though he was still out of her line of vision.

"I think you must be mistaken," she answered with mock outrage at the audacity of the claim he'd made on her.

Clay stepped from behind her then, his lopsided grin confident. "Nope. The deal was if my brother whisked away your sister tonight, you'd have dinner with me. And the whisking is under way," he said with a nod toward the courthouse entrance, where Cole was holding the door open for Trina. "So you're all mine."

Much too tantalizing an idea. Nia tamped down her thoughts and said, "Not necessarily."

"Oh, I don't know. Feels pretty necessary to me."

She laughed. But since her pulse was racing at breakneck speed just over their banter, she decided it was better to cool things off.

With that as her goal, she angled her gaze at the bronze statue in the center of the courthouse lobby and said, "What's your verdict?"

The statue depicted Hyram Heller perched tall and proud on the back of a horse, looking outward as if surveying all he would build, and Horatio Molner sitting equally tall and proud behind a desk, facing a different direction, just as their visions of Elk Creek had differed. But Clay didn't take his eyes off her to glance at it.

"The statue is nice, but I prefer this view. It's been catching my eye all night."

Heller charm. It had just the right mixture of humor and mischief to save it from being arrogant. And to make it all the more disarming.

"You look very city-girl chic," he added then.

Nia had worn a pantsuit she'd bought for her last trip to New York—a plum-colored crepe with straight-leg slacks and a funnel collar jacket that formed a V neckline before eight tiny buttons closed it down the front. Both the pants and the jacket had been altered to fit her every curve, and although she hadn't wanted to consider that—or the fact that Clay would see how it fit every curve—it *had* been on her mind when she'd dressed for the evening.

"City-girl chic?" she repeated. "Around here anything *city-girl* isn't automatically a good thing, so I can't tell if that's a compliment or not."

"Definitely a compliment," he said, letting his eyes wander all the way to the tips of her pointy shoes and back again to her face, so carefully made up with light, natural-looking cosmetics, and to her hair, caught on both sides with matching combs.

"You seem to have left behind your cowboy duds for the occasion, too," she observed, as if just noticing the fact, when in truth she'd stolen every chance she could to look at him since he'd arrived with Cole.

Clay had on a striped charcoal suit that Nia was sure had been handmade especially for him, a dove-gray shirt and a cranberry tie.

But her comment only made him flash a devilish smile and point one long index finger at the floor, where she discovered he was wearing cowboy boots.

She couldn't help laughing a second time. "Not what your tailor had in mind, I'd bet."

"Can't take the country out of the boy," he decreed. And then he returned to the discussion about their evening plans. "So, are we on for dinner? Because Margie Wilson's Café is our only choice and it's closing in about twenty minutes. If we leave now we can just get in under the wire."

"I am a little hungry," Nia admitted, as if that was the sole reason she was agreeing, when she'd actually spent most of the time during the unveiling speeches thinking about nothing but having dinner with Clay afterward.

"Let's go then," he urged, motioning toward the exit and waiting for her to precede him.

Nia did just that, making her way through what remained of the crowd until she and Clay were outside the courthouse in the pleasantly cool air.

"Did you drive?" he asked then.

"I did. Trina didn't feel like walking."

"I drove, too, I was in too much of a rush to walk. But since it's so nice tonight, what do you say we leg it over to the diner and back again later to get our cars?"

"Okay."

They weren't the only ones making the pilgrimage to Elk Creek's only family restaurant. Linc and Kansas Heller, Kansas's sister, Della, and her husband, Yance Culhane, and two of the McDermot brothers, Ry and Matt, and their wives, Tallie and Jenn, were heading in that direction, too. And even though they weren't going as a group, they all chatted as they walked, primarily about the mayor's long-windedness.

When they reached the café it was still about half-full, but despite the fact that it was so near to closing time, Maya and her mother welcomed them inside before flipping the sign in the window to Closed.

Most of the new arrivals pushed tables together to continue their discussion about the evening's events, but Clay subtly maneuvered Nia to a corner table where they could be alone.

Nia had a brief catching-up conversation with Maya, who surprised even Clay with the news that she was pregnant. Then orders were placed and food was served without delay—Margie Wilson's secret chicken salad sandwich for Nia and the house specialty, elk steak, for Clay. And finally they had some time to themselves.

Time Nia used to pull from her purse several sheets of paper, sliding them across the table to him.

"I don't know what this is, but it doesn't look like the next stack of journals for me to read," he stated.

"It's relevant excerpts from them."

"Relevant excerpts?"

"I've saved you having to read what you couldn't use, anyway, by making copies of what will finish out the supplements."

"What I *couldn't* use."

Nia pretended to scan the room. "Is there an echo in here?"

Clay ignored that question and asked one of his own. "What are you bringing me that I *can* use?"

"What Phoebe wrote about what happened between Hyram and Horatio after Maude and Jacob broke up. Things were never the same for the two fathers. There wasn't a family feud or anything, but the friendship suffered irreparable damage. They were barely civil to each other when they had to show up at the same town meetings and functions. They were never again on the same side of any issue or decision, and if they met on the street they didn't speak. But actually, their animosity helped the economy in some ways."

"How?" Clay asked.

"When one of them wanted a building or a piece of property, the other always put in a bid, too, hiking up the price. Not only did they end up pouring a lot of money into the town just out of spite, but—for instance—your cousin's wife, Kansas? Her family owned the land my family's house sits on now. They decided to sell it to build a small mercantile store, and by the time Horatio and Hyram were finished, Horatio paid about three times what the land was worth then. It allowed Kansas's family to build bigger than they'd originally thought they'd be able to, and a bigger general store was a benefit to the existing community and to town growth," Nia concluded. "I thought it made for a good ending to the supplements."

Clay's blue eyes bored into her for a moment and Nia took refuge in her sandwich, waiting for what she knew was to come.

"What about Phoebe catching Arlen kissing Maude? What came of that?"

"Nothing that had any effect on Elk Creek, so nothing that was relevant."

Clay's mouth stretched into a slow smile. "There's that word again—relevant."

"Worth repeating because it applies. You wanted the supplements to chronicle the growth of Elk Creek through Phoebe's journals. You added the romance between Maude and Jacob because they were the offspring of the founding fathers. You took it up to the point where Maude and Jacob ended their engagement. This ties it up by telling the story of what happened between the founding fathers after that and how it affected the town. Seems neat and tidy to me."

"But not as interesting as what must be in the rest of those journals."

Nia had had enough to eat and pushed her plate away.

"Are you honestly not even going to tell me what happened to Phoebe, Maude and Arlen?" Clay asked.

"And risk you publishing it? I don't think so."

"Oh, this must be good," he said with a laugh, pushing his empty plate away, too.

"Phoebe just made the best of a bad situation," Nia said truthfully.

"Did she ignore the kiss? Pretend it never happened? Have it out with Arlen and get him to promise never to do it again? Get into a catfight with Maude?"

"Even if any of that had happened, how would it be applicable to Founder's Day?" Nia reasoned.

"Human interest—the same reason I got you to agree to let me use the whole Phoebe-Arlen-Maude-Jacob romance element in the first place."

"Which you did, and it carried you through to a natural conclusion. One sister's husband kissing another sister is an ugly skeleton in the closet that doesn't need to come to light."

"Was that all it was—one kiss and nothing else?"

Nia rolled her eyes and then tried another small morsel of truth in an attempt to get him to drop it. "Maude left Elk Creek not long after that, and by a year later had moved to London, England, where she lived the rest of her life, as you know. Seriously, there just wasn't anything else that would have worked in the supplements."

"Then why not bring the journals to me and let me see for myself?"

"I know you're crunched for time."

"I'd be willing to stay up tonight and flip through them."

He was challenging her and Nia knew it. But she held her ground. "They're already put away. You got what you wanted out of them. Why would you want to lose a night's sleep going over material you can't use anyway?"

"Material I can't use because you won't let me."

"Tell me I'm wrong, that the breakup and subsequent dissension between Horatio and Hyram doesn't tie it all up perfectly," she said, trying a challenge of her own.

"You're not wrong," Clay admitted with a megawatt smile that showed how much he was enjoying their debate. "But *I* want to know the rest."

"But what *you* know everyone else might end up knowing."

"And it's such a deep, dark, ugly secret you can't take that risk," he added, making it sound very melodramatic.

"Exactly," Nia said facetiously, hoping that would convince him he was making something out of nothing. When he wasn't.

"It'll drive me crazy not knowing."

"Don't let it," she advised.

"So crazy I may have to dig up the information somewhere else," he warned.

"Where else *would* you dig it up?"

Clay merely smiled, as if he had an ace in the hole.

But Nia thought he was bluffing and called him on it. "Go ahead and dig. There's nothing to find out, anyway. Phoebe saw Arlen and Maude kiss, she was hurt but didn't let it destroy her marriage. Maude moved to England. Phoebe and Arlen stayed married until his death, living and working right here in Elk Creek for all to see."

Clay didn't say anything for a long moment, studying her, maybe hoping to make her uncomfortable enough to confess that there was more and spill it.

When it became clear he was going to keep her on the hot seat with his scrutiny, she glanced around and said, "Everyone else is gone. Maya and her mother could probably go home if we got out of here."

Clay chuckled as if conceding the loss of the battle, but not necessarily the loss of the war. "Guess we'd better go then."

He settled the bill with Margie while Nia chatted for a few more minutes with Maya. As mother and daughter walked them to the door and locked up, Clay's cell phone rang.

"I'm sorry, I thought I'd turned this thing off," he muttered, taking it out of his suitcoat pocket and checking the display. "It's only Cole."

"Answer it," Nia urged. "It might be something about Trina. Maybe she's looking for me. She might need something."

Clay did as he was told. "Hey," he said into the

phone a split second later. Then, after a moment of listening to his brother, he said, "Sure. I just need help moving the copy machine. I only said morning because I thought you could drop by on your way to the Molner house. But noon is fine—we can do it and then I'll buy you lunch as payment." Another pause. "Yeah. See you then."

Off went the phone, and Clay dropped it back into his pocket. "It wasn't anything about Trina," he informed Nia.

Except that Cole was making arrangements not to leave Trina too early in the morning, Nia thought. But she didn't say that.

She did, however, know what Clay was thinking as they headed down Center Street—that she was again being overly concerned with her sister. To get him off that track before he tried to explore it as he had on other occasions, she said, "So last night you told me about Cole's love life and you're obviously obsessed with the love lives of my great-aunts, but what about yours?"

Her goading tone did the trick and made him laugh. "*Obsessed?* You think I'm obsessed with other people's love lives?"

"Well, I haven't seen you peeking voyeuristically in bedroom windows or anything, but…" She let the sentence trail off.

"I beg your pardon," he said with another laugh.

"Come on, what's the scoop on you? Would it make a good human interest story?"

"Nah. It'd be boring copy."

"Okay then, bore me," Nia commanded. "For instance, have you ever been close to getting married?"

"Eight…no, nine times."

"Nine times?"

Her gullibility amused him. "Okay, okay, I've gotten more than close to getting married. I actually did it."

"Right—eight or nine times?" she said, thinking he was still kidding. With his looks, money and cosmopolitan lifestyle, marriage just didn't seem to fit.

"Really," he said, his tone more serious. "I was married. For about two years. I've been divorced for a year and a half."

"Were you married to someone from here? To anyone I'd know?"

"No to both questions. Shayna was a Texas girl. From Austin. She worked for me. Until we got married."

"What did she do?"

"She was the best executive assistant I've ever had."

"But she wasn't the best wife?" Nia guessed.

"To tell you the truth, she was too good."

At the end of Center Street where it looped around the park square Clay paused. "Shall we cut through or walk around?" he asked.

The temperature had dropped since they'd left the courthouse, and it was considerably farther to walk around than to cut through, but now that Nia had him talking about his past, she didn't want the abbreviated version. So she said, "Around. Unless—"

"I'm up for going around," he agreed.

As they headed that way, Nia returned to the subject of his marriage, hoping now that he'd begun to talk about it, he wouldn't have any qualms about continuing. "How was your wife too good?" she asked.

Clay didn't hesitate. "What made her a great assistant was that she anticipated my every need and dedicated herself to taking impeccable care of them all—" he looked at Nia from the corner of his eye "—and I don't mean my personal needs, if that's what you're thinking."

"Then you shouldn't have made it sound like that," Nia reprimanded jokingly.

"Everything was aboveboard—even though I was attracted to her—until she let herself be hired away by someone else. When she put in her notice she told me she was resigning because she was interested in me as more than a boss."

"Brazen hussy," Nia said to lighten the tone, since it was growing increasingly somber.

"It was pretty brave of her, since I'd been careful not to make even a hint of an overture to her. With sexual harassment issues the way they are, I knew better," he said, the serious note in his voice successfully tempered by the humor of her comment.

"Did she ask you out on the spot?"

"We talked about it, but she'd given me two weeks notice and we agreed not to start anything until she was on the other guy's payroll."

"But once she was…"

"Once she was, we started to date, and got married six months after that. When we did she said she didn't want to work anymore. I was okay with that. It wasn't as if we needed the income, and I wanted her to be happy."

"But she wasn't?"

"Oh, she was happy. For a while. Happy devoting her whole life, every minute of every day and night, to me."

Nia glanced at his striking profile. "That was a problem?"

"I know, it sounds like it shouldn't have been. And maybe for some guys it would be great. But what had worked so well at the office just didn't translate at home. I didn't want a handmaiden. I didn't *need* one—and that was a very big deal that I didn't anticipate."

"You've lost me."

"I didn't realize that part of why Shayna was so terrific at her job was that she *needed* to be needed. And at work I did need her. I needed a right-hand man—or woman—and she was it. In spades. But at home, I didn't have to have someone setting my alarm and laying out my clothes and my shaving gear and toothbrush so they were ready in the morning. I didn't have to have someone reminding me I should leave for the office in ten minutes, and checking the weather and road conditions to make sure I had an umbrella and took the most uncomplicated route to work. I didn't have to have lunch recommendations waiting on my desk when I got there, or reminders that the last time

I ate chili I'd put too much hot sauce on it—" Clay cut himself off, but by then his frustration was ringing loud and clear.

"This probably sounds petty," he said under his breath.

"Actually, it sounds kind of suffocating."

"That's exactly what it was," he agreed, seeming relieved that she understood what he was saying. "It was like we got married and all of a sudden she wanted me to revert to being a child so she could mother me. To death."

"You don't mean that literally?"

"No, of course not. She wasn't dangerous. Shayna is a kind, loving, caring woman. But like I said, she needs to be needed. In the extreme. And not only did I end up feeling suffocated, she ended up feeling unfulfilled and hurt because I balked at what was going on between us."

He paused for a moment and Nia wasn't sure he was going to finish what he'd been about to say.

Then, after another moment, he did.

"Shayna ended up finding someone else, who did need her."

He added that last part quietly, and while it seemed logical that the revelation had come out of pain, it was more as if it had come out of guilt.

"She cheated on you?" Nia asked gingerly, unable to mask her own surprise at the revelation that seemed uncharacteristic of someone who had poured herself into her marriage.

"She did, but it was my fault."

"How could it have been your fault?"

"At first I tried just telling her that she could relax, that she was my life partner, not my life assistant. Then I tried asking her flat-out not to do this or that. When nothing else worked, I even bought her a puppy, hoping that if she had something else to take care of, she might ease up on me a little…"

"What about kids? It seems as though she would have wanted a houseful of them to mother."

"You'd think, wouldn't you? But she didn't. Which, in hindsight, is probably a good thing, because I was so desperate I might have suggested it. But she didn't want any kids at all. She said she just wanted to focus on *her man*."

"And the puppy didn't provide a distraction?"

"No. So…I don't know. Little by little I just started…withdrawing. I stayed at work longer because it felt like the only place I could breathe. I traveled even more, and when I did, I padded the number of days I was gone. Or I piggybacked trips and went from city to city without coming home in between. And without giving in to her requests that I bring her along. Eventually, she got lonely and that need to be needed became *really* frustrated. I guess it stands to reason that she found someone else to fill the gap. Or someone else's gap for her to fill, you might say," he concluded.

"Did you know the guy?"

"Not personally. But I knew *of* him. She left me for her second boss."

"The man she'd gone to work for when she'd stopped being your assistant so you could date?"

"Yep. She'd apparently made the right switch because he not only liked her as an assistant, he married her and, as I understand it, loves having her undivided attention."

"So everything worked out for the best," Nia said, again trying to highlight the brighter side.

"It did work out for the best," Clay acknowledged. "But no one wants a failed marriage on their record."

"When things aren't right, they just aren't right."

"True," he conceded. Then he glanced over at her and smiled. "And how can I be having a good time talking about this, of all things?"

"Maybe it has to do with being out in the open and releasing old demons into the ozone," Nia joked, because she wasn't sure how else to respond.

"Or maybe it's the company and that's why I can't help coming back for more again and again."

They'd returned to the courthouse and headed into the parking lot, where their cars were the only two left. As they approached Nia's sedan Clay said, "What about your love life? Any blots on it or demons you want to release into the ozone?"

"Oh, it's too late to get into *that*," she said.

"You're just blocking me at every turn tonight, aren't you?"

Nia answered with only a smile.

He didn't seem to mind her nonverbal response because he just looked amused. "What about tomorrow night?" he asked when they reached her car.

Nia was suddenly not eager to end their time together, and rather than opening her door, she turned her back to it and faced Clay. "I don't know that I'll want to tell you about my love life demons tomorrow night, either. It's liable to end up in your newspaper."

"So it must be another meaty Molner love story?"

Nia shook her head. "I just don't want any more Molner love stories entertaining Elk Creek over morning coffee."

Clay was standing close in front of her, his big body providing enough heat to chase away the spring chill. She tried not to think about how much she liked having him there as she gazed up into his handsome face, lit by the glow of the parking lot and courthouse lights.

"Actually, when I said how about tomorrow night I wasn't lookin' for a story," he explained.

"What were you *lookin'* for?" she asked, teasing him by mimicking the way he shortened words every now and again.

He wasn't phased by her jest at his expense because he repeated it. "I was *lookin'* for a date to the banquet tomorrow night. I'm feelin' a little cut off from you since you banned me from the journals, and I can't say I'm ready for that," he confided, almost as if he were reluctant to feel the way he did, let alone admit it.

His confession warmed her even more. From the inside out this time.

"So what do you say?" he persisted. "Will you let me take you to the banquet?"

She wanted to leap right in and say yes. Yes! Yes! Yes!

But she hesitated as an internal voice warned her she shouldn't, that she was supposed to be keeping this man at a distance. And that at that moment not only wasn't he even an arm's length away, he was asking her on a genuine, straightforward, no excuses or pretenses date.

"Come on," he urged in a deep, enticing voice. "Abandon your charge. Neglect your sisterly duties. Go out on a limb—"

"I get the idea," Nia said with a laugh. Clay obviously misinterpreted her hesitation and apparently thought Trina was the reason for it.

"Just say yes," he added anyway. "Besides, odds are highly in favor of Trina going with Cole."

That was true. And then either Nia would be left to go alone or Trina would feel she had to turn down Cole so Nia wouldn't have to. The last thing Nia wanted was to be an obstacle to them spending time together, getting to know each other and eventually making a home for their baby….

A domino effect.

Nia knew she was rationalizing. But it provided just the impetus she needed to give in. When giving in was such an appealing thought.

"Okay," she heard herself say.

Her answer surprised them both. Clay's eyebrows

arched even as he smiled down at her. "Okay? No kidding? You're saying okay without checking with Trina first, or putting me off just in case she might not approve, or making stipulations for a bail clause if Trina has plans for you?"

"Have I been that bad?" Nia asked.

"Not bad, just awfully accommodating of your sister."

She shrugged. "I think you're right and she'll go with Cole, so I should be free."

"To go with me," Clay finished for her.

"To go with you," she confirmed, even as that voice of caution warned her again that she shouldn't.

But the week was coming to an end, and within a few days she'd be leaving Elk Creek, returning to Denver and rarely if ever seeing Clay again. So what harm could there really be in going to an event with him that most of the town would be attending? It wasn't a big deal unless she made it one. And she wouldn't. She'd merely treat it like what it was—a nice invitation by one of Elk Creek's most prominent citizens to escort a visitor to a community event.

And it pleased him, because there he was with that ruggedly handsome face, smiling down at her once more.

"Great," he murmured.

Either of them could have said good-night then and put an end to the evening. But neither did. Instead they stayed like that, his intense eyes peering into hers for a moment longer before he leaned forward with slow intent and kissed her.

It had happened twice before, so there was a cer-

tain amount of pleasant familiarity to it, and yet there
was so much more to it, too. His lips were parted right
from the start and hers were relaxed, as well, but
tonight his arms came around her to pull her to him.
To envelop her in the warmth of his body, as one big
hand cradled her head so he could deepen the kiss.

His lips didn't stay only slightly parted tonight.
They opened more, coaxing hers to, as well, to make
way for his tongue when it came to test the waters.

By then the waters were just fine. Nia's eyes were
closed, her own hands were flat against the hard wall
of Clay's chest, and her head was a bit dizzy from the
clean scent of his cologne and the intoxication of that
kiss, of being held in those arms. The waters were fine
enough for her to meet the tip of his tongue with her
own. To invite him all the way in to frolic and play a
sensuous little game of cat and mouse.

Mouths opened wider still and tongues grew braver,
more demanding, as Clay held her even closer, pressing her backward at the same time so that she was
against the car, pinned between the sedan and the man.
But in a good way. A *very* good way.

Her breasts were flattened against his chest, and her
nipples hardened in response.

While one of his hands remained supporting her
head, the other hand was splayed against her back, and
she could feel the strength in them both. A strength that
inspired in Nia a growing craving to have them on her
breasts. To have them unfasten the buttons of her top
and find their way inside. To have them unhook her bra

and mold themselves to her, cup her and caress her and learn every contour….

But even as that craving became ever more demanding, she suddenly remembered where they were. Out in the open, in the courthouse parking lot. Like two teenagers after a civics club meeting. And anyone in town could walk or drive by and see them.

Clay didn't seem to have the same qualms, because even after she'd eased out of that kiss he dropped lower and continued kissing the hollow of her throat exposed by her funnel-necked jacket.

"Isn't there an ordinance against public displays of affection in a place like Elk Creek?" she joked in a voice raw with all he'd aroused in her.

"Probably," Clay answered, as if he couldn't care less, flicking his tongue against her skin and electrifying her nerve endings.

"You'll have to report the story if we get arrested," she warned, undermining the conviction in her own tone by letting her head fall even farther back to allow him free access to her arched neck.

"It might be worth it," he said, in a voice as husky as hers was raw.

Still, they were in the *parking lot,* and now that that was uppermost in her mind, she couldn't lose sight of it. Or of how they really couldn't go on with this. No matter how much she might want to…

"And isn't that window on the side of the building part of the sheriff's office?" she pointed out.

Clay groaned with that reminder, but finally

stopped kissing her, rising up to look at her again and sighing before he smiled a deliciously evil smile. Then he aimed his chin toward the rear of the courthouse. "We could go in back," he suggested, with a lascivious inflection to his whisper.

Nia laughed. "I don't think so."

"Damn," he muttered, clearly aware that she never would have agreed, anyway.

Then he kissed her again, more like he had the night before, and let her go, stepping far enough back so she could open her car door.

"One last chance," he said, casting another glance at the rear of the courthouse.

"Sorry," she murmured.

"Okay, then how about one last chance to tell me what was in Phoebe's journals so I can get it into the Founder's Day supplement?" he suggested, stretching that evil smile into a full-fledged grin.

"Sorry on that count, too," Nia said, laughing as she slipped behind the wheel and started her engine.

"I think you probably will be. Sorry, I mean," he predicted sagely.

"For which? Not going behind the courthouse or not telling you what was in Phoebe's journal?"

"Both," he said emphatically, making her laugh.

"I'll just have to risk it."

"If you change your mind give me a call. Even if it's hours from now."

"If I change my mind about going behind the courthouse or about telling you what's in the journals?"

"Either one."

"I'll give it serious consideration," she said facetiously.

"Good," he declared, as if she'd meant it.

"Good night, Clay," she said then.

"'Night, Nia," he countered, closing her door.

Then he took another step back so she could pull away, staying there to watch her as she drove off.

But even as she did, even as she left the parking lot and lost sight of him in her rearview mirror, Nia was still thinking about the kiss that could very well have gotten her into trouble. Trouble greater than any repercussions for being caught doing it out in the open.

Because it had probably been kisses like that that had gotten her great-aunts into such a mess so long ago....

Chapter 7

"Sorry this had to be a fast-food lunch," Clay said to his brother. They were each carrying a tray of hamburgers, french fries and drinks to a hard-seated booth at the local Dairy King the next day, after Cole helped Clay move the copier at his office. "Some payment for hard labor, huh?"

"I'm fine with burgers," Cole assured him. "What time do you have to be over at Jackson's place?"

"I have about an hour."

"And he's flyin' you in the helicopter to Cheyenne to see the old man?"

"Right. Want to come?" Clay asked, since the "old man" Cole referred to was their grandfather.

"I would, but I need to work this afternoon. Say hey for me, though."

"Will do," Clay assured him, as they both set out their lunches.

"You're hopin' you can get him to remember something about what went on between Jacob and Maude Molner?" Cole asked, just before taking a bite of his first double cheeseburger.

"Sort of," Clay said. He hadn't told anyone that he and Nia had discovered Maude Molner had kissed her sister's husband, because he wasn't sure whether or not he was going to print that information. Until he made a decision, he was just letting what was in the supplements speak for him. This morning's had taken the relationship between Maude Molner and Jacob Heller to the breaking point.

"What made you decide to talk to the old man, after all? I read the paper this morning. Seemed like you had the whole story. What else do you want to know?"

"I just have a couple of questions," Clay said, not wanting to go into the tussle he and Nia were engaged in over her withholding the remainder of the diaries and the information they contained. He didn't want to give Cole any indication of how much he was enjoying even tussling with Nia. How much he was enjoying—and liking—everything about Nia. How much he was enjoying her, and thinking about her all the time, and wanting to be with her. How much he wanted to be with her every waking moment because he found her stimulating. And beautiful. And funny. And sexy beyond belief.

"Well, good luck gettin' the old guy to tell you anything," Cole said.

For a split second Clay wasn't sure what his brother was talking about—that's how far and fast his mind had wandered to Nia. But then he realized that it was his and Cole's grandfather they were discussing. That Cole was wishing him luck with the old man's lucidity.

"Thanks, I'll probably need it," Clay said. Then he changed the subject.

"How'd last night go with Trina? Must have been pretty good if you weren't figuring on getting out till noon."

"It kind of surprised me that she was willin' to stay the night. I think it was sort of an experiment to see if she could stand my place."

Clay washed down a fry with a drink of soda. "What makes you say that?" he asked, grateful for the chance to focus on his brother's relationship with Trina to keep his own head out of the Nia-cloud.

"Just a feelin' I had. She was checkin' the place out. Seemed like she was making a pro-and-con list in her head."

"Yeah? How do you think you did?"

"Me, personally?" Cole asked with a cocky, telling grin. "I did great."

Clay laughed. "So that goes in the pro column. What went in the con?"

"I'm not sure. I built her a fire in the fireplace and we sat in front of it talkin' and…well, you know. Anyway, she said it was cozy and she liked it there, and I thought that was good. But then she woke up kind of sick this mornin' and I was in shavin' and she freaked out a little that there was only one bathroom."

"Sick?"

"Yeah, man, she was white as a ghost, couldn't even stand the idea of toast or crackers, needed the bathroom in a hurry. She was in bad shape. But it was goin' away by the time her sister came out to get her."

A couple of questions popped up in Clay's mind at his brother's words, causing Clay to stop eating and sort through them. "She was feelin' all right last night?"

"*Late* last night. We didn't end up gettin' to sleep until about four."

"And she was okay then?"

"Better than okay," Cole confirmed with another of those pleased-with-himself smiles.

"And after a few hours sleep, she woke up sick?"

"Right."

"And why did her sister come out to get her?"

"I wondered the same thing," Cole said. "I told her if she wanted to get home, I'd take her. And it would have been quicker. But, I don't know, maybe things are just still too new between us and she didn't want me seein' her that sick. She seemed a little panicky, said she just needed Nia to pick her up."

"And of course Nia came running."

"Sure. But it still would have been faster for me to have taken Trina home. Plus I was goin' there anyway, to work."

"And then Trina got well?" Clay asked.

"By the time her sister got there Trina had stopped runnin' for the bathroom. And I was at the Molner house about half an hour after Nia picked her up, and Trina was fine. It was just like she hadn't been sick at all."

"You didn't feed her any of those leftovers you like to keep around until they grow fur, did you?"

"Nah. She's been real finicky about what she eats since she's been here. She says food's been tastin' funny to her. Smells bother her, too—I had a scrap of cedar wood I tossed on the fire last night and she hated it so much we had to sit on the porch until it'd burned away and the place was aired out."

"Huh."

"What?" Cole asked as he polished off his first burger and started on his second.

"It all seems a little strange," Clay observed.

"Strange how?"

Clay shrugged, telling himself that what he was thinking was far-fetched and overly suspicious. But still he said, "How long ago was it that Trina was here last?"

Cole took a drink of malt. "I don't know. Six, seven weeks, I guess. How long ago were you in Chicago?"

"'Bout that. And you, uh, did *great,* then, too?"

"Yeah. I told you," Cole said a touch defensively.

"I'm just tryin' to get the whole picture," Clay answered. "And when you did, uh, *great* six or seven weeks ago, you used something, right?"

He saw light dawn in his brother's eyes. "You're not thinkin'—"

"I'm thinkin' that Nia said Trina was under the weather a couple of days ago, and then she was all of a sudden well again, too. But it could be just a coincidence. Or that she's fightin' off a bug of some kind that comes and goes."

"Or not," Cole said, frowning so fiercely deep creases appeared between his eyebrows. "Come to think of it, she's been weird about drinkin' alcohol this time around, too. Last time it was a bottle of wine that put us both over the edge, but she hasn't touched a drop since she's been here. And I had a bottle of her favorite chilled and ready to uncork last night."

"It's probably nothin'," Clay said.

"But what if it isn't nothin'?"

That wasn't a question Clay could answer for him, so he didn't try.

"You think that's why she's back?" Cole said then. "That's why she's tryin' so hard to like me? To adapt to the way I live? To *settle*?"

"Whoa!" Clay was quick to say. "I don't see that she's *trying* to like you. Looks to me like she definitely likes you. She spent the night with you last night, didn't she? And you both had a good time—"

"Yeah, but mine was genuine. Maybe hers was—"

"Come on," Clay urged. "You're jumpin' to all

kinds of conclusions when there might not be a single thing to any of it."

"Or there might be."

"But there probably isn't."

"That night six weeks ago—we, uh, didn't sleep much then, either. We started out safe, but used up all I had left in the box. We both knew we should have quit then, but you know how it is—things got out of control and we didn't. But last night…" Cole shook his head ominously. "She didn't bring up the issue at all. Not even for the first go-round. Like maybe it's already too late."

"Okay, so even if there is something to that part of it, that doesn't mean she's having to work at likin' you or tryin' to settle."

"That's what Marilou would have had to do if she'd turned up pregnant unexpectedly. She'd have had to try to resign herself to bein' stuck with somebody not up to her standards." Cole had apparently lost his appetite, because he pushed away his tray without finishing the rest of his food. "Damn."

"Look, I was just thinkin' out loud," Clay said, trying hard for damage control and wishing he'd kept his mouth shut. "Could be there's nothin' to any of it. Even if there is, you're crazy about Trina, right? And from what I've seen she shows all the signs of being crazy about you, too. If she is pregnant—and that's a very big if—it could be she's here testin' the waters with you, scared silly how you might react."

That seemed to help. But only slightly.

"She has been pretty edgy off and on," Cole conceded.

"But it still might be nothing," Clay insisted. "Why don't you just feel her out?"

Cole clamped his eyes shut and shook his head a second time at that choice of words.

Clay chuckled and amended what he'd said. "You know what I mean. Ask a few questions. Take a closer look. See what unfolds. Are the two of you going to the banquet tonight?"

Cole opened his eyes. "Actually, she suggested we just stay in. I know the banquet is in honor of the two founding fathers and their families, but she said Nia could represent the Molners, and I figured that since there'll be plenty of Hellers there, no one will miss me. She wants to come to my place again and bring a picnic supper she's havin' Fran fix, so we can be alone."

"I don't know about nobody missing you, but that sounds nice. And it's not as if she's really upset about having to spend time with you."

Cole didn't agree or disagree with that. He didn't say anything at all. But Clay noticed that all the color had drained from his brother's face.

"What if she is pregnant?" he asked, finding his own appetite suddenly gone. "Would you be okay with it?"

Cole's eyebrows arched high at the question. "I don't know," he confessed solemnly. "It's not something I've even thought about."

Clay nodded. "Well, just do some subtle digging. Don't borrow trouble if you don't have good cause."

Cole nodded as if he were taking the advice to heart. "Guess we're both off to do some diggin'," he said then.

"I guess we are," Clay agreed, silently reminding himself how complicated relationships could be and why he should be guarding against the intense pull he felt for Nia.

It was just that it would have been easier if that pull wasn't quite *so* intense.

When Nia dressed for Friday evening's banquet it was with the previous evening in mind. The *end* of the previous evening and the kiss she and Clay had shared.

That kiss, along with the two that had preceded it, should never have happened. And clearly, with each kiss having gotten increasingly hotter and hotter, she needed to put a stop to them. So prim and proper was what she was going for when she chose tonight's outfit. Prim and proper while still being dressy enough for the occasion that, though not formal, wasn't a jeans and T-shirt event the way the actual Founder's Day festivities on Saturday would be.

She didn't want to look dowdy, though, so despite the fact that she opted for a pair of black slacks and a long-sleeved white lace turtleneck that was fully lined for modesty's sake, both were formfitting and showed off every curve to the utmost.

When it came to makeup she applied only mascara and blush, and she merely brushed her hair, leaving it to fall free and unadorned around her shoulders.

She did wear a pair of sexy three-inch heels, but she didn't think the shoes were so sexy that they would negate the high neck, the sleeves whose scalloped edges reached an inch below her wrists, or the fact that, except for her face, hands and the top of her feet, she was showing no skin whatsoever.

Prim and proper.

"And no kissing tonight!" she ordered her reflection when she took one final look at herself in the mirror before leaving her room.

She'd purposely started getting ready a little early so that she finished with a few minutes to spare. A few minutes she had every intention of using to talk to Trina. Nia was worried about her. Not only had her sister been sick again this morning and called Nia to pick her up from Cole's house, but the minute Nia had pulled away from the front of the small home, her sister had burst into tears and sobbed inconsolably through the entire drive back to town.

Trina had refused to tell Nia what was wrong, had composed herself only moments before Cole had arrived to work on the remodel, and then she'd gone to bed for the remainder of the day with nothing but a mention to Nia that she and Cole were spending this evening at his place again rather than attending the banquet.

That was the last Nia had seen of her sister, and as she left her bedroom with every intention of going to Trina's to find out what had happened to cause her morning breakdown, she instead came face-to-face with her twin in the hall.

"You're finally up," Nia said in greeting. "I was beginning to think you'd gone into hibernation."

Trina's smile was weak and she was still slightly pale, but there weren't any other remnants of either her morning sickness or her morning distress.

"I was just coming to see you," she responded.

"How are you?"

"Fine. Now. You know how it is—one minute I want to die and then it's over for the day. I couldn't remember if I'd thanked you for coming out to Cole's to get me this morning or not, but I really appreciated it. I was so sick I didn't know if I could keep from throwing up in the car, and I didn't want to be with Cole if I did."

"I assumed it was something like that when you called. But then, when you were so upset on the way back, I wasn't sure," Nia said, getting to the heart of what had her the most concerned. She knew one or both of the Heller brothers could be arriving at any minute—Cole to pick up Trina, and Clay for her—and beating around the bush risked leaving her still not knowing what was going on or if her sister was all right.

Trina shrugged and looked forlorn. "I'm not too sure myself."

"Did Cole do something to hurt your feelings?"

"Oh, no," she answered quickly. "He couldn't have been nicer about my being sick. He was considerate and compassionate and he really cared. He gave the bathroom over to me and finished shaving in the kitchen, and he kept knocking on the door, asking if I needed anything or if there was anything he could do or get for me. He wanted to call the local doctor—he was jumping through hoops for me."

"So nothing bad happened between you two?"

"No. And nothing bad happened before I got sick, either."

"Were you just upset because you got sick again this morning after yesterday's reprieve? And in front of Cole?" Nia guessed.

"There was more to it than that. When he was being so sweet I started feeling guilty for lying to him about why I was sick, and then wondering if he'd be so sweet if he knew what was really making me sick and...I don't know, Nia. I was just a mess."

"And you're going back for a return engagement tonight?" Nia asked, confused.

"I guess I am," Trina confirmed with a laugh.

"Are you staying until morning again?"

Trina smiled. "Probably. I know I shouldn't. Especially when it could mean a repeat of today. And I'd like to say there's absolutely no way that I *will* stay. But I also know that I'm so weak when it comes to this guy. Last night was...wow! Better than it was the last time I was here. Better than I even remembered it."

"That's good," Nia said. "So maybe—"

"I still don't think I'm ready to tell him. Or make a decision—that was some of what had me crying in the car today. I mean, why can't I get off the fence about this? Why can't I make a decision? Cole is wonderful and I can't even begin to tell you how much I want him every minute we're together. So much I just can't stop myself. But then there I was in his bathroom this morning, considering telling him I'm pregnant, and I just couldn't do it."

"But you were leaning toward telling him?" Nia said hopefully, thinking that was at least a small step in the right direction.

"A little. Then I looked around at his old, dinky bathroom—the only one he has, and—"

Nia laughed. "So add another bathroom."

"I know it doesn't make sense," Trina said defensively. "*I* don't make sense. Even to me. But it wasn't only the…let's be kind and say *rustic* accommodations. I also started thinking what if I told him about the pregnancy and he hated it? Or hated me because of it? What if he felt trapped and said he wasn't ready for that in his life? What if he said it was one thing to have some fun together, but a *baby*? What if he said no thanks, and there I'd be, not knowing what to do, and…I told you, I was a mess."

"So are you going to spend another night out there trying to make sense of it all, or trying to work up the courage to tell him about the baby?"

Trina shrugged. "I don't know."

The doorbell rang then, putting an end to their brief conversation.

"Just don't get too far from a phone in case I need another rescue," Trina said as they both headed in the direction of the steps to go downstairs.

"I won't. You know you can even call me in the middle of the night, before you go to sleep, if you're afraid to risk waking up there sick again."

"Thanks," Trina said as they reached the foyer.

It was Clay who had rung the doorbell, but just as Nia opened the door, Cole pulled up in front of the house in his truck.

"I might as well go out," Trina announced before anyone had had the opportunity to even say hello, and the moment Clay stepped aside, that's just what she did.

Nia and Clay both watched her leave—Clay slightly longer than Nia. He went on looking in that direction even after Cole had gotten out of the truck to help Trina climb into the passenger side and the brothers had called greetings. He went on looking until Cole drove off.

Nia was curious as to why Clay was so interested. And because she could only conclude that it was an interest in Trina, she felt all the more certain that she needed to nip in the bud whatever might be developing between herself and Clay.

"Would you like to come in or should we just get to the banquet?" she asked with an edge of formality as his gaze followed his brother's truck all the way down Molner Circle before he turned to her.

"I better come in," he said, confusing her with the somewhat serious tone in his voice.

Nia took a step backward to allow him across the threshold, and once he was inside he closed the door.

Then he leaned against it, taking what appeared to be his first real glance at her.

And even though there was obvious appreciation in his freshly shaved, handsome-enough-to-be-dangerous face, Nia worked to tamp down her flattered reaction, reminding herself of his scrutiny of her sister.

"You look fantastic," he said.

Nia muttered a thank-you under her breath. "You don't want to get going?" she pressed, thinking that the sooner they got to a public place, the better.

"Not yet," he said. But that was all he said as he went on giving her the once-over, as if he couldn't get his fill of the sight of her.

Nia wasn't happy to note that he looked terrific himself. He was dressed in gray slacks that hinted at the muscular mass of his thighs, and a black mock-turtle cashmere sweater that glided over his broad shoulders and chest like water over rock. Of course, the cowboy boots he wore diminished the cosmopolitan flair, but somehow, on him, it all worked to sexy perfection.

"I don't think it would be good to be late, since I'm the only Molner representing the family," she said then, feeling far too many stirrings to go on standing in the entryway alone with him, admiring the pure potency of his masculinity.

"We'll make it in time," he said. "I need to talk to you before we go."

"Oh?"

"I went into Cheyenne today. To see my grandfather. He's in a care facility there."

"I didn't realize one of your grandfathers was still living," Nia said, beginning to realize he genuinely did have something to tell her. Something that was keeping his expression sober.

"My Heller grandfather—Jack. Jacob's younger brother."

Nia had had no idea Jacob Heller's brother was still alive. And a potential source of information.

"Oh?" she repeated, not knowing what else to say but wanting to urge Clay to go on.

"He's eighty-three and frail, and if you don't catch him on a good day, he's pretty out of it. But today was a good day, and on those he's himself. You can have an ordinary conversation with him and what he says can be enlightening."

It was sinking in for Nia that she'd made a tactical error in thinking that the journals alone told the story from the past. The journals she'd hoarded in order to protect the people involved.

"You went to ask your grandfather if he knew anything about Phoebe, Maude and Arlen, didn't you?" she said, cutting to the chase for the second time in the last half hour.

"I did. You left me hanging—not a good thing to do to a newspaper man. I have those digging instincts and I had to give it a shot. If it had been one of the old man's bad days, I wouldn't have gotten anywhere. But as it was…"

"You did get somewhere," she finished for him.

Clay nodded his head slowly.

"But how reliable is information you get from your grandfather even on the good days?" she reasoned, to plant the seed of doubt.

"This time I think it's pretty reliable. All the pieces fit."

Nia only arched her eyebrows, daring him to prove it.

And his almost-sad-to-admit-it partial smile left her no doubt he believed he could, even before he said, "Maude and Arlen didn't stop at that one kiss we read about before you cut me off from the journals. They had an affair—a pretty hot one that led Arlen to confess to Phoebe, to tell her that he was in love with her sister and wanted out of his marriage."

Clay held up a hand to stop the denial he must have seen coming.

"I know," he said, before Nia could get a word out. "It was a very big deal to Phoebe to keep the family secrets quiet, and you're thinking no one could know about the affair for sure, that I'm bluffing, that maybe there were rumors at the time or conjecture, and my grandfather just repeated them to me today. But you'd be wrong. Phoebe made a desperate attempt to get Jacob and Maude back together. To try to convince Jacob to change his ways, to make up with Maude. And Jacob told it all to his brother—my grandfather."

"Maybe Phoebe just *tried* to get Maude and Jacob back together, and the rumors and conjecture came from that, as a way to explain why she was trying to patch up her sister's relationship with a not-very-nice guy."

Okay, so Nia knew better. But what she didn't know was how much *Clay* knew. And on the off chance that he didn't know everything, she wanted to add what doubt she could.

But it didn't have much effect, because Clay went on undaunted. "Phoebe was desperate and determined enough to pour out her heart to Jacob. She told him that Maude and Arlen were having an affair and that she'd do anything to save her marriage, to avoid a scandal that would ruin the Molner name, that would cause dissension among the Molner and Fitzwilliam families, and hurt a lot of innocent people."

Nia merely raised her chin, making sure to keep her own expression blank.

"Jacob wasn't interested," Clay said anyway. "Not only had Maude broken up with him, he didn't want a woman who was involved with another guy. But even without Jacob's help Phoebe prevailed—although I'll admit I don't know how. Arlen and Maude ended the affair, and Arlen and Phoebe stayed married. But—"

"Not to say I'm confirming any of this," Nia stated, interrupting him. "But for argument's sake, let's say you've garnered a few more details about a brief, hurtful romance that happened a long time ago. Did it change the course of anything in Elk Creek?"

"No," Clay conceded.

"And it's Elk Creek's development and progression to the present that are what the Founder's Day supplements are supposed to be about. So what difference does any of it make—even if it were true? And I'm not saying it is."

Clay didn't respond to her question; he just finished what he'd clearly been about to say. "Then Maude realized she was pregnant."

Nia closed her eyes and turned her head away as she resigned herself to the fact that he really did know the whole story.

"Phoebe made a second try with Jacob, offering him a boatload of cash to marry Maude and pretend the baby was his. He wouldn't have any part of that, either, and then both Maude and Phoebe left Elk Creek for London. A year later Phoebe came back with the baby. Maude's and Arlen's baby. Curtis—the son Phoebe and Arlen raised as their own."

"Maybe he *was* their own," Nia said, attempting one more bluff. "Just because Maude was pregnant doesn't mean Phoebe wasn't, too. Maybe—"

"Curtis wasn't Phoebe's," he said, cutting her off. "Phoebe made one more visit to Jacob to ask him to keep the secret that Curtis was really Maude's child. Jacob kept her secret—except from my grandfather, who said telling me was the first he'd spoken about it to anyone but Jacob. From there Jacob and old Jack could only guess what went on, but Jack said no one could overlook what a cold, distant, withdrawn husband Arlen was to Phoebe the whole rest of their lives. Jacob and Jack assumed that Arlen was always in love with Maude. Everyone else around here couldn't figure out why he treated her the way he did, but they felt sorry for her. They thought she'd been shortchanged, used to bring two banking families together to build an empire and left to rot in a loveless marriage to a man who acted as if he hardly knew she was alive. Widely held opinion was that she deserved better."

"Better than a sad and lonely life knowing her husband was pining for her sister," Nia heard herself say, before she even realized she'd opened her mouth.

Still, the words didn't do any more damage, since it was too late to try keeping anything from Clay.

"So it *was* one of the old man's good days," he concluded, letting her know only then that he hadn't been as certain as he'd pretended to be.

It was too late for her to attempt to refute any of it, but she didn't give it her stamp of approval, either. Instead she said, "But again, this story has nothing to do with Elk Creek. Which means there's no reason to expose it now."

Clay's brilliant blue eyes stayed on her. Intently. "It's an interesting ending to a story everyone in town has been following."

"Today's supplement read like an ending—Maude broke up with Jacob, it caused a rift between the two founding fathers. Tomorrow's supplement can tie up how Horatio and Hyram's relationship played out for the rest of their lives. We already talked about this."

"But now I know more and I could let my readers know what happened during the rest of Maude's and Phoebe's lives, too."

"When we went into this you said you wanted information on the early days of Elk Creek," Nia reminded him. "That's what you got. Leave it at that."

Once more she could tell this debate was an intellectual stimulant for him, because one eyebrow rose as if he were accepting a challenge. "I also said I wanted some human interest. And this is that."

"You agreed not to print anything that makes my family look bad."

"Actually, I agreed not to print anything that makes *Phoebe* look bad."

"A loophole? You're using a loophole?" Nia demanded, her voice raising an octave.

Clay put his hands up, palms outward, as if to ward off her outburst. "I'm just saying that *technically* that's what I agreed to. And Phoebe *doesn't* look bad. She forgave her husband his infidelity. She raised the child who came from that infidelity as her own. It could even be argued that she did something heroic, if you consider that maybe if she hadn't held it together, if your family and the Fitzwilliams had come to some sort of parting of the ways after joining their financial concerns, the bank here might have suffered or even closed. And that would have done damage to the economy and future of the town."

"Still, Maude *wasn't* heroic, and I want her protected just the same as I wanted to protect Phoebe."

"I understand that. But all we have here is human weaknesses and the consequences of them. And they were all set into motion by *my* family, by Jacob being a jerk. Maude reacted to that, turned to Arlen for comfort and ended up having an affair with him. Phoebe must have seen it that way or how else could she forgive her sister?"

Nia was absolutely not going to comment on *that*. She also realized that she and Clay could go on arguing this all night unless she put a stop to it.

"So are you printing this or not?"

Clay didn't answer immediately. And when he did, it wasn't much of an answer at all. "Tomorrow's supplement is already written and in the works."

"And?"

"Who would be hurt if I've printed the whole story?" he countered, without letting her know whether or not he had. "Maude, Phoebe, Arlen, Jacob, even Curtis— who died without leaving a family of his own behind to care—are all gone. Business at your family's bank certainly isn't going to slow down because of this. No one is going to snub you or Trina or your folks on the street when you come to town. It's history. Not quite ancient history, but history that, while it's interesting and adds identifiable human frailties and a more personal angle to my supplements, does no harm to anyone."

"It harms the memory of my great-aunt. Of Phoebe's husband, who was a respected member of the community here and shouldn't have his reputation tarnished now, after his death," Nia said, holding fast to her side of this issue.

"I don't know about harming anybody's memory. It just lets everyone know they were flesh and blood people like the rest of us."

"So you used it," Nia said accusingly.

"Maybe. Maybe not. Maybe you'll just have to wait and see."

"Wait and see if you respected my wishes and *didn't* print it?"

"Or if I wrote it up in a way that made it all understandable, forgivable, and with Jacob at the heart of it and to blame."

"And you're not going to give me even a hint of which it is."

"No, I'm not."

Nia took a deep breath and then sighed.

But before her frustration with him could find voice, he came to stand directly in front of her.

"One way or another," he said in a suddenly soothing tone, "what you *could* do is trust me. But I get the feeling that might be asking too much of you."

"It might be," she agreed. He had no idea just how much *too much* it was asking of her.

"Why is that?" he mused then, studying her.

Nia tilted her chin. "If you can leave me wondering, I can leave you wondering, too."

That made him chuckle—a sexy, throaty sound.

"Okay, I earned that and I'll accept it. For now," he added, as if he were warning her that he wouldn't accept it for long.

Then he took her upper arms in his two big hands, massaging them and successfully easing her anger and frustration despite her best efforts to hang on to them.

He leaned forward only slightly so that he could

whisper in her ear. "No matter what, you might as well let it go. It's too late now. Whichever direction I went, the ball is in play—the third supplement will hit the stands tomorrow."

"Then I guess our affiliation is over, too," she said, fighting to raise her chin in a show of defiance when all she really wanted was to meet him halfway, to lay her hands against his chest, to tilt her head so he had access to her earlobe….

"Our *professional* affiliation may be over," he answered. "But I'd be derelict in my duty as a citizen of Elk Creek and as a Heller if I didn't escort the visiting delegate from the Molner family to this banquet tonight."

"I'm relieving you of your duty," she said, not intending that to sound flirtatious, and wondering how it was that this man could bring that out in her even when she was miffed at him. How could he be bringing out so many things in her that shouldn't be there at all.

Her comment only inspired another chuckle. "There are a lot of things I'd be more than happy to have you relieve, but my duty isn't one of them. So if you're even thinking of not going with me tonight to this banquet, think again."

"Is that so?"

"That *is* so," he decreed. "Don't make me pick you up and carry you in there tonight, 'cause I'd do it."

Nia half believed he would. But that wasn't what convinced her to go through with their date. Heaven help her, even in the midst of a test of wills with him—a test of wills she might well have lost—there was still a part of her that wanted to be with him. A part so strong it overrode everything else, including her better judgment.

She wouldn't cave in and let him know it, though.

"If I read that supplement tomorrow and find out you did the wrong thing, I'm not going to be a happy camper, and you'll answer for it," she threatened, putting as much force into her words as she could muster.

"Bring it on, baby."

That was just too macho for her not to laugh at. And when Clay straightened up to peer down at her again he was smiling in a way that let her know that had been his intention.

"Where did you come from to torture me?" she asked.

"I was a special order."

"Customer service will have to hear about this."

"Great, save the complaints for them, so you and I can just have a good time tonight." He let go of her arms and took one of her hands instead. "Now come on before we're late."

"I'll bet you were a bad, bad kid," Nia remarked as he ushered her out the front door.

"The worst. My mother had gray hair by the time she was thirty."

"I don't doubt it!"

And Nia didn't put up any more resistance.

* * *

The banquet was held in the church basement, where Nia had attended many a summer potluck supper and bingo game with her grandparents when she'd visited Elk Creek. It was decorated more formally tonight, with linen tablecloths covering the round tables that filled the space for the occasion, with red roses and baby's breath centerpieces, and chairs camouflaged in white cloths tied with red sashes.

Nia and Clay sat with the rest of the Hellers at the table nearest to the raised platform. There was a podium and microphone for speeches from some oldtimers honoring Horatio and Hyram, and for presentations to Nia, as well as to Linc Heller—the oldest of the Hellers present.

The speeches seemed to go on and on, but they were given during a lovely meal of roasted chicken, country mashed potatoes, corn casserole, rolls and salad. Then everyone was left to mingle and talk.

For Nia it was yet another opportunity to renew old acquaintances and catch up with people who might have only been summer friends, but who she thought highly of nonetheless.

She particularly liked seeing more pictures of the babies and small children so many of those friends had now, and was very interested in a conversation she had with Megan Bailey. Nia had met Megan outside of the childbirth class the evening Nia and Clay had taken their walk around town. Megan was married to the local sheriff, Josh Brimley, and was eight months pregnant with their first child, a girl, according to what Megan announced that evening.

That night on the street Megan had borne the brunt of teasing because she'd inquired about painkillers. But tonight when Nia talked to her, she learned that Megan intended to rely on acupuncture to ease the discomforts of labor and delivery, and had arranged for a friend she'd trained with to come into town to perform it on her. Megan's sister, Nissa, who was a massage therapist, was also on board to aid the process, and Nia thought that both ideas could be recommended to Trina.

The banquet cake was served at nine o'clock. Many of the attendees were also going to be in the Founder's Day parade or needed to put finishing touches on floats for it, so once dessert and coffee had been enjoyed people began saying good-night and leaving.

Nia and Clay were among the last to leave, but it was barely ten-thirty when she took the plaque honoring Horatio Molner and she and Clay went back out into the night. And even though Nia knew she should be glad for an early end to the evening and to being with Clay, she wasn't.

Yes, he'd aggravated her by digging up the rest of the story about her aunts and Arlen Fitzwilliam, and she was going to be upset with him if he printed it in the next day's supplement. Because of that, she should have been happy to bid him a chilly farewell at her door.

But once they reached it she just wasn't inclined to do that.

Apparently neither was he, because rather than saying good-night and letting her go inside, he stretched an arm across the open doorway and grasped the jamb, effectively blocking her entrance as he said, "You seemed uncommonly interested in Megan Bailey's birth plan tonight. Any special reason for that?"

Nia shrugged. "I might have a baby someday and want to explore alternatives."

He was studying her intently again, even more so than he had earlier in the foyer, as if he were trying to read between the lines. For some reason, Nia had the impression he doubted her answer. Or that he was suspicious of something.

But after a moment he seemed to let that go.

"You want kids of your own, then?" he asked.

"I do."

"Twins?"

"I don't know about that. Two kids, maybe, but it might be nice to have them one at a time, get to know them in their own right."

"Don't you like being a twin?"

"It isn't that. There are a lot of things I like about it. But there have also been times when I've wished I wasn't one of a pair. When I've wanted to be seen as an individual, as just myself."

"I can understand that," he said, still studying her and giving her the impression that he was very much seeing her for herself.

It pleased her. And for a moment Nia got lost in feasting on the sight of him, too. On those sharply angled features. On the way they all worked together in such harmony to produce a face she thought she could stare at for an eternity and never tire of. Complete with a body that couldn't be overlooked…

"What about you?" she said, dragging herself from the slight trance she'd lapsed into. "I know you said your former wife didn't want kids, but do you?"

"I do." He repeated her words. "I was more in a take-it-or-leave-it frame of mind when I was with Shayna—probably because it was a time in my life when I was buried in my work. But now that I've changed my course, my priorities, and settled in Elk Creek, I've discovered that family is more important to me than I realized. So I know for a fact that I want to have kids. Just with a balance to things."

Meaning that he didn't want to have kids in an unbalanced situation like the one he'd been in before, Nia thought. But she didn't say it. Instead she said, "Balance—Megan Bailey said that's what Chinese medicine and acupuncture strive for. Maybe you should look into it."

"When I go into labor?" he asked with that smile that knocked her socks off.

"I think it's only the wife who wants to stick needles in the husband at that point," she answered, playing along with his joke.

"Kind of like you wanted to do to me before the banquet?"

"Kind of."

That just made him laugh again. "How 'bout now?"

he asked in a voice that was quieter, deeper, more intimate.

"I'll tell you tomorrow. After I see the supplement."

"But right at this minute you don't want to poke needles into me."

She could think of some things she wanted to do to him now—along with some things she wanted him to do to her—but none of it had anything to do with needles.

"No, maybe not right at this minute," she admitted, her own tone different, too. An involuntary response to the awakening of senses that were all tuned to him.

"Glad to hear it," he said, as he leaned forward slowly and kissed her.

They were soft, warm lips that met hers. Gently. Without much pressure at first. But only at first. Only for a moment before they parted and enticed hers to part, too.

Nia knew on some level that she shouldn't be doing this, allowing this, that she should put a stop to it right then, in no uncertain terms. But everything in her was screaming to do exactly what she was doing—kissing Clay. Matching his every movement with one of her own. Opening her mouth even wider. Meeting his tongue with hers. Playing every game his initiated. Dancing every dance. Following every lead. And so that was what she did.

She also wanted to raise her hands to his chest, so she did that, too. She pressed her palms against that broad, honed expanse encased in cashmere, and absorbed the feel of his strong, powerful body through her skin.

She wanted to move in closer to him, hoping he got the message that she needed the feel of his arms around her, to be held against him. And when he did that, she sighed in approval, in encouragement, letting him know it was just what she'd had in mind.

Yes, on some level she knew she shouldn't be doing this, but she'd disconnected from that level, from the thoughts and cautions that went with it, and simply floated along, giving as good as she got when mouths opened wider still and tongues fenced hungrily.

Her hands followed the breadth of his shoulders to his biceps before following a path under his arms and around to his back so her breasts could find their place against his chest. Breasts that felt full enough to strain against her lacy bra. Breasts whose nipples were hard with demands of their own. Breasts that yearned for the touch of those big hands massaging her back, those strong fingers digging into her flesh in a way her breasts were envious of.

Nia slipped her hands underneath Clay's sweater when the desire to have skin-on-skin became too great. Silken skin over hardened steel muscles that expanded as she traveled upward from the base of his back to his shoulder blades.

He pulled her closer, tighter, and she felt those muscles roll beneath her hands. Muscles she clung to, kneaded the way her body craved to be kneaded in return.

Mouths clung, as well, in kisses that tested every limit, that were uninhibited and abandoned and wild, suffusing Nia's entire body with passion, enlivening every nerve ending and awakening every inch of her.

One of Clay's hands stopped caressing her back and began a journey that lit sparks as it went, trailing downward and around, resting on her side for a moment, as if waiting to see if she would let him go farther.

Not only would she let him, she wanted him to. So badly that she couldn't contain the tiny groan of regret when that hand stopped.

And then it started to move again and her nipples tightened even more just at the possibility that that was where he intended to go. Her shoulders drew back. Her spine arched. And if he hadn't finally reached one of her breasts with that massive hand, she might have cried. But reach it he did! He curved his palm around her flesh, and it felt so good her knees went weak and she leaned even farther into his grasp.

Good. It definitely felt good. Just not good enough. Not with the lace of her turtleneck and bra and the turtleneck's underblouse between them. It wasn't enough just to have her hands on his bare skin. She wanted his hand on hers, too.

And then it was.

She didn't know if he'd read her mind, or if he just wanted it as much as she did, but he wasted no time insinuating that hand under her shirt and her bra, reclaiming her breast exactly as she'd yearned for him to.

And no, it didn't just feel good. It felt great. Her nipple beaded in his palm as his whole hand molded to her again, as his fingers gently but masterfully fondled her flesh, working it, kneading it, building within her an even more intense hunger to feel his hands everywhere on her body, to feel every inch of him against her, to feel the press of that entire glorious body to her own....

Inside. They needed to go inside. Upstairs. To her bedroom. To her bed...

But that thought brought her back to that level where she knew she shouldn't be doing this. And on that level she realized she'd forgotten where they were. Who they were.

She'd forgotten that they were in the doorway where earlier she'd watched Clay watch Trina. With interest.

She'd forgotten that she was Trina's sister. And that Clay was a man who'd had something going with Trina. Who'd had an infatuation for her, an attraction. Something that made this a really big no-no for Nia.

"Wait," she heard herself say in a breathless voice as her head fell back, breaking the kiss that had gone on and on and on.

Clay pressed his lips to the arch of her neck, just above the scalloped edge of lace that encircled it. And to make matters worse, he squeezed her breast, reminding her just how much she didn't want him to stop.

But she had to. He'd been so interested in Trina such a short time ago....

"No, really. No more," she insisted.

He squeezed again and drew those long fingers in a caress that went slowly to her nipple, holding it for one moment like a flower bud about to be plucked, before he let go of her and dropped his hand to her side.

"No?" he asked, his voice tempting her to rethink the decision.

But she couldn't let herself do that, and instead shook her head, unable to speak as she fought the urges he'd so skillfully brought to life in her. Unable to even open her eyes as she battled for the strength to resist him and what her own traitorous body was still crying out for.

"No," she repeated when she could, only managing a whisper.

She swallowed.

She heard him draw in a deep breath and breathe it out as if he were deflating an inner tube.

And when Nia finally did open her eyes it was to find signs of his struggle to conquer his own arousal. His oh-so-handsome face was tilted toward the stars as he obviously worked to compose himself before he looked down at her again.

"It boggles the mind to think of what might have happened if you *weren't* mad at me," he said then, joking. But his voice was so ragged with emotion there was no doubt he'd been as overwhelmed by what had been going on between them as she had.

Nia couldn't help smiling as she straightened up and pressed her spine to the doorjamb to gain a little distance from him.

He took her lead, pulling away and taking a step backward.

"I guess this is good-night, huh?" he said.

Nia nodded, staring up into those blue eyes of his and wondering if they were darker now because only the porch light illuminated them or if it was an effect of unsatisfied desires.

He took another deep breath, sighing it out this time and nodding himself.

"You're probably right," he said. Then, without warning, he leaned forward and, close to her ear, added, "But I can't say it *feels* right."

Another smooth move brought his mouth to hers for one last kiss before he muttered a genuine good-night and left her standing there.

Which was where she stayed, watching him get behind the wheel of his SUV, start the engine, wave and finally drive away.

Watching him as intently as he'd watched Trina.

And trying not to forget the fact that he *had* watched Trina, while everything in Nia's body was shouting for her to do just that so she could have what she wanted more than she wanted air to breathe at that moment.

So she could have Clay…

Chapter 8

"I'm sorry about this, Nia. When you offered to come out and pick me up in the middle of the night you probably didn't think I'd really make you."

It *was* the middle of the night—2:36 a.m. on the dashboard clock—when Trina slinked out of Cole Heller's house and into the passenger seat of the sedan Nia had just driven up in.

"It's okay, but keep your fingers crossed that we don't get a flat tire. I'm not dressed," Nia said, attempting to add a hint of levity to the moment. It was true, though, that underneath her raincoat she was wearing pajamas. Plus her face was washed free of makeup and her hair was haphazardly caught in a clip.

"Were you sleeping?" Trina asked. "It didn't sound like it."

"No, I was in bed, but I wasn't sleeping. I guess I have insomnia tonight." That was true, too. She hadn't so much as drifted off because she hadn't been able to stop thinking about Clay. About how close she'd come to making love with him. About what it might have been like if she had. About how much she'd wanted to. About how much she'd gone on wanting to…

"Are you sick?" Nia asked her sister, who had given no explanation for the late-night call for a ride home.

"No. I haven't been to sleep yet, either. My stomach must not know it's morning."

"Is that why you decided to have me come get you? So if you wake up sick after you do sleep Cole won't know?" Nia asked, hoping that was all that was going on.

"No," Trina answered with a voice full of emotion. "It's too late to worry about that. I told him."

They were on the dark country highway that led back to Elk Creek from the outlying farms and ranches, and Nia took her eyes off the road for a moment to look at her twin.

"You told him you're pregnant?"

"He'd more or less figured it out himself. I was wondering why he was so… Well, it isn't like he's rough or anything. He isn't. But last night, there was something different about things right from the start. He was being extra careful, extra gentle. And he was paying more attention to details—like he realized I'm bigger up top than I was before, and he seemed to be checking out my stomach once…."

"Do you think it just struck him last night, or did your morning sickness give it away?"

"The morning sickness. And the fact that I felt so much better by the afternoon. Later, when we got into it all, he said it made him start to think about some other things that have been going on with me."

"So did *he* tell *you,* or did you tell him?"

"It just sort of evolved into a question he asked me. He was a little on the quiet side all evening but I didn't think much of it. I mean, as usual, we couldn't keep our hands off each other from the minute we got to his place, and that doesn't inspire a lot of conversation, anyway. Like I said, the biggest difference I noticed was in the lovemaking, but that was nice, too, so I didn't think much of it. But then about an hour ago we got hungry—"

"You didn't come up for food until an hour ago?" Nia asked with a glance out of the corner of her eye.

"No. And that was when he started asking me things."

"Things like what?"

"Like if I still felt all right and if there had been a lot of episodes like yesterday morning and if I was prone to being sick and then getting well again that way. He asked if he was only imagining it or had some parts of my body changed from before, and weren't some of those same parts more sensitive."

"And from that the pregnancy came to light?"

"That was where the questions led—to the big one."

"And you confirmed that you're pregnant."

"I weighed whether to lie and go on hiding the fact, or tell him the truth. And then…I don't know…I looked at him and thought about how this week has been and I just decided to take the plunge and see what happened. So I said yes, I'm pregnant."

The fact that Trina had ended up calling Nia to come get her and that her tone was so shaky didn't leave Nia the illusion that the conversation had gone well from there. Still, not wanting to jump to any conclusions, she said, "And then?"

"He asked if it was his." Trina began to cry.

Nia took her hand off the steering wheel and squeezed one of her sister's. "I know, it's not the first thing you wanted to hear. It isn't the first thing anyone wants to hear. But he was probably just making sure. After all, you were married almost right up to the time you came to Elk Creek six weeks ago. He might have thought the baby could be Drew's."

"I know. It's just that none of it went the way I was hoping it might if I told him."

One more squeeze and Nia released Trina's hand, reaching into the glove box for a tissue to give her sister.

"How *did* it go from there?" she said.

"He didn't do or say anything rotten," Trina admitted. "After I told him that, yes, the baby was his, that there was no one else whose baby it could be, he didn't deny it or say he wanted proof or anything. He wanted to know if I was okay. How bad the morning sickness is. If I'm well otherwise. If I've seen a doctor."

"He was concerned for you—that's good."

"And he was shocked. Even if he had had suspicions of it before, until I confirmed it I don't think it was really real to him. He looked like he'd seen a ghost or something."

"You didn't accept it yourself even after three positive home pregnancy tests," Nia reminded her. "And once you did, that was when the anxiety attacks started."

"I know," Trina said once more. But she didn't sound as if that knowledge helped anything.

"What else?" Nia inquired, based on the assumption that there had to be more.

"He asked if I was happy about it, and I kind of skirted the issue. I just said it was a surprise, and he agreed with that. In fact, he went on for a while about how much of a surprise it was, shaking his head the whole time as if he couldn't get it to sink in."

"He was probably just *working* at getting it to sink in," Nia said.

"Then he wanted to know if the pregnancy was really why I was back in Elk Creek."

"Did he say it the way you just did? That ominously?"

"He didn't say it ominously, no. It just turned out to be such a sore spot...." Trina's shoulders shook with a fresh onslaught of tears.

"A sore spot with Cole?" Nia said when it seemed as if she might be able to continue.

Trina nodded. "It was a sore spot that the pregnancy might be the *only* reason I'd come back, that if I wasn't pregnant he wouldn't have ever seen me again."

Nia could understand how that would be a sore spot, all right. But she didn't say so. "What did you tell him?"

"I couldn't say what I might or might not have done had this not happened. Now, in hindsight, maybe I should have told a little white lie and said I absolutely would have come back. But I didn't *want* to lie to him, so I didn't address it at all. I just said that I came back to Elk Creek to spend time with him—which is true. To see if what had happened between us six weeks ago was a flash in the pan or if it was more than that. And that I thought there could be more because of the way things have been between us since I've been here."

"That doesn't sound bad," Nia hedged, because her sister's tone still hinted that it hadn't been good.

"No, except that he noticed that I hadn't answered the real question."

"About whether you would have come back at all if you weren't pregnant."

"Yes. And when he pushed it, I had to tell him that I didn't know. That I'd thought about him nonstop after I left Elk Creek six weeks ago, so maybe I would have. But I also said that I have a whole other life in Denver and I might have gotten caught up in that again and—"

"He didn't find that too reassuring," Nia guessed.

"No. Because he knows, Nia. Maybe he senses my doubts, or it's a holdover from that Marilou person who wouldn't marry him because she said he wasn't good enough for her. But he knows I've been worrying about the differences between the way he lives and the way I do. He said he was hoping that I had come back just to be with him again, but since I didn't say that, he could see it wasn't the case. That he was hoping that what happened six weeks ago hadn't only been a fling with the hired help. That I'd missed him. That I'd wanted to see him again—even though he's just a rancher and a handyman. But apparently, if I hadn't ended up pregnant, that would have been it for us."

Trina was sobbing by the time she finished, but she went on anyway, recounting what seemed to have been the worst of the confrontation, as if now that she'd begun, she couldn't stop. "I said maybe we should just look at this last week we've had together and go from there. At the fact that we genuinely have hit it off. That we have such a good time when we're together that we lose track of everything and everyone else. That no matter how long we're together, neither of us wants it to end. But that didn't seem to be enough. He got *really* quiet then. Closed off. He said I should go to bed, get some sleep, that I looked tired and needed my rest. Only he wouldn't come with me and I knew that was a bad, bad sign. So when I got to the bedroom I decided to call you, and then I got dressed. He was still in the kitchen when I left."

"You didn't tell him you were going?"

"I know, you're thinking it was like before and I shouldn't have done it again, but I was too afraid to say anything else to him. I was afraid I might cry." Which she was doing, even harder now. "I was afraid I might even grovel and embarrass myself and—" Her voice caught on a bumpy breath. "And make it all worse than it already is."

They'd reached home and Nia turned off the engine. By then Trina was bent over with her face in her hands, and Nia didn't think her sister was aware that they'd arrived at their destination. She didn't point it out because what she and Trina were talking about was more important.

"Why would you have groveled and embarrassed yourself and made it worse?" she asked.

"I didn't realize until the end just how much I didn't want Cole to pull away. How much I was hoping for a better ending—for something that wasn't an ending at all. I'm afraid I love him, Nia, and I've blown this whole thing," Trina wailed in abject misery.

"Maybe not, though," Nia said, reaching an arm around her sister's shoulders to give her a hug. "You said yourself that Cole was shocked tonight. He has to be feeling confused and worried and all the things you've been feeling since you found out about the baby. He might just need some time to get used to the idea. To think about how things between you *have* been this last week. To realize you *do* care about each other and have the foundation for a future together."

"That's a lot to hope for," Trina said dejectedly. "Especially when he's thinking that I wouldn't have ever come back to him if I hadn't gotten pregnant. I keep remembering how he looked, how far away from me he stayed in that tiny kitchen. That he wouldn't go back to bed with me... It was almost like a part of him hated me. It was awful."

"Still, T, give him the chance to digest everything. It doesn't seem to me that he's slammed any doors. Only that he's shaken and needs to regain his equilibrium a little. Maybe once he has, you just need to convince him that no matter what might or might not have been the case before, your feelings for him have grown. That with or without the baby, you'd want to be with him now—even if there are differences in your lifestyles that you need to iron out. With some encouragement he may come around and this could work out, after all."

Trina raised bloodshot, flooded eyes to her. "You think so?" she asked, with such raw hope in her voice that Nia's heart ached to even consider that she might not be right.

"I think so," she said with conviction, despite the fact that she had no idea one way or another how this would end. "But for now, let's go inside and get you to bed. Cole was right—you do need some rest. Everything will be better in the morning."

"When I'm throwing up?" Trina said, managing a weak laugh.

"Maybe you won't be throwing up," Nia answered

lightly, deciding that if she was going to nurture one hope that might be unfounded, she might as well nurture two.

But then she added what she honestly did believe. "It'll all work out the way it's meant to, T. You'll see."

"Only now I'm counting on it working out so that I end up with Cole, and not going home to Denver to have this baby and give it away."

Nia's own eyes grew instantly moist. "I'm counting on that, too," she told her sister, giving Trina one more hug before they both got out of the car to go inside.

The Founder's Day parade was scheduled for eleven o'clock on Saturday. A coin toss had decided that the Molner float, on which Nia and Trina would ride, would be the parade's leadoff, followed by the float that would carry the entire Heller family.

When she'd finally gotten back to bed at 3:00 a.m., Nia had doubted that Trina would be ready by then and well enough to participate. But sheer determination born from the hope that she would see and talk to Cole made Trina rally for the event.

They were a little late being dropped off by Fran and Simon where the floats were loading at the train station, though, and so were hurried onto their perches without seeing or talking to anyone but the parade coordinator.

The floats were all set up on the backs of flatbed trucks. Both the Molner and the Heller floats were adorned with red and white carnations surrounding papier-mâché replicas of the brass sculpture of the founding fathers that had been unveiled at the courthouse on Thursday evening. The Molner float held chairs for Nia and Trina at the foot of the somewhat rudimentary reproduction, and the moment they were seated, the signal was given to begin the parade.

Once they were under way Nia could finally glance at the float that followed. Because there were considerably more Heller descendents, some were seated, while others stood.

Clay was standing to one side and just behind the flatbed's cab, allowing him to look over the top at her. And wave to her.

Nia knew it was crazy that such a small thing should send a little thrill of delight through her, but it did. Provoking a smile and a wave in return. Even as she reminded herself that at that exact moment there could be copies of his newspaper revealing her family secrets in spite of the fact that she'd tried to prevent the exposure. And all because of that man.

That tall, lean, broad-shouldered, staggeringly handsome man dressed in cowboy boots, a pair of hip-and thigh-hugging jeans, and a black crew-necked T-shirt under a rough-and-tumble jean jacket that made him look as if he'd come straight from riding roughshod over a herd of cattle.

"He isn't there!"

Trina's whispered lament brought Nia out of her absorption of Clay, and reminded her that what she had on the line today was nothing compared to what her sister did. And with that reminder, Nia did her own head count of the Hellers on the float.

Linc and his family were present and accounted for, as were Jackson and his, and Beth and hers. Savannah and Ivey and their entire contingent were in attendance. And of course Clay was there. But Trina was right, Cole wasn't on the float.

It didn't seem to be a good sign.

"Maybe he just slept through his alarm and didn't make it," Nia whispered back to her sister. "I'm sure you'll see him after the parade."

Except she wasn't so sure.

But there was nothing either of them could do about it from the float, so, trying to keep her attitude cheery, Nia added, "Just smile and throw the candy to the crowd the way we're supposed to and it'll be over before you know it."

Nia took her own advice, dipped a hand into the ribbon-decorated basket on her lap and tossed soft toffees to the onlookers lining the curb of Center Street. But one glance at Trina doing the same thing let her know that her twin was barely holding herself together.

Even at a snail's pace, the trip down Center Street, around the square and to the school parking lot that marked the end of the parade only took half an hour. But that was as long as Trina could maintain her composure, and the moment it was possible to get down from the float, she announced to Nia that she needed to get home.

Considering that her sister's morning sickness might rear its ugly head, Nia had made provisions for a fast escape at the end of the parade route. After having Fran and Simon drop them off at the train station, she'd asked that they drive the car to the school, where the older couple could cross to the tents, stands and festivities set up in the park, and leave the sedan for Nia and Trina.

Nia spotted the car in the lot as planned and pointed it out to Trina, following her sister's quick flight in that direction just as the Heller float pulled into the lot.

"Are you sure you don't want to wait a minute? I can ask Clay if he knows where Cole is," Nia suggested.

"No. I just want to get out of here," Trina insisted, prompting Nia to take the driver's seat and do as her sister wanted.

It was no easy task, however, to avoid Center Street and the parade. To do that Nia had to drive out of town, catch the highway they'd been on in the middle of the night coming home from Cole's ranch, and use a turnoff that circled around the western side of town so they could reenter Elk Creek near the train station and follow the tail end of the parade to Molner Circle.

To where Cole Heller was waiting in his truck in front of their house.

Seeing him, Nia thought Trina might be relieved. But instead that initial sight of man and vehicle seemed to shoot panic through her sister.

"Don't leave me alone with him," Trina half commanded, half pleaded.

"It could be good," Nia said encouragingly, even though the solemn-in-the-extreme expression on Cole's face wasn't altogether heartening as she pulled to a stop beside his truck.

"But if it isn't I can't face it by myself. Please!" Trina insisted.

"Whatever you need," Nia said, thinking that this was no time for Trina to be any more upset than she already was.

Cole was out of his truck before Nia and Trina left the car, and the moment they had, his intensely blue eyes zeroed in on Trina.

"Can we talk?" he said, forgoing any greeting.

"Okay," Trina agreed in a quivery voice.

Uncomfortable to be in on this, Nia went ahead of them and unlocked the front door, holding it open for Trina, who was nearly in tears, and giving Cole a weak smile as he came in, too.

"I want Nia with me," Trina announced the moment they were all inside. She led the way into the living room as if she were going to her own execution.

Cole didn't respond to that, and Nia wasn't even sure the demand for her presence had registered as he followed Trina. Or that anything much beyond whatever he'd come to say could.

He didn't appear to have slept much, if at all. His face was shadowed with beard, and his wild mane of hair didn't look as if it had been combed by anything but the fingers he drew through it as he moved to within a few feet of Trina and stopped. Even his usually straight shoulders were hunched slightly to accommodate his other hand, which was jammed into the rear pocket of his jeans.

Wishing she could run up the stairs and hide rather than be witness to what was about to happen—good or bad—Nia slipped into the living room, too. But just barely, stopping at the archway from the foyer and standing with her back pressed to the wall as if she might blend into it, making herself as unobtrusive as possible.

"I couldn't believe you just left last night," Cole said right off the bat.

"I thought it was for the best, since you didn't seem to want to be with me," Trina said, raising her chin with a hint of defiance that Nia knew was really an attempt to keep from breaking down.

"It wasn't that I didn't want to be with you. I just needed to think. To sort through things. A lot of things." Cole jammed both hands through his hair this time and then put them in his back pockets. "Look, I know I didn't handle the news well. I should have. I saw it coming. But when it did, it still hit me like a ton of bricks."

"Me, too," Trina said, and Nia was glad her sister had opened up to Cole.

"I also know that it can't be what you had planned for yourself. For your future," he continued. "I mean, I'm not some bigwig mogul like Clay. Like you're used to. My hands get dirty every day. I break my back to make a living and I'm happy doing it. I'm pretty sure I'm not the guy who would have been your first choice to have a baby with."

Nia's heart ached for him, for the old wound this so obviously touched on, for the fact that he seemed to so deeply believe it was true. And even from a distance she thought she saw her sister's eyes fill with tears.

Before Trina could say anything, Cole went on. "But here we are. There's a baby and I'm its father and I had to think about where that left us. All three of us."

He stalled for a split second, shook his head and then said, "I don't know what you think of me, Trina. Or how you feel about me. Or if this last week has been just a damn good demonstration of your acting ability. But after thinkin' about things all night long, I can tell you this—I have feelin's for you. Deep ones. I've been afraid of 'em. Afraid they were gonna get me into trouble. And I sure as hell hope that isn't what they're doin' right now. But there they are, anyway. I'm in love with you. And if you'll let me, I'll do everything I can to be what you want me to—"

"No, Cole," Trina said, taking a tiny step toward him.

Nia didn't know what her sister was rejecting and apparently neither did Cole, but before she could go any further, he stopped her with a raised palm.

"Let me finish. You didn't say what your plans are—about the baby and the future—but I'm figurin' if you hadn't thought to have it, you'd have already taken care of that. And I don't want you havin' my baby without me. Any more than I want you doin' anything else without me—that's what I came to know for a fact today about dawn. So I'll sell my place here and move to Denver. Clay has plenty of connections—he can put me in touch with a lot of people who could hire me. Or I can use the money the ranch brings to start a business of my own—something white-collar. I'll live wherever you want to live. I'll do whatever you want me to do. But I want—I *need*—to be a part of this. To be in your life. In my kid's life. I want us to be together, Trina. You and me. You and me and our baby."

"No, Cole," Trina repeated.

Nia wanted to shout a no of her own at her sister. How could she turn this man down? This proud man who was standing before her with his heart on his sleeve?

As both Nia and Cole watched Trina, she took another step closer to him.

"I don't want you to be anything but what you are," she said then. "I've done a lot of thinking since I left your house, too. More thinking, almost, than I've done since I found out about the baby. Since I've been in Elk Creek again. *Clear* thinking, finally. You were right—I was worried that you're different than anyone I've ever been attracted to. Not that working with your hands is a bad thing, just different. But then it occurred to me that what I feel about you is different, too. Different than anything I've ever felt for anyone else. It isn't just on the surface."

Trina laughed wryly and cast a glance at Nia then,

who'd thought both her sister and Cole had forgotten she was there.

"I'm sorry, Nia. Sorrier than I was even before to discover that I wreaked such havoc for you, too, over feelings that don't compare to what I feel now." Trina returned her glance to Cole and continued. "But what I came to know this morning is that no feelings I've had before have been so deep. So real. That's what I feel for you, Cole. Love. Long-lasting, genuine love. The kind that lives are built on. And it doesn't matter what you do or what color your collar is or where you do it. All that matters is that we're together. That we can have our baby and raise it, and share that life."

Nia felt a wave of relief and saw the tension drain out of Cole, as well. He took his hands from his pockets and reached for Trina, holding her by the shoulders without pulling her to him, keeping her at arm's length to study her as if he needed that to absorb what she was saying.

"I don't want you to leave Elk Creek," Trina added. "*I* don't want to leave Elk Creek. And I definitely don't want you doing any other kind of work when I know the work you do is what you like."

"What about my place?" Cole asked. "One bathroom—that seemed to upset you…"

Trina laughed. "I hate that," she admitted. "And as soon as you finish remodeling this house, you're going to have to start work—a whole lot of work that I can finance—on the ranch house. But that's not important—unless you have a problem with it…."

Cole grinned, apparently finally grasping that Trina had thought through everything, that she meant what she was saying. And he was happy about it. Too happy to allow details like bathrooms to bother him.

"I don't have a problem with anything. Not now," he said.

And then he did pull Trina into his arms to kiss her. A kiss that was not intended to be witnessed by a third party. Her sister's need for moral support had come to an end.

Nia pivoted around the archway's edge into the foyer and then tiptoed across the hardwood floor to escape and allow the couple their privacy.

But as she climbed the stairs, relief settled over her. Relief so great she realized only then just how worried she'd been that this might not work out as it had. More worried than she'd been fully aware of.

But it *had* worked out. In the best way it could have. Because not only would Trina have the baby now, she and Cole would keep it. And Nia would get to know her niece or nephew. She'd get to have the child in her life, too—what she'd been hoping for all along.

Thank you, thank you, thank you, she thought, sending her gratitude out into the universe as she went into her room and closed the door.

"And now on to the next order of business," she muttered after a moment of absorbing her relief.

The next order of business being the *Elk Creek Gazette*'s final Founder's Day supplement. And whether or not Clay had revealed the sordid details of her aunts' rocky romances with Arlen Fitzwilliam.

Nia hadn't had time to locate a copy yet, so she made that her goal. But first she needed to change out of the designer suit she'd worn for the parade.

She'd already decided what to wear for the Founder's Day festivities and so wasted no time hanging her suit in the closet and putting on the long-sleeved cardigan sweater that sported mauve flowers on a navy blue background, and ten buttons that went from the ruffle-edged hem at her hipbones to the low U of the scoop neck. Then on went a pair of low-rise jeans before she hurriedly stepped into blue leather mules that provided convenience and comfort for the long day ahead.

Lastly she ran a brush through her hair, twisted it in back and clasped it just below her crown, leaving a spray of wavy ends to frolic above it.

One final glance at herself in the full-length mirror warned her that she was showing a bit more cleavage than she'd planned. But rather than considering whether she should put on a T-shirt or blouse underneath it, she thought of Clay.

Clay and the previous evening.

The *end* of the previous evening…

It was phenomenal to her that that was all it took to feel once more all she had last night. To want again all she'd wanted. To wish all over again that what hadn't happened might have.

But in the cold light of day she willed every bit of

those feelings back into submission with the reminder that, while things might have worked out for Trina and Cole, nothing had changed when it came to the fact that Clay had been attracted to Trina in the past, and that Nia could never completely trust that he wasn't still attracted to her now. Or wouldn't be again. With the reminder that she didn't altogether trust him when it came to what he might be printing in his newspaper, either.

The newspaper she was about to go on a quest to find.

Nia took a deep breath and blew it out slowly to clear her head.

The next order of business, she silently repeated to herself.

But deep down she hoped that that next order of business turned out as well as the business between Trina and Cole had.

And then maybe she could actually have some rest and relaxation, and enjoy Founder's Day.

And Clay, a little voice whispered in the back of her mind.

But she tried to ignore it. Knowing that despite what the man could arouse in her, he was the one person she really shouldn't—and couldn't—let her hair down with.

Or her guard.

Chapter 9

Elk Creek had gone all out for the Founder's Day Centennial celebration. The usual booths, stalls and stands that were set up for Labor Day, Memorial Day and Fourth of July festivities were there, but as Nia approached the park square she could see that for this occasion extra lengths had been gone to to make it more special.

Carnival rides had been brought in—a fair-size roller coaster, a Ferris wheel, a merry-go-round and a Tilt-A-Whirl among them. There were pony rides and a petting zoo for the younger kids, and arcade games for the older kids and adults. There were several cooking contests and an entire tent set up by the 4-H Club to show off animals being raised and hybrid plants being experimented with. There were tap-dancing, baton-twirling, band and singing contests, and pig calling and catching competitions for which prizes and trophies were being awarded. There was food galore, entertainments scheduled throughout the day and evening, and so many people had come in from other small towns nearby and even from cities farther out, that it looked more like a state fair than a small town Founder's Day.

Nia had left home on foot and stopped at every newspaper box on Center Street, but by the time she reached the park square she still hadn't come across a single copy of the *Gazette* or its supplement. Her only option was to find Clay and ask why. So she headed into the crowd, assuming that was where she'd find him.

When she hadn't come across him an hour later, she was beginning to get frustrated. But just as she spotted Linc Heller several yards in front of her at a juice stand, and headed for him to ask if he knew where his cousin was, a big hand closed around one of her shoulders and stopped her in her tracks. And then, above the din of the many voices around her, the familiar deep tones that alone had the power to make everything inside her sit up and take notice, said, "What do I need to do, lasso you to get you to hold up?"

Clay. There he was suddenly, right beside her.

"I've been following you and calling your name for five minutes now," he added.

"There's so much noise I didn't hear you," she an-

swered, raising her own voice and pretending she
hadn't been looking for him all along.

"Let's get out of the way," he suggested, tugging her
from the flow of pedestrians to a more quiet spot between a booth where plastic fish could be caught for
trinkets and another where milk bottles stacked in pyr-
amids could be knocked over with beanbags to win
stuffed animals.

"You're a hard woman to pin down," Clay complained once they were more or less alone. But the
complaint came with a smile. "I thought I'd see you
at the end of the parade, and instead you'd disappeared
by the time our float got to the school. Somebody said
they thought they'd seen you and Trina drive off, and
I figured you must have gone home to change clothes."

His eyes dropped to what she was wearing and he
seemed to approve.

"Apparently I got that right. Anyway, I had to make
a stop at the office for some last-minute details on today's
paper, and then I went to your house, and Cole and Trina
said I was too late, that you'd already come back here."

"Actually, I came looking for today's paper," she
said pointedly.

He grinned. "Didn't find one, did you?"

"Obviously you know I didn't. But *why* didn't I?"

"Because they aren't out yet. I'm doing today's
issue as a special edition—higher quality paper and
ink, splashier ads, the whole bit. They aren't coming
out until this evening, and then they'll be all around
here, souvenirs to commemorate the occasion."

"And I won't know until then what's in the supplement?"

"Nope."

He was pleased with himself, and Nia had to wonder if the delay of the paper's release honestly was because of the upgrade in production or if Clay had done it purposely, just to vex her. Or possibly to put off having to deal with her when she discovered he'd printed what she wanted him not to.

But she was sure he wouldn't admit that even if it were true, so she didn't bother to ask. Instead she said, "So why were you looking for me? Is something wrong?"

"Things seem to be pretty right—I understand there's a joint Heller-Molner project in the works. A baby, huh?"

"You're going to be an uncle," Nia confirmed. But he still hadn't told her why he'd been so determined to get to her, so she asked again.

"I thought maybe we could do this together today," he said, pointing his chin toward the crowds. "I was going to suggest it last night but you, uh, distracted me and I blanked it out."

Just the mention of the distraction of the night before caused goose bumps to erupt on Nia's arms and again made her remember all too vividly what it had been like to have his hands on more than just her shoulder.

"What do you say?" he asked then, nodding once more toward the festivities. "Together? Can we do it up right? Celebrate our pending aunt- and unclehood, and Founder's Day, and the work on the supplements being finished? We can have the whole day to ourselves, doing nothing but having a good time."

"Before I know what's in the supplement," Nia said suspiciously.

"Yep," he confirmed, sounding cocksure.

"Was that the plan?" she asked, voicing her earlier curiosity, after all. "To put off releasing the paper until you had me where you wanted me?"

He flashed another grin, blindingly engaging and enticing as only Clay's smiles could be. "Right where I want you—plied with corn dogs and beer, your defenses weak," he joked.

Her defenses always seemed weak when she was with him. She didn't need to be plied with corn dogs and beer.

"What do you say?" he demanded when she hesitated. "Give yourself over to me for just one day and let's have some fun."

Every day with him had been fun in its own way, but Nia didn't say that, either. She did, however, weigh the wisdom in agreeing to what he was asking.

But even though she knew the wise move would have been to turn him down, she just couldn't make herself do it. Not when he was standing right in front of her, emanating such warmth and appeal. Not when all she wanted was to spend the day with him.

"I hope I don't regret this when the supplement comes out," she said, more to herself than to him.

But Clay took it as agreement, grinned even more widely, and said, "Corn dogs and beer it is," as he draped an arm around her shoulders as if he had the right, and brought out a fresh crop of those goose bumps Nia had fought back moments before.

Nia couldn't help having fun as the afternoon progressed. Clay was open to trying and doing everything, so there wasn't a single event they missed out on. And it was Elk Creek, so even though the ranks were filled with strangers who had come to town for Founder's Day, there were still countless familiar faces to share in the amusements and make them all the better.

At six that evening, for a nominal fee, a box supper was served from the biggest of the tents. Most people were weary by then and gratefully took their food to sit at tables, on benches or on the ground, resting and recharging before the kickoff of the dance scheduled to begin at eight o'clock.

There were blankets to be borrowed for those who ended up on the ground, and Nia and Clay were among that group. They spread a plaid flannel throw on the park square's lawn and sat there to enjoy a thick pot roast and vegetable stew served over mashed potatoes and accompanied by thick slices of hot, homemade bread.

Once most folks were fed and merely lounging in the aftermath of a busy day and a heavy meal, a horde of boys appeared from out of nowhere. They were all dressed in knickers and caps like old-fashioned news-boys, each of them carrying stacks of the *Elk Creek Gazette*'s special Founder's Day edition. Hawking them as if they were for sale, the boys passed them out free of charge to everyone who would take one.

"Very cute," Nia said, laughing and enjoying the spectacle Clay had arranged.

"In keeping with the theme," he said, stretching out to lie on his side on the grass, and bracing his weight on one arm to face Nia as she accepted a copy of his paper.

"The hour of reckoning is upon you," she said, sit-ting cross-legged beside him.

"Maybe I should take off now so I can get a head start," he said in mock trepidation as she sifted through the paper to get to the supplement.

Nia just cast him a glance from under her eyebrows and began to read.

He gave her the courtesy of not watching her as she did. Of looking away so she wasn't uncomfortable. She appreciated that. But not as much as she appreci-ated what was in the supplement. Or actually, what *wasn't* in the supplement.

"You didn't use the family skeletons," she said when she'd finished, and the only mention of Phoebe, Maude, Arlen and Curtis were in summary, as she'd suggested—outlining where they'd lived out their lives, how and where they'd died and the contributions Phoebe and Arlen, in particular, had made to Elk Creek.

"It would have made for good reading, though," he responded.

"Thank you for not airing the scandal."

The relief that washed over Nia for the second time today must have sounded in her voice because he said, "You didn't trust me right up to the end, did you? You thought I'd go against your wishes and print it."

"You're a newspaperman. I thought that was what you guys did."

"I think there's more to it than that," Clay insisted. "I think this was something personal. Something that came from you and whatever it is that taught you to be so *un*trusting."

"I'm just glad you didn't spill the beans about Maude and Arlen and Curtis," Nia hedged. "Phoebe made a lot of sacrifices to keep that secret. She would have turned over in her grave to know that it was all out there for everyone to know now."

Clay sat up and faced Nia. "Now for my reward," he said, tapping the supplement she'd set in her lap. "You beat around the bush with me yesterday as payback because I wouldn't tell you what I'd printed. But since your wondering is over, mine should be, too. So come on, play fair—tell me what happened to make you expect me to take the low road."

Nia supposed that *was* what she'd done. And he was right, he hadn't done anything to deserve it, so maybe she should tell him why she'd reacted the way she had. Maybe he had earned an explanation as compensation for being unjustly distrusted.

Besides, it wasn't as if it was a secret.

"Does it have something to do with Trina's ex?" he guessed. "Did knowing he cheated on her turn you skeptical, too?"

"Drew," Nia said, deciding at that moment to be honest with Clay. "Trina's ex-husband's name is Drew. Drew McGrath. And he gets the blame for turning me skeptical, yes. Only he accomplished it before what he did to end his marriage to Trina."

"Yeah?" Clay said, lifting his eyebrows. "How'd he do that?"

"He was engaged to me."

The eyebrows dropped and came together in confusion. "Your sister married the guy you were engaged to?"

"She did."

"I have to hear this story."

And since she'd come this far, Nia was willing to go the rest of the way and tell it. So that's what she did, although without looking directly at Clay, because that made her feel somehow more vulnerable to the old wounds she was revealing.

"Drew was someone I met through the museum," she said. "His family is very wealthy—they made a fortune manufacturing some of the first rubber tires. When his grandfather died, he left a substantial art collection that they wanted to donate to the museum. I met Drew when I went to assess the pieces."

"Uh-huh," Clay said, encouraging her to go on.

"Drew was charming and attractive and we seemed

to click." Not unlike the way she saw Clay. Something she told herself she should keep in mind….

"Anyway, we dated and got more and more involved and then he asked me to marry him."

"And you said yes."

"I did."

"Without reservation?"

Nia smiled. "Most people don't say yes to a marriage proposal if they have reservations about it. I didn't think I had blinders on, though, if that's what you mean. I recognized that Drew was sort of spoiled—even more spoiled than Trina and I had been. He was an only child in a family that pampered him like royalty—the heir to the throne—and I knew he'd never been denied anything in his life. But at the time that didn't seem like a character flaw, just a fact of his life."

"Uh-huh," Clay said again.

"I'd met his family before we got engaged, but he hadn't met mine. We'd only dated for about four months, and Trina and my parents had been in and out of the city during that time so it just hadn't worked out. But I arranged for a dinner."

"If this were a movie I think we'd be hearing dramatic music right about now."

"Dun-duh-dun-duh…" Nia provided, trying to add some levity to the moment even though recalling this didn't make her lighthearted.

"So Tire Guy came to dinner."

"And met my family."

"Including Trina."

"Including Trina."

"And…"

Okay, maybe Nia was stalling a bit. It was just always difficult for her to get into this part.

But she took a deep breath and plunged ahead. "And they liked each other. Of course I thought they just liked each other as about-to-be-in-laws—you know, the way Phoebe saw things between her and Arlen and Maude and Jacob. I thought Drew was fitting into the family, that we could all go on to have a nice relationship, enjoy holidays together, a vacation here and there, that sort of thing."

The sarcastic inflection that had inadvertently crept into her voice made Clay flinch. "But things between Trina and Tire Guy were a little too nice?"

"Love at first sight—that's what Trina believed it was. She said she'd resisted his attentions and her own attraction to him as long as she could, but in the end…" Nia shrugged.

"In the end Trina couldn't resist him?"

"I honestly think she tried. But I also think that that made Drew want her all the more. Remember that spoiled part I told you about? How he was never denied anything? Well, when he was faced with it for the first time, he couldn't accept it. He decided he absolutely *had* to have Trina. No matter what."

"So she got the full-court press."

"I'm not sure what that is, but if it means that Drew did everything he possibly could to win Trina over, then yes, the full-court press."

"How did you find out?"

"I started getting a little suspicious about a month before Trina confessed. Things just looked too friendly once or twice when I came into a room they were in. And there was something about the way Drew looked at Trina, talked about her, that began to make me wonder. But when I asked him, he said I was imagining things."

"And then Trina told you otherwise, not Tire Guy?"

"I was never sure if Drew would have said anything at all, or if he might have actually married me and just kept on seeing my sister on the side. But Trina was guilt stricken and finally came to me. She told me how in love they were, that they wanted to be together, but that neither of them wanted to hurt me." Again, the facetious tone tinged her words. "It was a little late for that, but—"

"You stepped aside."

Something about Clay's statement chafed and Nia finally glanced at him. "I suppose that's one way to look at it," she admitted. "But even if Trina had bowed out of the picture I wouldn't have gone on to marry Drew once I knew what had been going on behind my back. I would have been crazy to. And reading Aunt Phoebe's journals only confirmed that she knew that after what had happened between her sister and her husband, Arlen never felt for Phoebe what he'd felt for Maude. Phoebe spent the rest of her life knowing she wasn't who he wanted. Long before learning this, I knew better than to marry someone who loved my sister more than he loved me."

"So Trina married him instead."

"Yes, Trina married Drew instead," Nia confirmed.

"And when you said poor Phoebe got a lousy pay-back for supporting Maude through her breakup with Jacob, you must have been thinking about yourself some, too. What a lousy payback you got for all that mothering and watching out for and babying of Trina because of her heart problem."

Okay, maybe that *had* been what she'd been thinking when they'd discovered Maude and Arlen's affair in the journals and she'd voiced her sympathy for Phoebe. But it surprised Nia that Clay not only recalled that, but had put two and two together.

"This whole thing hit close to home for you, didn't it?" he said then.

"Sort of," Nia answered.

"But Maude left the country and stayed away, with the exception of a few visits here and there over the years, so obviously she and Phoebe weren't close afterward. Yet here you and Trina are…."

"It wasn't easy getting to where we are again," Nia said. "Trina and Drew eloped and lived in Europe for a year. We didn't see each other and didn't speak at all during that time."

"So you were angry," he guessed, sounding happy to hear it.

"Angry, hurt, betrayed—I wasn't happy, that's for sure."

"But you got over it?"

"Not in the blink of an eye, no. When they first

came back to Denver I let it be known that there was
no way I'd ever be in the same room with Drew again,
and I still tried to avoid Trina. But that wasn't easy and
I didn't want to make ugly scenes every time I had to
see her, so I was…coolly civil. But Trina had made up
her mind to mend fences with me, and so she gave me
the full-court press—as you say."

"Were you open to that?"

"Not initially. But she kept at it. Time passed, and
I guess that helped to blunt the damage, too. Plus, she
is my sister. My twin sister. As angry as I was, as hurt,
there was still a part of me that missed her. After a
while I decided to work at trying to remember the way
things had been between us before Drew, to actually
think of the Trina who was my sister as someone different than the Trina who had ended up married to my
fiancé."

"That couldn't have been easy."

"No, it wasn't. And I can't say I was always successful at it. Sometimes I didn't take her calls, or half
an hour before I was supposed to have lunch with her
I'd get angry all over again and cancel, and not see or
talk to her again for a couple of weeks."

"But eventually?"

"Trina persisted and eventually it got better. And
then her marriage began to come apart at the seams and
my eyes were opened even more to what a smarmy jerk
Drew really was. By the time she found him in bed with
someone else I'd already come to the point where I felt
as if I'd dodged a bullet not to have ended up with him."

"But there's still the baggage that made you figure I'd do the worst when it came to the supplements."

Nia gave him a chagrinned smile but took the offensive rather than the defensive. "You could have just told me what you were doing."

"I could have, but what fun would that have been?" he said with a smile of his own. "So, is all the baggage aimed at men? Isn't there any left when it comes to Trina?"

Nia grimaced. "I'd be lying if I said I didn't have a twinge of resentment here and there. But on the whole? I think we actually have a more normal relationship than we did before."

"Normal being you mothering her, sacrificing for her?" he said, as if he didn't agree with her definition of normal.

"No. Normal meaning that since the whole Drew business there hasn't been any of that. At least not until lately. In a way the fiasco with Drew showed me that Trina isn't weak or fragile anymore. It showed me she was strong enough to hurt me," Nia added somewhat wryly. "That changed things. For the better, in that I was forced to really see each of us as individuals. And by the end of her marriage, and after having gone our separate ways, we sort of came back together as ordinary sisters. That's how it is now. Well, usually. I will admit that since Trina found out she's pregnant her emotions have been intense, on top of her being miserably sick, and she's needed help. So some of the old patterns have been in force again."

"So that's why you've been fretting about her and making sure you're at her beck and call."

"Yes."

"But still, you like being needed," he said, as if his words were some kind of test question.

"It's more that I've been hoping if I gave her all the support I could, things would work out the way they have and not… Well, not some other way that we all might have been sorry for."

"So, unlike Phoebe, you wouldn't have adopted Trina's baby to keep it in the family?"

"To tell you the truth, that had actually occurred to me even before reading the journals. I was surprised when I read that that's what Phoebe had done and how similar some things in our lives were. But I'm glad it won't be an issue now."

The sound of music starting up not far away gave her the perfect out then.

"Have we been sitting here talking for that long?" she asked, referring to the fact that the dance wasn't scheduled to begin until eight o'clock.

"Looks like it," Clay said, glancing around as if he'd been so involved in their conversation he hadn't noticed it getting dark, either.

But apparently he wasn't quite finished talking yet because his focus returned to her. "Is that everything? One engagement that didn't pan out, no marriages and no other close calls I'd want to know about?"

She wasn't sure why he wanted to know about her past at all, but rather than question it she said, "That's it. Now you know my own whole sordid history and the whole sordid history of my family."

"You're a colorful, hot-blooded bunch," he said, making her laugh and easing the tension that had grown through the telling of her story.

Clay stood and held out a hand to her. "And now that you know that you don't have to be P.O.'ed at me for the supplement, and I know all the skeletons in your closet, what do you say we go back to having some fun? Let's dance."

Once again resisting his appeal was beyond Nia's grasp. His hand wasn't, though, and she accepted it, reveling in the warm strength that wrapped around hers when she did, and marveling at yet another wash of relief coming over her. A total relief that gave her a sense of complete freedom. A sense that she really had earned the right to let her hair down tonight.

"I'm not sure you're good for me," she muttered as he pulled her to her feet.

"Yeah, but sometimes bad is better," he whispered into her ear as they followed what seemed to be a horde of other people who were also answering the call of the music.

The Founder's Day dance took place in the big tent that had earlier been used as a dining hall. The tables had been replaced with a raised platform for the band, a wooden dance floor that covered the entire center, and folding chairs around the perimeter. Space heaters had also been added to chase away the spring evening chill, and the top of the tent had been strung with lights.

There had been dances in Elk Creek at other times when Nia was there but she'd either been too young to be allowed to attend them or, as a teenager, had had other pursuits that she'd preferred. But tonight she learned why her grandparents, and her parents when they were in town, had refused to miss one. This was no stuffy country club cotillion. This was a plain, down-home good time.

Everyone danced, even the few children who were there were on the floor, mimicking the adults or dancing with their parents. Several couples Nia would have believed too aged and infirm left behind ailments and aches and pains to kick up their heels, too. There were no wallflowers; everyone was included even if it meant threesomes dancing here and there.

Nia herself never lacked a partner. Although she was happiest dancing with Clay, they were cut in on numerous times by his cousins and cousins-in-law, as well as by the Brimley brothers and, it seemed, half the rest of the male population of Elk Creek.

Nia had never had an evening quite like it. The music was mainly country and western but ran the gamut from fast to slow, to two-steps to line dancing and everything in between. Everyone on the floor was game to try anything and to learn from anyone who knew steps they didn't.

All in all it was just a grand time and Nia found it hard to believe it was already 1:00 a.m. when things wrapped up and those who were still left—a not insubstantial number—had to call it a night.

Clay walked Nia home but it was amid a whole contingent of Elk Creek's citizens, so it wasn't a solitary stroll. But that was nice, too. Weariness seemed to inspire even more camaraderie, and jokes and comments and gossip were passed along and laughed at and enjoyed.

And for the first time it occurred to Nia why Clay had been willing to change his lifestyle so drastically to move to this small town. It really was like one great big family comprised of open, down-to-earth, unpretentious people who seemed to like one another. She could see the draw.

Then Nia and Clay turned off onto Molner Circle and went the rest of the way to her house alone. And while she felt a twinge of regret to call good-nights to so many of those old friends she'd reconnected with and the new acquaintances she'd just made on this trip, she didn't regret finally being alone with Clay as they walked side by side up the middle of the paved avenue.

"Cole's truck is gone," Nia observed when the house came into view. "He and Trina must have gone to his place again."

"They never did show up at the celebration, did they?" Clay said.

"I never saw them if they did."

"I thought they might at least come to the dance tonight—Cole does a mean two-step."

Nia couldn't imagine her sister doing that but didn't say it. Instead she just kept optimistic that that, like so many other things about Cole, would be something Trina would adapt to.

"I hope not showing up doesn't mean Trina was too sick to come."

Clay chuckled a bit under his breath. "If I was going to put money on it I'd say they just had a more private celebration of their own."

Nia smiled, thinking how true that probably was, but didn't comment as they stepped up to the front door.

She opened it but didn't go inside. The walk from Center Street up Molner Circle had seemed shorter than ever before and she knew that she wasn't ready yet to say good-night—possibly goodbye—to Clay.

She just wasn't sure what she *was* ready for.

"I know it's late, but would you like to come in?" she heard herself ask before she even knew she was going to, still without a clear idea of exactly what she was requesting. Or suggesting.

The porch light was on and they were standing beneath it, face-to-face by then, and Clay seemed to have no similar confusion. He just smiled at her, a perfectly serene, one-sided smile.

"For a nightcap?" he asked with a voice full of mischief.

There was an idea—she didn't know why she hadn't thought of it. "The bar is well stocked," she said, as if that were what she'd had in mind all along.

Clay nodded his handsome head, but it seemed more as if he were thinking over what she'd said, not agreeing to it.

"I could do that," he answered noncommittally.

"Or if you're hungry the refrigerator is always stocked, too," she added.

Again the nod, lazy and ruminative. "I could do that, too," he said, his blue eyes locked onto hers with a self-assurance that seemed to convey that, unlike Nia, he knew exactly what he wanted.

"Or we could even watch a movie or something, if you aren't tired."

His smile broadened. "Aren't you tired?"

She'd thought she was after all that dancing. But now? She just didn't want him to go.

"No, I'm not tired," she answered.

"Hungry or thirsty?" he asked.

"Not particularly."

"Then instead of a nightcap or food or a movie, I'd rather do this…."

His hands came to her shoulders, holding her steady as he leaned forward and kissed her.

And that was when Nia knew exactly what she wanted. Right then, with his lips parted over hers and the faint scent of his aftershave going to her head and the whole essence of the man himself all around her. It wasn't only that she didn't want the brief minutes they'd finally gotten alone to end. It wasn't only that she wasn't ready to say good-night or goodbye to him. She wanted much more than that. Much more than a nightcap or a sandwich or to watch a late movie.

She wanted what she'd wanted the night before and denied herself. She wanted what she'd wanted all through the sleepless hours after he'd left, and the moment her eyes had opened this morning. She wanted what she realized, just at that moment, that she'd wanted all day and all evening. She wanted him.

She lifted her hands to his chest, laying palms to honed pectorals and absorbing his heat. His arms came around her then, pulling her closer as his mouth opened wider over hers and his tongue urged her mouth to open wider, too.

It occurred to her that she might not be thinking clearly. That after the week she'd just put in and all the stress over Trina's pregnancy, after Trina's indecision over Cole and all the uncertainty of how things might turn out, after all the work on the journals and the test of wills between herself and Clay, after the long day and night she'd just enjoyed and the fatigue that had set in, her thinking might be clouded. That she might be losing sight of things she shouldn't lose sight of. That she might be in a prime position to do something she could regret.

But it just didn't seem to matter. This moment, this man and the way he made her feel, was all that seemed important and she just couldn't force reason to take over.

One night, she thought. *What harm could there be in that?*

And since she couldn't think of an answer, she ended their kiss, took Clay's hand and led him over the threshold and into the house.

He went willingly and closed the door behind them,

but then took control again, leaning back against the oak panel and using their clasped hands to carefully yank her toward him.

"I don't want food or booze or movies," he repeated with a warning note in his voice.

"Neither do I."

"I want to take you upstairs and do what I wanted to do last night—*all* of what I wanted to do last night."

"That's where I was headed," she whispered, as if there was someone else who might hear.

"What happened between last night and tonight to make things different?" he asked, demanding to be convinced that she actually would go through with this.

Nia shrugged. "It…just never went away," she said, unsure whether or not he would understand that the *it* she was referring to were the desires he'd aroused in her. The desires that had been growing in her since she'd set eyes on him.

But he must have understood because he grinned at her in the dimness of the foyer and said, "Kind of amazing, isn't it—what happens between us?"

Nia nodded.

"And you're sure? Tonight you're sure you don't want to fight it?"

She nodded again, staring at his features in all their angled, rugged glory, and just wishing he would kiss her again.

He didn't, though. Instead he straightened and said, "Say it. Say you're sure."

Nia didn't hesitate. "I'm sure. I'm absolutely positive."

For another moment he studied her, judging just how certain she was. But then he smiled the sexiest smile she'd ever seen, and, continuing to hold her hand, led her up the stairs.

Nia could only assume that he knew which room was hers from being in the house when his brother was working on the remodeling, and she was right. He took her there, closing that door behind them.

And then they were not only alone, they were alone in her room, bathed in the silvery glow of the moonlight coming in through the open curtains.

If Nia had had any lingering doubts, they disappeared the moment the door was closed. What remained was nothing but her desire for him, running free and rampant at last. Pure, sensual indulgence—that was what this was, and for once in her life she was willing—she was driven—to simply give in to it. To give herself over to it. And that's what she did.

She kicked off her shoes and unfastened the top two buttons of her cardigan.

But Clay grabbed her wrists and stopped her before she could do the rest.

"Let me," he ordered, releasing her long enough to remove and toss aside his own boots and socks. Then he caught her wrists all over again, pulling them to rest atop his shoulders so he could circle her waist with his arms and bring her closer to him. Close enough to reclaim her mouth with his.

But it wasn't an at-the-door good-night kiss. Now it was open and sensual. Now tongues fenced and jockeyed and courted and wooed boldly as Nia's hands went to Clay's neck and rose into the bristly shortness of his hair. Clay's arms wrapped her tighter and held her against him where her nipples could nudge his chest.

Nipples that wanted to be unleashed along with the rest of Nia's body.

It occurred to her that he'd stopped her from divesting herself of her clothes, but as much as she wanted to shed her own she wanted his gone, too. And there hadn't been any edicts about that.

So she leaned back enough to make way for her hands to drop to his chest, underneath the jean jacket he still wore, sliding them again up and over his shoulders to rid him of the denim coat.

There were no complaints about that, or about yanking his T-shirt out of his jeans and rolling it up and over his head, interrupting their seeking mouths for a split second to accomplish it.

But Nia broke away again once the shirt was off and she realized his chest was bare. That it was right there for her to see.

She gave him two consolation kisses before stepping back enough to feast on the sight of his naked torso. And despite the fact that she still longed for his mouth, it was worth it to see for herself his broad, broad shoulders, his honed pectorals, his washboard abs and the dark line of hair that led from his navel to disappear behind the low waistband of his jeans.

His torso was so spectacular that she couldn't force her hands not to explore it, not to learn the feel of it, the textures and tones. From boulderlike biceps to the dip of his collarbone, her fingers and palms roamed, high and low. She brushed her fingertips across his nipples on her way to the sides of his waist, all the while letting her gaze devour him.

He really was like a living, breathing work of art, and she memorized every line the same way she memorized every line of the sculptures she worked with.

Clay didn't seem to mind her scrutiny because his attention was where she'd wanted it in the first place—he was unbuttoning her sweater. Taking it off and then oh-so-softly kissing each shoulder in turn before sliding her bra straps down her arms and leaving them to dangle at her elbows while he reached around to unfasten the hooks in back.

The lacy cups stayed partially in place even then, until Clay kissed a trail down the uppermost mound of one breast, nuzzling her bra off with his nose so he could press another kiss to her nipple before taking it playfully into his mouth.

Nia let the bra fall to the floor as she got lost in what he was doing to her. As her eyes closed and her chin pointed toward the ceiling.

Hot. Wet. Wonderful. His mouth and hands performed a blissful torture of both breasts. Caressing. Kneading. Tugging and titillating and tormenting her with the awakening of even greater desires. Desires that rippled downward from breasts that seemed to swell and strain as he managed to turn her nipples into tiny pebbles of pleasure before releasing them.

She found the waistband of his jeans then, propelled by a craving so intense she could hardly stand it. Bringing her head forward, she rested her brow against his chest, opening her eyes to scant slits as she began to unfasten the buttons of his fly, watching his jeans spread an inch at a time, revealing the rest of his flat belly and more. So much more…

He didn't have anything on underneath the jeans and the burgeoning proof of his need for her was there in a magnificence all its own. A magnificence Nia couldn't resist clasping her hand around to test the steely length and strength of.

A low groan rumbled from Clay's throat, and the pressure of his mouth on her breast increased tenfold to kick up Nia's own yearnings another notch.

He took his turn at unfastening her jeans then, causing them and her panties to fall around her ankles before discarding his own jeans as if he couldn't wait to be rid of them.

While Nia kicked the last of her clothes away, Clay captured her mouth with his again in a hungry, wide-open kiss, plundering her as his hands filled themselves with her breasts. She went on exploring him, learning just how to drive him to near frenzy—near enough to skip from her mouth to her breast again, wrap one arm around her back and the other under her knees, scoop her up in his arms and whisk her to the bed.

He laid her there to watch as he retrieved his jeans in a hurry, returning with protection.

Nia sat up as he knelt beside her, taking a turn herself at kissing him, at teasing his mouth and tongue with hers while he made sure they were both safe. Then he pressed her flat again so he could stretch out half beside her, half above her.

Once more he deserted her mouth, returning to one of her breasts to draw it into that velvety cavern. To circle her nipple with his tongue. To tug on it with gentle teeth. To flick and fondle it as his hand began an entirely new course from where it worked the engorged flesh of her other breast—down her stomach, down her thigh and around to the back of it, raising it with his forearm and reaching from behind to find that spot between her legs where need had been mounting all along.

Nia's breath caught at that first touch. At that first entrance of a thick, adept finger into her while his thumb found that most sensitive cleft farther forward and left her every focus on the wonders he was working, on sensations more potent than anything she'd ever experienced before.

He seemed to know just how much she could take without losing herself, and on the very brink, he stopped, let her leg fall to the bed and came over her. Bracing his weight on his hands on either side of her head, he fitted himself between her thighs to find that same juncture with the part of his body she'd marveled at before.

Long and thick, he slipped into her, filling her with heat and power, pausing only a moment before he began to move within her, slowly at first, pulsing, flexing. Then gaining speed, moving in and out.

Nia pressed her hands to his broad shoulders, meeting him, drawing back, keeping up with the rhythm, the pace, as every nerve ending, every sense, every inch of her came awake, alert, alive.

Faster and faster he thrust into her, deeper, harder. And as she kept up with him something began to take shape within her. Something that almost felt like a ball of energy, growing bigger, stronger, hotter and hotter until it could be contained no longer and burst into a wild spree of color and light that swept her away with it even as Clay stiffened in his own climax. Color and light that sapped all thought from Nia, all will, all ability to do anything but cling to him as wave after wave of keen, exquisite ecstasy rushed through her, over her, all around her.

Only after an eternity did the colors begin to dim, to fade. And when they did they took with them every ounce of strength Nia had ever possessed, leaving her muscles, her joints dissolved into a sultry liquid she could do nothing more than languish in.

For a time Clay was very still above her, inside of her, his body melded to hers and weighing her down in a way that felt better than good. And then he raised his upper half onto his forearms and looked down at her.

"Last night I said that it boggled the mind to think of what might happen between us if you weren't mad at me. But even my mind-bogglings couldn't compare to this," he said in a ragged voice.

He inched forward so he could kiss her again, a kiss that seemed to seal what they'd just shared and somehow bind them, before he slipped out of her and rolled them both a full turn so that Nia ended up lying completely on top of him, her head pillowed by his chest.

"Say you're still sure," he commanded, one arm wrapped around her while the fingers of his other hand combed through her hair.

"I'm still sure." Nia complied in a quiet, raspy voice of her own.

He took his hand from her hair and pulled one of her hands to his mouth to kiss it before holding it to his chest, where she could see that big, powerful mitt around hers. Then he gave a satisfied sigh that raised his chest and her along with it, and she felt him relax so completely beneath her that she knew he was falling asleep.

But Nia was too spent herself to care. Or to be able to fight off slumber for long.

And so she drifted in that direction, too, thinking about nothing but how incredibly right it felt to be lying with her body following every rise and fall of his.

Chapter 10

There were times in Clay's life when his instincts had served him well. There were also times when they hadn't. And that was one of the things he was thinking about the next morning, lying in Nia's bed.

It was a few minutes before nine and he'd been awake about half an hour, watching Nia sleep.

He knew she would probably hate it if she found out, but he was lying very still so as not to wake her as he sorted through all the things going on in his head.

She was on her side, facing him, curled up into a tight little ball. Her hair was fanned out on the pillow in waves of silky auburn splendor. Her skin looked like fresh cream. Her long dark eyelashes rested against pale pink cheeks, and those lips he was crazy about kissing were parted only a slit and curved upward slightly at the corners, as if she were having a pleasant dream.

Or maybe it was in response to the night they'd just had together and the two rounds of lovemaking that had rocked his world.

Clay preferred believing the faint hint of a smile was due to the lovemaking.

It had sure as hell left him feeling good.

So good it had actually changed things for him. It had opened his eyes—figuratively as well as literally this morning, when wanting her again had roused him out of sleep. It had made him start thinking about what else he wanted. What he didn't want. What his instincts were telling him and whether or not he should listen to them.

Clay was lying on his side, too, but he had one arm on his pillow so he could brace his head on his hand and get the full view of Nia. The view he'd been thinking he'd like to wake up to every morning.

Which was another thing that had made the wheels in his brain start turning.

She'd be leaving town anytime now—that had occurred to him right off the bat. And when she did, not only wouldn't he have that view to wake up to every morning, he might not ever wake up to it again. And he'd discovered that he hated that possibility. That he didn't want it to be a possibility at all.

Which led him to think about exactly what he did—and didn't—want.

Obviously he wanted Nia; it hadn't taken much to come to that. And given that fact, he definitely didn't want her to get in her car and drive away. Not today or tomorrow or next week or the week after that. He didn't want there to be any chance that he might not see her again or that he might only see her on rare occasions when she came to visit her sister. And he didn't want some long-distance relationship with her, either—where they talked on the phone or e-mailed each other more than they saw each other. Where they only got together when they could manage it.

So what *did* he want beyond Nia? he'd asked himself. What exactly did that mean over and above the fact that he wanted her right where she was at that moment?

It hadn't been all that tough to come to that, either. He didn't merely want her in bed. He wanted her in the bigger sense, too. He wanted not only to see her every morning when he woke up, but all through the day. All through the evening. Every day and evening. He wanted her around. Around town. Around his house. Around him. He wanted her near enough, always, to be able to do nothing more than open a door or cross a street to see her. He wanted her in his life— that's what he'd finally concluded. He wanted the whole nine yards.

Coming to that conclusion had felt right, too. His instincts even now were telling him to go for it. And when it came to business, his instincts had never steered him wrong.

The problem was, when it came to relationships with women, his instincts had told him to go for it with Shayna, too.

And that was where his thinking hit a logjam. Because not only had his instincts pointed him in Shayna's direction, there were some similarities between Nia and Shayna that weren't altogether good.

How many times had something Nia said or done in the past week made him think of Shayna? he asked himself now. How many times had something Nia said or done set off his alarms?

Too many to deny it. Too many to ignore it. Especially when it might mean he was on the verge of ending up with another mother hen. Another woman who needed to be needed to such an extent that it drove him out of his mind.

But as he continued to watch Nia, something about her and that mother hen thing didn't exactly ring true for him.

Yeah, she'd mothered Trina. Right from the first day they'd arrived in Elk Creek, when she'd waited on her sister hand and foot, as if Trina were a child. And yeah, there had been all those times when plans he'd wanted to make with Nia had been put on hold until she was sure Trina was occupied—as if Trina required a baby-sitter. And yeah, there had been that night coming out of Margie Wilson's Café when his cell phone rang and Nia had insisted he answer it in case it was Trina or something to do with her. Plus Cole had told him that Nia had actually driven out to his ranch in the middle of the night to pick Trina up—as if she were a five-year-old who hadn't been able to stay at a sleep-over.

At the time those had all seemed like signs to Clay. Bad signs of a smothering, suffocating person like Shayna had been. A person who honed in on another and made that individual her life's work, the center of her universe, blocking out everything and everyone else.

But what if he'd been reading the signs wrong all along? he asked himself now. What if it really was the way Nia had said it was when she'd told him about Trina and Nia's former fiancé? What if everything he'd seen as signs that Nia was like Shayna had been Nia simply responding to her sister's pregnancy and emotional state? What if the signs didn't amount to anything more than Nia being a supportive sister?

A supportive sister wasn't the same thing as a mother hen. It wasn't the same as someone needing to be needed. It didn't translate into suffocation. It could just mean that Nia was a caring, compassionate person. Which was good. It could mean that family and family closeness were important to her, which was also good, since family and family closeness were things Clay was all for. Certainly he didn't want an uncaring and un-compassionate woman who didn't want any connection with her family or anyone else's. *That* was Shayna, who had wanted them both isolated from everyone else so she would have the illusion he was dependent on her, and that no one besides her filled any need he might have.

But could he be sure that the mother hen stuff *was* Nia simply being a supportive sister and not another Shayna?

As Clay studied Nia one of her eyebrows arched, apparently in response to something she was seeing in her sleep. It made him smile. But it also reminded him of something else. It reminded him of the dynamics of their working relationship as they'd gone through the journals, and of the arguments they'd had over what he was allowed to print from them.

From day one Nia hadn't been there to assist him— the capacity in which Shayna had been employed, and the role she'd been so good at because it fed her need to be needed. Nia had approached their reading the diaries together as equals.

She'd also presented him with a challenge from the very beginning. There hadn't been anything nurturing or self-sacrificing in that. Nia had done battle with him over what he could and couldn't print, all the way to the end. Even after things had begun to heat up between them.

By then, in that situation, Shayna would have accepted even a hit to her own family in order to meet his needs, to make herself more valuable to him in the hopes that it would make him rely more on her.

But not Nia. She'd come in setting the rules and she'd stuck to them. And he knew for a fact that had he written about the Phoebe-Maude-Arlen scandal in that last supplement he would have had some answering to do.

No, there hadn't been any indication that Nia was inclined to mother anyone but Trina. Or any indication that Nia would feel unfulfilled because he didn't need or want her to make him the center of her universe. She was her own person and expected the same from him—even if what she'd ultimately believed of him hadn't been too flattering.

But he couldn't fault her for not completely trusting him over the supplements. Hell, here he was, not completely trusting her, either. Or at least having to hash through his own mistrust to get to the truth.

He thought he *had* gotten to the truth, though. Now that he weighed it all. When Nia had told him about Trina's affair and marriage to Nia's fiancé, she'd told him how that had altered their relationship as sisters. He didn't doubt that it would. And since he hadn't seen any other evidence of Nia playing mother hen, any evidence that she'd gotten any kind of thrill out of it— the way Shayna had seemed to be in her glory when she was bending over backward for him—he didn't find it so difficult to believe that Nia's actions had been a temporary throwback to old training. Something she'd done because it *had* to be done and not the way things were under normal circumstances. Not the way Nia even wanted them to be.

And if he didn't believe that Nia was a suffocating mother hen, then he couldn't see a single reason why they couldn't make this work out between them. Why he couldn't have Nia in his life.

If she was willing.

And damn, did he hope she was willing…

Because even though his instincts might have failed him on the romance front once before, he was going to listen to them again now.

He had to. What he felt for Nia, what they had together, was just too overwhelming to be ignored. Too overwhelming not to act on.

Too overwhelming not to work out…

"Knock, knock! Rise and shine! I only have a few minutes and… Whoops! I didn't know you had company."

Nia was jolted out of sleep by her sister's boisterous entrance into her room. She sat up, realized a split second later that not only wasn't she wearing anything, she also wasn't alone.

Something Trina realized at about the same time, making a hasty retreat and closing the door again as Nia snatched up the sheet, holding it to her naked breasts.

From beside her, Clay chuckled. He seemed to be the only one not shaken by his presence. "I had a more subtle plan for waking you up, but I guess that did the trick."

Adrenaline rushed through Nia, and it took her a moment to get her bearings. Sunday morning. Yesterday was Founder's Day. She and Clay had made love….

But before she could say anything to him, Trina's voice came from the hallway just outside the door, sounding more amused than shocked now.

"Sorry about that. I guess we know why we haven't been able to get you on the phone at home, Clay. Cole is downstairs in the living room and we only have a few minutes before we're supposed to meet Bax Mc-Dermot at his office so he can do our blood tests. But we wanted to talk to you two. Could you, uh, come out?"

"We'll be right there," Clay called back, his own tone filled with humor even as he added to Nia, "Are you okay?"

She nodded, not quite sure what to say.

Clay sat up and out of the corner of her eye she saw his bare chest—as spectacular in daylight as it had been in moonglow—and a sudden wave of the same desire that had gotten her into her current position rippled through her.

But this was no time for a third taste of Clay's charms, so she wrestled that renegade burst of desire into submission.

"Looks like we'd better get up and throw on some clothes," he suggested. "But I have some pretty important stuff to talk to you about myself, so even if they try to enlist us in something, let's see if we can buy ourselves a little time alone first, huh?"

Curiosity finally allowed Nia to find her voice. "What kind of stuff?" she asked, hazarding a direct glance at him and finding she even liked him with the scruffy beard that had appeared overnight, shadowing the lower half of his face.

He gave her a wicked smile from amid those rugged

whiskers. "Just some stuff," he answered enigmatically as he rolled in the other direction and got out of bed.

Okay, so about the last thing she needed at that moment, when she was already struggling with uninvited urges and disorientation, was to get a look at his naked derriere. It should have been a crime for any man to have a butt that terrific, and seeing it only increased the intensity of those cravings she was trying to keep at bay.

But knowing that her sister and Cole were close by, waiting for them, she also knew she had to get some control over herself. Nia bent both knees under the sheet and dropped her head to them.

"You get dressed and go down. I'll be right behind you," she said, her voice muffled by the sheet.

"Feeling a little shy, are we?" he asked, chuckling again.

She could tell by the sound of his voice that he was facing her, and as much as she wanted to look up at the daylight view of his front half, she knew it was just asking for trouble. "A little," she confirmed.

"Ah, but for the time to chase that away..." he mused.

Nia heard him pulling on his jeans and a moment later felt his weight on the end of the bed.

"I'm decent if you want to un-bury your face," he said then.

She only peeked, finding that, while he had put on his jeans and was in the process of donning his boots, his upper half remained bare and beautiful, making her hands itch to touch him.

Then, while she was still spying, he shrugged into his T-shirt in a movement that was so sexy it sent shivers along the surface of her skin.

"That's okay," she said a bit belatedly, closing her eyes and pressing her face to her knees again.

Another chuckle preceded the release of the mattress as he stood and said, "Okay, that's it for me."

"I'll see you downstairs," Nia answered.

Once more the mattress was depressed—apparently by his hands bracing his weight as he leaned from the bottom of the bed to kiss the crown of her head. "Remember, we have to talk."

She nodded but refused to look up again until she heard the door close behind him.

Then she took a deep breath and blew it out in a gust that still didn't help to quell all that had been so suddenly aroused at just the sight of him.

But she knew if she lingered much longer Trina would be back, and Nia didn't really want her sister there, looking at the rumpled bed where she and Clay had made love. So she got up and quickly put on her own discarded clothes from the day before, because they were the nearest at hand.

Then she glanced in the mirror above her vanity, dragged a brush through her hair and blessed unsmudgeable mascara for being invented, then followed Clay downstairs.

On the way she fought embarrassment at the

thought of coming face-to-face with his brother under these circumstances. But that embarrassment disappeared on its own when she went from the foyer into the living room.

Because that was when she came upon Clay with his arms around Trina.

The sight stopped Nia cold in her tracks under the archway.

Trina was in Clay's arms….

And no matter how innocent it might have been, it was like a bucket of cold water thrown in Nia's face to actually see them that way.

"Hey, break it up," Cole said jokingly from where he was standing beside Trina. "You had your chance with her and blew it. She's mine now, so hands off."

"Oh yeah, right, I forgot," Clay joked back before saying to Trina, "Congratulations and welcome to the family." Then he released her to extend his hand to his brother and combine a hug with a handshake.

"Nia! There you are," Trina said, catching sight of her then.

"Looks like we're having a wedding," Clay announced, unaware of the impact seeing him embrace her sister was having on Nia.

"As soon as possible," Trina added with a laugh. "That's why the hurry with the blood test. We're getting the waiting time waived, too, so we can have the ceremony tomorrow. Cole wants Clay to be best man and I want you as my maid of honor—that's why we were trying to track the two of you down this morning. Not that I expected to track you both down in your bedroom. Sorry, again, about that."

Nia didn't address the comment or the apology that went with it, and instead stepped up to hug her sister and offer her own congratulations.

"I told you it would all work out," she added in a whisper for Trina's ears alone.

"Maybe some things are working out for you, too," she whispered back happily before their hug ended.

When it did, Trina went on to talk very fast about the fact that she'd called their parents in Europe to tell them the news, and that she and Cole were trying to make arrangements to actually have the wedding the next day, and what they were doing to accomplish that.

"And I even got a reprieve from the morning sickness today," she added almost giddily.

"But we still got a later start than we should have," Cole pointed out. "So we'd better get going. Bax is coming in just to do this for us. We don't want to keep him waiting."

"I know," Trina conceded. She gave Nia a second hug. "I'll be back later, though, to fill you in," she said.

"I'll be here," Nia assured her, watching as Trina linked an arm through Cole's and shot him a beaming smile.

"Later for us, too, huh?" Cole said to Clay.

"Sure."

Cole led Trina out then as Clay and Nia looked on.

"That's nice," Clay said as the front door closed behind their siblings. "But I'm jealous."

Coupled with the scene she'd walked in on only moments before, his comment stabbed Nia.

"Of Cole," she said.

Clay laughed. "No, not of Cole," he corrected. "I'm jealous of the two of them. What they've found together."

He stepped up to Nia then and circled her waist with his arms, bending over to kiss the side of her neck. And while Nia knew the effect that would have had on her half an hour ago, it didn't have that same effect now. Now it only served to stiffen her entire body.

To such a degree that Clay loosened his grip just enough for her to slip out of it and put some distance between them.

"It can't be easy to lose your former girlfriend to your brother," she said, unable to keep the challenge from her tone.

Clay's expression pulled into a confused frown. "*Former* being the operative word here. And actually, it was pretty easy. I didn't have any problem with it at all. I have other things on my mind."

Nia suddenly did, too. But not much of it was good anymore.

"You wanted to talk," she said, assuming that whatever he'd wanted to talk about was what was on his mind.

Clay's frown deepened. "Are you okay? Did you not want them to get together?" he asked, misinterpreting her cool tone and not much warmer reception of him.

"They're having a baby, so of course I wanted them to get together," Nia insisted. "I've been rooting for it all along."

"Then you're okay with that, but something else is bothering you. Is it me? Last night?"

Both. And wondering if she'd let herself lose sight of things she shouldn't have.

She didn't say that, though. Instead she said, "I'm fine," but without much conviction. "What did you want to talk about?"

He didn't answer immediately. He stared at her, studied her, as if gauging whether or not to believe she was fine, and go on, after all.

But in the end he decided to take the plunge. "I wanted to talk about you and me."

Nia only raised her chin as encouragement for him to continue.

"I was awake a long time before Trina charged in. Awake and thinking," Clay said.

"About you and me?"

"About you and me. And where we're going from here."

"Apparently we're going to a wedding," she stated, more flippantly than she felt, for the stinging effects of seeing Trina in his arms lingered just beneath the surface.

And suddenly the distance she'd put between them wasn't enough, so she turned as if she'd developed an interest in a piece of lint on the high back of the chair nearest to her, and went to remove it.

"What about after the wedding?" Clay asked then. "Where are you and I going from there?"

"Back to work, I guess," Nia answered.

"Which, for you, means back to Denver."

"That is where I work."

"Well, that's what I realized I didn't want—you going back to Denver. Our not seeing each other, or only seeing each other sporadically. Not having you here, with me."

It was on the tip of her tongue to say, *You'll have Trina here, though....*

But she didn't.

And Clay didn't wait for her to respond before he went on.

"I want what they have," he said, nodding in the direction Cole and Trina had just gone. "I know this has all happened fast, but when it's right, it's right. And my gut instinct is telling me that it's right. *We're* right. I haven't wanted to do anything but be with you since the day you got here. Every minute I've been with you has been better than the one before and I haven't wanted it to end. And last night... Last night was...well, it sealed the deal for me. I woke up this morning knowing that I want us to be together. I *need* for us to be together."

They were nice words. Nice sentiments. They just weren't powerful enough to erase the images in her mind. Not only the image of walking into the living room to find him holding Trina, but also the image of Trina with Drew—an image Nia had never had to witness, but had pictured too many times for it not to seem real. And all she could do was shake her head.

"I know," Clay said, guessing what she was thinking. "You love your job at the museum. You've worked to be where you are since you were a teenager. But what if you and I bring art to Elk Creek? Money is no object. We could open a gallery, put in the highest tech security so we could attract even exhibits of grand masters and private collections. I know people everywhere. You have connections in the art world. We could—"

Nia shook her head again, more firmly this time. Firmly enough to stop him.

"It isn't my job," she said in a quiet voice.

"Then what is it?" he asked. "You don't like me?"

He'd added that last with a slight chuckle, as if he knew better. And of course, he should have. The night they'd just spent together couldn't have left him with any doubts that she had feelings for him. That she could be carried away by those feelings. She just couldn't let herself be carried away by them anymore.

"I was Phoebe once. I won't be again," she said then, ignoring his question about liking him.

Confusion returned to his features. "I can see how you were in Phoebe's shoes when Trina and your fiancé fell in love the way Maude and Arlen did. But how would you be Phoebe in any scenario with me?"

"You were involved with Trina. Attracted to her. Interested in her—"

"A lifetime ago."

"Twelve years is not a lifetime."

"It might as well be," he insisted. "And I don't know how *involved* it was—we dated a little one summer when we were barely more than kids."

"You dated because you were attracted to her, interested in her."

"You make that sound like more than it was. I liked Trina well enough. I still like her. That doesn't mean—"

"What it means to me is that I've done something I swore I would never do again. I let someone get close who isn't completely impervious to Trina. It's just that this last week I've gone back and forth between remembering that that's who you are and forgetting it. Although it's crazy that I kept forgetting it when the reminders have been right in front of my face."

"What reminders?"

"The times when I came into a room and found the two of you talking and laughing together. There was Friday night, when you picked me up for the banquet and spent so long watching Trina go out to Cole's truck—as if you couldn't take your eyes off her. There was just now, when I came down and found you hugging her—"

"There wasn't anything to any of that. So we talked and laughed—that doesn't mean a thing. I talk to a lot of people. I laugh with a lot of people. So do you. So does everybody. And my watching Trina go out to Cole's truck on Friday night wasn't because I couldn't take my eyes off her. It was because Cole and I had guessed she was pregnant and I wondered if I could tell just by looking—that's all there was to that. And just now..." He blew out a miffed sigh. "That was a congratulatory hug. I gave one to my secretary when she got engaged to the minister, too."

"The point is, I couldn't help wondering. I couldn't help worrying. And I can't be in a situation that will always make me feel that way."

"Okay then, I'll never hug her again. Or anyone else, for that matter, if it makes you feel better," he said as if she were being petty.

"This isn't a joke to me," she said.

He pressed his fingertips to his temples and shook his head. "This just isn't reasonable, Nia. Basically, the only thing that went on between your sister and me is that I knew her. I didn't sleep with her. We didn't even hit it off enough to write letters when she left that summer. We didn't hit it off enough to keep in touch."

"Apparently you hit it off enough for her to have fond memories and come back here looking for you a few weeks ago."

"Because of some teenage romance fantasy she thought would boost her ego after the blow of finding her husband in bed with someone else? Realistically, what do you think would have happened if I *had* been here?"

Nia shrugged. "It might be you getting a blood test with her right now rather than Cole."

Clay shook his head vigorously. "No, it wouldn't

be. Trina and Cole connected because they clicked. Trina and I didn't click enough twelve years ago for it to go anywhere, and we wouldn't have clicked weeks ago had I been here. We just plain don't click in that way. We didn't before. We don't now. We won't in the future."

"You can't say that for sure—about the future," Nia accused.

"Yes, I can. I've had a lot of girlfriends and known a lot of women—one I married—and none of them are relevant now or will be relevant in the future. They're in the past. Just the way anybody you've dated or been involved with is in *your* past. Would I need to wonder and worry about you if you happened across any one of them? I understand you went on a hayride with my cousin Jackson once when you were thirteen—should I worry that he could tear us apart now? Or that one day five years from now your eyes might meet his and what attracted you enough for you to agree to go on that hayride with him then will reignite and be the end of everything for us?"

"Of course not."

"But you'll condemn me for what amounts to that."

"I'm not condemning you. I'm just saying that it's a risk I can't take. I can't risk history repeating itself—twice, since it happened to Phoebe, too. Maybe it's the Molner curse."

"You can't believe that," he said. But when she didn't deny it he shook his head again, his hot neon gaze boring into her. "Nia, I don't have any feelings

for your sister. I will never have any feelings for her
that aren't a hundred percent brotherly. It's you I care
about. It's you I want. Don't—"

"I can't, Clay," she said, cutting him off before he
went any further. "There's been a precedent set and I
just can't. Not and ever relax. Not and ever not have
it in the back of my mind that at any time one of you
could come to me the way Trina did before and let me
know you've rekindled an old flame. My eyes have to
be open from the start. From now."

"Then open your eyes and look at this—at me—the
way you *should.* I'm a better bet than anyone. I've already been *involved* with Trina—I use that term
loosely—and it didn't go anywhere. That should make
me *more* worthy of your trust, because I've proved that
I don't want her. You said yourself that this Drew guy
fell for her the first time he laid eyes on her. Who's to
say that the next guy you fall in love with and bring
around to meet her doesn't do the same thing?"

He had a point. But it wasn't a point that changed
the mental picture still tormenting her, of coming
downstairs to find him and her sister in an embrace. It
wasn't a point that changed all the times during this
last week when she'd wondered if a conversation he
and Trina had had, or a look Clay had cast her way,
had meant something. It didn't change all the times
Nia had wondered if he'd been wishing he were in his
brother's shoes, if Clay wasn't still attracted to her sister.

And all she could think about was how badly it had

hurt when she'd lost Drew to Trina. All she could think was how empty her aunt's life had been, how Phoebe had had to spend it with a man who had wanted Maude more than he'd wanted her. All Nia could think about was that being with Clay, fully opening up her heart to Clay, letting Clay in completely, would be only asking for trouble.

"It just doesn't work for me," she said with a catch in her throat as she looked at his whiskered face, which was no less gorgeous scraggly than clean-shaven. At the body that had fit so perfectly with hers...

"It doesn't work for you because you won't let it," he accused in a deep, gravelly voice.

"I can't," she repeated flatly.

"It's funny, you know?" he countered humorlessly. "I was afraid you were too self-sacrificing. Now I'm getting punched in the gut by the opposite—you're so damn self-protective that you won't even listen to reason."

Nia didn't have an answer to that, so she merely raised her chin a second time.

But it must have been enough for him to see just how deeply her heels were dug in, because after another angry shake of his head, he walked out.

Chapter 11

To Nia's amazement, in Elk Creek a nice wedding could be given with one day's notice and still draw a houseful of guests. With blessings sent from Nia and Trina's absent parents, all the Hellers, Culhanes, McDermots and Brimleys came for Trina and Cole's 7:00 p.m. ceremony on Monday, along with Fran, Simon and several other townsfolk. Everyone brought gifts, and food for the reception afterward, and an impromptu wedding cake was produced by the local bakery.

As Trina and Cole stood before the minister in the Molner living room, which had been cleared of furniture, Nia tried to focus on the wealth of warmth, affection and friendliness that permeated the occasion, and not on her own feelings.

Because she felt pretty awful.

Not about the wedding. She and Trina had had a long talk as she'd helped Trina dress, and Nia was convinced that her sister could—and would—be happy with Cole. Trina had conquered all the doubts she'd had about the great-looking cowboy, and Nia honestly believed that even if her sister weren't pregnant, she and Cole would still be there, tying the knot and eager to embark on a life together.

Trina had even laughed off Nia's question about how she was going to feel having Clay as a brother-in-law. It wasn't going to bother her in the slightest, she'd assured her.

"That whole thing with him was like cotton candy," Trina had said. "Remember how much we loved cotton candy when we were kids, and then had it again that time we went to Disneyland to make ourselves feel better when the dog died? That was the year after college graduation and we were determined to do something we'd enjoyed when we were kids—right down to eating cotton candy, remember? But the cotton candy just didn't taste as good to us as it had when we were little. We ended up throwing most of it away, and you know neither one of us will ever eat it again.

"Well, Clay is cotton candy to me. I was trying to recapture something from a long time ago to make myself feel better. But it wouldn't have worked. I see him now as just a nice guy, but not someone I'm attracted to. I see Cole and—I know this will sound strange because on the surface we seem so different, but we aren't—when I'm with him I'm so much more comfortable in my own skin that I know I can handle anything. I'm stronger and better and more centered, and I don't ever want to be without him."

No, Nia hadn't been left with any concerns about Trina marrying Cole after that, and so the wedding wasn't what was making her feel bad.

She felt awful because of Clay. She'd felt awful since the previous morning, when he'd walked out. Even though it was her own fault that he had. Even though it was what she'd been aiming for—an end to what had been happening between them before it went any further.

But accomplishing what she'd told herself was for the best had still left her miserable. And that misery wasn't aided by having him standing only a few feet away right then, on the other side of Cole and Trina.

Nia hadn't ventured a full look his way, but she'd surreptitiously glanced at Clay, enough to know that he and Cole were both wearing dark suits, white shirts and dark ties—forgoing tuxedos for the informal affair.

As always, Clay looked incredible. Nia couldn't keep from thinking about how he'd looked the morning before, too—with the night's growth of beard roughing up his jaw, his hair in wilder disarray than usual, his body in all its naked glory after a night of lovemaking like nothing Nia had ever experienced before.

Lovemaking that had left her satiated and wanting so much more at the same time. Lovemaking that had left her still able to feel his hands, his mouth, his body on hers...so vividly she couldn't curb the craving for it all again. And again. And again...

It just wasn't fair, she thought as the minister sermonized. It wasn't fair to want someone who wasn't good for her, let alone want him with such intensity she didn't think she was ever going to be able to completely rid herself of it. And if she didn't, how would she be able to be with anyone else? To have a relationship with anyone else? A future? What was it going to take to stop remembering? To stop reliving? To stop longing for it all—for everything they'd shared in the past week? Was it going to take Clay actually having an affair with Trina?

Nia wouldn't wish that on Cole and she chastised herself for even thinking such a thing.

Besides, the more she thought about Trina, the more she came to believe her twin would never do anything to hurt anyone again the way she'd hurt Nia with Drew. Trina had endured too much guilt. She'd worked too hard to make amends. She'd learned her own harsh lesson in what had happened with Nia, and then in suffering that same kind of betrayal when Drew had cheated on her.

Looking at it more objectively suddenly, Nia felt certain that once her sister had made the commitment to Cole, Trina wouldn't ever venture over the boundaries with Clay.

So that sort of left Clay free and clear....

Nia wasn't sure where that thought had come from, but she resisted the inclination to consider Clay free and clear for her. He might be free and clear, but for someone else....

And he *should* have someone else, she thought. He was a good man. He deserved someone who would appreciate that. Who would treat him well. Someone unlike his ex-wife, who had used him for her own neurotic needs. He deserved someone who would make him happy.

Someone he'd bring to events like the christening of Trina and Cole's baby. Where Nia couldn't help but see him...

That image hurt so much it nearly made her gasp.

Clay with someone else.

Someone Nia would inevitably meet. Someone she'd encounter at holidays and events when both families got together...

But then, maybe after a while, she really would get over wanting Clay, she told herself. Maybe she'd get over comparing other men to him. Maybe she'd find someone, too—some guy who was just as nice as Clay. Just as sexy. Someone she liked just as well...

But thinking that didn't make her feel any better. In fact, it made her feel worse.

It only threw a big, bright light on the reality that she didn't want anyone else. That she couldn't even fathom being with anyone else now that she'd been with him.

No, deep in her soul she knew that no one else could ever fill his shoes.

So what was she going to do? she asked herself in a surge of panic she could only hope didn't show on her face, standing as she was in front of a roomful of people.

She took several deep breaths, keeping them subtle enough not to be seen and willing herself to calm down. To be rational. To think clearly.

But she'd assumed that rational, clear thinking would lead her to recall all the reasons she *didn't* want Clay. All the reasons she'd turned him down in the first place.

Only that wasn't what happened.

Instead, as she began to gain some control, her mind went off in a different direction. She started to consider the possibility that she'd gone overboard when it came to Clay and the fact that he'd once been involved with Trina. Overboard when it came to being so sure that because of that former involvement, something could develop between Trina and Clay again.

Had she gone overboard? she asked herself gingerly, almost afraid to entertain the possibility.

The idea of something developing between Trina

and Clay again was still tantamount to pouring salt into an open wound for her. But just how much of a chance was there that it would happen? she wondered now.

She already felt certain that Trina wouldn't hurt Cole that way. But what about Clay? Just how sure was she that *he* would do something that meant hurting his brother? Hurting Nia, if they were together?

Clay doing something that would hurt her, hurt his brother?

It just didn't fit.

When Nia learned that Drew had seduced Trina, that they'd had an affair behind her back, it hadn't been difficult to believe. Such a thing wasn't out of character for spoiled, pampered Drew, who always thought of himself first, who had never been denied anything he wanted and certainly had never denied himself anything his heart desired.

But Clay? That wasn't Clay. Not even with the financial means to provide what Drew's family had provided him would Clay live that kind of life. And Clay wasn't the hedonist Drew had been. Clay had a clear view of what was important to him, and indulging his own whims regardless of what kind of repercussions they might incur wasn't part of the picture. If he was like that he would have printed the rest of the Phoebe-Maude-Arlen story. And no, Nia couldn't envision him ever doing anything that would cause the kind of pain, of havoc, that Drew had. Not for his brother, whom

Clay had changed his entire lifestyle to live near, to have a close relationship with. And maybe not for Nia, either.

Of course, that still didn't mean he couldn't have feelings for Trina. It didn't mean that if he was with someone else and that old attraction to Trina resurfaced, the person he was with couldn't end up the way Phoebe had—with a man who was outwardly loyal but who actually loved someone else.

Although suddenly Nia recalled what Clay had said the day before, really giving it some thought now. Some consideration.

Clay had pointed out that he already knew Trina, that he'd already had a youthful fling with her and hadn't taken it any further. And it was true. Clay *did* know Trina. He'd known her for a long time. And nothing had come of it. He'd never made any overtures to her. He'd never tried to contact her, to rekindle their summer romance of years and years ago. And if he hadn't wanted Trina before, wasn't it unlikely that he would want her in the future?

So maybe Clay was right, that not only was he a safe bet, he was a safer bet than a man who hadn't met Trina before.

Suddenly, thinking of Clay as a safe bet—as if that were his biggest selling point—almost made Nia laugh. Clay was so, so much more than that. He was kind and sweet and fun to be with. He had integrity and strength of character. He was confident and cocksure, in a way that was endearing and entertaining. He was intelligent, witty, charming. And he was sexy enough to almost make all the rest of his qualities incidental.

He was also trustworthy—that was something Nia finally admitted to herself.

It had been difficult for her to trust any man since Drew's betrayal, but despite the fact that she *hadn't* trusted Clay, he'd proved himself when he'd respected her wishes not to air her family secrets in the newspaper supplement. When, out of deference to her, he'd forfeited revealing a juicy scandal that might have gained him even greater readership.

As Trina and Cole exchanged rings and made their vows, Nia stole another glance at Clay, and realized something else: her own feelings for him wouldn't let her continue on her current course. They were too powerful not to force her to deal with her fears the same way Trina had had to deal with her doubts about Cole.

And in that instant, Nia knew that she had to conquer her fears, put her own bad experience behind her and trust that regardless of whatever infatuation Clay and Trina had had for each other in the past, it *was* in the past and would remain there.

Because the alternative was to not have Clay in her life at all.

And in spite of the fact that it had taken her some time to realize it, that just wasn't an alternative Nia could live with.

"I now pronounce you man and wife, and, Cole, you may kiss your bride," the minister announced then.

Nia took her eyes off Clay to watch the end of her sister's ceremony, thinking that it might not bode well for her decision that Clay had avoided her as much as she'd avoided him this evening, and that he seemed totally disinclined to even look at her.

Not that it wasn't what she deserved after yesterday, she reminded herself. She just hoped it wasn't an indication that she'd so thoroughly disgusted him he'd written her off completely.

After their kiss, Cole and Trina turned from the minister and gave a comical little bow in response to the applause. Then they retreated down the makeshift aisle that formed as the crowd of onlookers parted.

The entire wedding had been informal, so as soon as Cole and Trina reached the other side of the living room, the guests began to mill around, most heading for the newlyweds to give their best wishes.

Nia stayed where she was, waiting for Clay to finish shaking hands and thanking the minister, hoping that when he had, he might finally make eye contact and give her the opening she was hoping for.

But that didn't happen. Once he and the minister finished chatting, Clay turned the other way.

This wasn't going to be easy.

Still, Nia couldn't give up, so she followed him,

managing to get close enough to softly call his name just before he reached the Brimleys.

He turned to her, but while his expression and raised brow questioned what she wanted, his eyes remained cool, aloof.

It was enough to tell her that not only wasn't this going to be easy, it also wasn't something she could do with a crowd around.

So rather than saying any of the dozens of things she'd thought she might, she said, "Could you stay tonight until after everyone is gone?"

"I *could*," he answered, without letting her know whether or not he would.

"Will you?" Nia pressed. She had too much at stake not to.

"Is there a reason?"

"Now *I* need to talk to *you*," she said simply.

For a moment that lasted long enough for Nia to worry he might refuse her, Clay merely stood there, staring.

"Okay," he finally conceded—although not with any enthusiasm.

"Thank you," she whispered.

His only response was to raise both eyebrows, which left her thinking that while he'd agreed to stay so she could talk to him, he might not be too open to what she had to say when he did.

Then he turned around and made his way over to the Brimleys, leaving Nia not feeling encouraged in the slightest.

Still, she refused to accept defeat before she'd even attempted the battle, and so she went through the reception with a stiff back and a smile on her face, holding fast to her determination to try to clear up the mess she'd made of things.

But it seemed as if the party would never end.

It was midnight before the last of the wedding guests relayed their good wishes to Trina and Cole and finally left. As with everything else, people had been pitching in all evening to clear the food and drink debris. While the house was going to need some straightening, it wasn't in complete upheaval, so Nia sent Fran and Simon on their way, too, promising that the three of them could do everything else the next day before she was scheduled to leave for Denver.

Then she turned to the happy but obviously tired Trina and urged her and Cole to go to his place to begin their wedding night.

But when Nia was finally alone with Clay—who stood statue stiff in the center of the foyer after having said good-night to his brother and Trina—an instantaneous attack of nerves made her heart beat so fast it pounded in her ears. And suddenly everything she'd considered saying to him flew out of her mind, leaving her at a loss over how to broach the subject she so desperately wanted to talk to him about.

The only thing she could come up with was, "I have your jacket from Founder's Day. I'll get it."

Then she fled up the stairs to her room.

Clay's jacket was the denim one she'd stripped from him Saturday night. After shoes, boots and socks, it was the first article of clothing to be discarded before they'd both ended up naked and in bed together.

Nia had spent too many hours since yesterday morning clutching it to her and crying, and now that she'd retrieved it from her closet she only got halfway to the door before pausing to once again hold it to the front of her. She closed her eyes and wished on it as if it were the first star of the night. Wishing for strength and the words she needed to say. Wishing for Clay to be receptive to those words...

"If you like it that much you can keep it. I have others."

The deep, rumbling voice came from her doorway and startled Nia. Her eyes flew open and there Clay was, leaning a shoulder against the door frame.

He'd used the time since she'd left him in the foyer to remove his tie—now wadded up and dangling from one of his suit coat pockets—and to unfasten the collar button of his shirt.

"Is that why you wanted me to stay until everyone else was gone?" he asked when Nia still hadn't thought of what to say to him. "So no one would see you give me my jacket?"

"No," she managed to reply in a small, uncertain voice.

"You wanted to ask me if you could keep the coat?" he said with a sardonic nod, as Nia continued clasping it to her.

"I was making a wish on it," she confessed then, walking toward him.

"It's magic and I didn't know it?"

"I hope so," she muttered, more to herself than to him.

"What were you wishing for?"

"A good way to tell you what I want to tell you," she confessed.

"A good way would be just to spit it out."

His flippant attitude wasn't helping, and Nia had to remind herself that he had every reason to be peeved at her. But curt or not, she decided to take his suggestion.

"I was an idiot," she announced.

One eyebrow went up. "Yeah? How so?"

"Yesterday morning… I reacted to things that exist in my own head more than in reality."

"Things?"

"Things like not believing you when you said there wasn't anything between you and Trina—and wouldn't be ever again—just because you dated a long time ago."

"Uh-huh," he said, clearly waiting for more.

"It's not easy when your sister and the man you're engaged to end up together. It just seemed logical that to avoid it ever happening again, the last thing I should do was get involved with someone who already had a history of liking her."

Clay nodded, and Nia wondered if she were imagining it, or if he was softening somewhat.

"I can see where that would seem logical at the start," he agreed. "Just not as time went by and you got to know me and see that nothing was happening between Trina and me. I mean, I went into this seeing you treating Trina like an infant and figuring you were doing the whole mothering thing Shayna had done to me. I started out figuring I should steer clear of you for that. But when I looked at the whole picture, thought about what you'd said along the way, put two and two together…I decided that wasn't true."

"But your own baggage gave you a skewed perception until you worked it out," Nia said, gaining some steam. "That's where I've been, too—I had a skewed perception based on my baggage and now I've worked it out."

His eyebrow took wing again. "What, exactly, have you worked out?"

"That Trina was like a new car you took for a test drive and didn't buy. You aren't likely to get back behind the wheel of it twelve years later."

Apparently he liked her analogy, because a hint of a smile tweaked his lips. "Was that my biggest plus?"

"Hardly. It was just the part that made enough sense to me to break through the skewed perception."

"Uh-huh," he said again. "And once you broke through, then what?"

"Then I came to the conclusion that I could have what I want…. Well, dependent on you…"

"What is it you want?"

Okay, now he was enjoying putting her on the hot seat.

Still, Nia thought she had that coming, too, after so unreasonably rejecting him the day before.

But she wasn't about to admit what she wanted without a bit of challenge of her own. She raised her chin boldly and said, "You."

"Me? You want me?"

"That's what I decided."

"Uh-huh," he said, as if it wasn't a foregone conclusion that she could have him. Even though from the mischief in his handsome face now, she thought it was.

"In what way do you want me?"

This time Nia smiled, and she couldn't keep her eyes from dropping from his face to his body. But then she dragged them up to his face again and said, "In every way."

"As a part of the family? Or do I need to stay a hundred feet from Trina at all times?"

"I think as a part of the family."

"You *think*?"

"Uh-huh." She mimicked him.

"You'll give up your museum and move here permanently?"

"Maybe," she said, turning the tables on him a little.

"You'll open a gallery and bring art to Elk Creek?"

"Maybe."

"You'll marry me and have babies and forget I ever so much as said *boo* to your sister?"

"Maybe."

"To the marry me part? The having babies part? Or the forget I ever so much as said *boo* to your sister part?"

"Definitely to the forget you ever so much as said *boo* to my sister part."

She could tell that he knew she was toying with him; the lazy, lopsided smile that lit up his features was full of devilry.

Then he used his shoulder to push himself off the doorjamb, hooked his jean jacket over the knob and came to stand in front of her.

"And the rest?" he demanded. "Because be warned, you don't get the body without the commitment."

Nia laughed. "I don't recall that being in the agreement Saturday night."

"It was in the fine print. I let you skate on that the first time—"

"And the second time that night, too," she reminded him.

"But not tonight. Tonight the fine print is in effect. You want the body, you make the commitment."

She pretended to think it over only so she could feast her eyes on the body.

And oh, what a body it was!

Then she slipped her hands under his suit coat and slid it off his shoulders, letting it fall to the floor behind him. "I should see more of the body before I decide."

"It hasn't changed since yesterday," he said, as if he was more serious than she'd thought about not letting her have him physically unless she said she'd marry him.

"Whatever it takes," she declared, opening the next two buttons of his shirt before he took her wrists in his hands and stopped her.

"Say you'll marry me," he ordered.

Nia raised her eyes to his and smiled. "I'll marry you."

"And have babies."

"I'll do what I can."

"And forget the whole Trina business."

"Already agreed to," she reminded him.

Clay looked over her shoulder. "I still don't know

if I can trust you. Now that we have the minister warmed up, maybe we should go get him."

Nia decided to call his bluff and took a step backward to put some distance between them even as he went on holding her wrists.

"Okay, if you want to wait…"

That made him laugh as he tugged her close again. "Maybe a more compliant woman isn't such a bad thing."

"Tough luck. Now you're stuck with me," she countered just before he captured her mouth with his in a kiss that wiped away all the misery Nia had felt since the morning before and made everything right again.

Right enough to bring back to life all that had brought them to that bedroom Saturday night.

Only this time mouths didn't need any encouragement to open wide, tongues didn't hesitate to meet and greet. Clothes came off in record time so hands could seek and find—hers pressed to his hard chest to go from there on a journey of discovery over massive shoulders to magnificent biceps to a broad, broad back, while Clay found her breasts, complete with knotted nipples making demands of their own.

Demands his hands, his fingertips and then his mouth were only too willing to meet as Clay began to inch toward Nia's bed, taking her with him every step of the way.

And like lovers too long separated, once they'd reached it they couldn't wait to come together, him into her. To join bodies and souls to seal the claims they'd just made on each other, the promises. To truly put to rest all their anxieties, all their fears, everything that had kept them apart. To give new, stronger life to what lay ahead of them with the explosion of ecstasy that united them and left them, in its aftermath, euphoric and exhausted as they rolled to their sides, front to front, legs entwined, arms around each other.

When his breathing eased Clay kissed the top of Nia's head, sighing warm air into her hair. "You won't change your mind in the light of day again, will you? I don't want another surprise like yesterday," he said in a deep voice ragged from passion.

"I won't," she assured him without hesitation.

"Because I couldn't take it, you know? I love you too much."

Nia looked up at him, at that sharply angular jaw line, at the perfect planes of that face she never tired of gazing at. "I don't think it can be *too* much," she said, craning up enough to kiss him. "And in case you're wondering? I love you, too."

"I wasn't wondering. I knew," he said with a smile that warmed her to the very core. He dropped his brow to the spot on her head he'd kissed moments before. "What do you say that tomorrow we roust Bax McDermot for another round of blood tests and repeat tonight's wedding the next day?"

Nia laughed. "This poor town will think the Molners and the Hellers have gone completely crazy."

"Or just that they're finally answering their destiny.

Either way it'll be a good story to tell for years and
years. And Elk Creek loves a good story."

"Since I deprived them of the end of Phoebe's, I
guess I owe them this one."

"You do," Clay confirmed.

"Then I'd better give it to them," she said, thinking
that destiny really might have had a hand in bringing her
and Clay together.

Destiny and her great-aunt Phoebe.

And as Nia breathed in a deep breath and basked in
the love she knew without a doubt Clay had for her, she
offered a silent thanks to Phoebe for leading her to this
man she knew would be hers—and hers alone—until the
end of time.

*Everything you love about romance...**and more!***

*Please turn the page for Signature Select™
Bonus Features.*

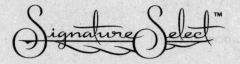

BONUS FEATURES

Her sister's keeper

EXCLUSIVE BONUS FEATURES INSIDE

Character
PROFILES

Isn't it great when you read a book, and you've been so pulled into that world that you want more of the characters you've grown to love? Here are some more character tidbits to satisfy your curiosity.

4

Nia Molner
Despite an enviable family fortune, Nia Molner has many elements of the girl next door. She's down to earth, practical, loyal and has strong family ties. And with her wavy, deep auburn hair and vibrant hazel eyes, the art acquisitions expert has both brains and beauty, too. She's also capable and responsible, and although she may only be five minutes older than her fraternal twin, Nia is every bit the big sister when it comes to putting Trina's needs first.

At least until Nia's needs—and desires—demand a little attention of their own. It's just that the man who inspires those needs and desires happens to have a history with her sister and that makes him off-limits to Nia. If only her heart would listen and respect those boundaries.

Trina Molner
Sable-haired, doe-eyed Trina is very much the baby of the Molner family. An early health condition demanded that she be pampered and cared for, and while her heart problem was solved in early adolescence, old habits are hard for her, and everyone around her, to break. And while she sits on the board of directors for the Molner banking concerns, she's still the more fragile sister. The sister who was indulged in childhood and now isn't good at self-restraint or self-denial. Not even when it isn't wise to indulge because it may hurt those she loves most.

It's something that's gotten her into trouble in the past and again now. Trouble with one Heller brother when it was the other Heller brother she came looking for.

Clay Heller
Astute business and media mogul Clay Heller may have his head in his professional pursuits but his spirit is all cowboy. This rugged, passionate, hot-blooded cowboy is wrapped up in a drop-dead gorgeous package complete with mile-wide shoulders, short sun-streaked hair and neon-blue eyes that can bore right through a person.

And although he's simplifying his life and settling in the small town of Elk Creek, Wyoming, where everyone he passes on the street knows his name, that doesn't change the fact that he's determined and stubborn and won't be denied what he wants no matter how many obstacles stand in his way. Unless the obstacle also happens to be a woman he might want more than what she's protecting.

Cole Heller

The strong, silent type, Cole Heller is more comfortable out on the range than sitting behind a desk. That's obvious in his untamed mane of golden hair, his tan skin and his toned outdoorsman's body. But even though he may be somewhat of a loner, roots are important to Cole and he's moved to Elk Creek to put them down in the small town where he spent his best summers, where he can be near his brother and his cousins.

Still, like his brother, the fires of his urges burn bright and red-hot. It's just that his intense pride makes him question whether or not a Molner heiress could ever settle for a man with nothing more to offer than a small ranch in a one-horse town.

The Writing Life

Ever wonder how authors spend their days? Here's your chance to peek inside the life of author Victoria Pade, who shared her description of a day in her writing life.

Hmm. Back to Elk Creek? Bigger book? Multiple romances? Sounds like fun. And a challenge. I always like that.

Have to come up with an idea and a proposal on the double, though. What about that Post-it on the inside of the desk cupboard door with the others containing snippets of ideas that have popped into my head from who knows where—from wondering why a movie didn't do this instead of what it did, from a news story that made me wonder, from remembering someone I met somewhere who said something that aroused my curiosity, from out of the blue....

I've read the Post-it enough times to know what's on it—*old love letters that track a long-ago romance, heroine finds them, returns to sender, meets hero, their romance seems to follow the same path.*

Every time I see this Post-it and consider writing the story, I think I need more than the length of a Silhouette Special Edition novel to do it. But this new book *needs* to be longer. And the idea has multiple romances built in—the old one through the letters and the present-day one. Okay. That could work.

But adding some letters isn't going to give me another fifty to eighty pages. How about a third romance? But between whom? And why? And what about Elk Creek? Are all these romances happening between people who are already there? Do some come into town, and some live there?

Better get out of bed, check the Post-its. Look over the other books. See what I can build from...

Okay, to the floor with pancakes and warm lemon water in hand to check out the Post-it. Hoping it might have friends—sometimes I get lucky and find a few companion thoughts stuck behind the original note that expanded the idea when I first had it.

But no, not this time. Just one lonely Post-it hanging out with a bunch of others that don't have anything to do with it.

There is another Post-it, though, that says "Founder's Day" on it. It was a thought I had for the new small-town series—Northbridge Nuptials. But now I'm thinking back to Elk Creek. *Old* love letters. Founder's Day seems tailor-made for this. I'll use it here.

Founder's Day—keep that in mind while thumbing through the previous Ranching Family books. The Heller family was *one* of the founding families. So who else was in on it?

The old Molner mansion—that gets mentioned in every book. The longer I wrote the series, the more I started to wonder who the Molners were. So who *were* they?

The Molner family could be cofounders of Elk Creek. Brought back to town for the celebration. They'd have a history with the Hellers. Maybe someone from the Hellers and someone from the Molners might have exchanged love letters....

I like that.

So who's who? Who are the heroes? Who are the heroines?

Even though there were several Heller women, I'd rather do the Hellers as men. Tough guys from tough stock—they make good cowboys. Good, hunky cowboys. Good, hunky heroes. That means the Molners need to be my heroines. So who are the Molner women and what's up with them?

Take them along while I get ready for the day before someone catches me still in my pajamas at nearly noon....

I'm always thinking about the dynamics of people. What shapes them. What makes them tick. Where their strengths and weaknesses lie, and why. Who takes the lead. Who follows.

People stick in my head. I'm rotten with names, good with faces and even tiny details that can come out when I meet someone or talk to them for the briefest time. Plus, my brain just automatically gives everyone a story—sometimes seeing someone walking down the street spurs a whole imaginary scenario. I don't know why. It just happens. And then there are the people I know or hear about. Pieces of all that go into the characters. Along with a little of me. So over lunch I'm thinking about the Molner women, wondering who they are, what their stories are.

Sisters—they're sisters, that just seems to be a given. And they're both returning to Elk Creek. Why did they leave in the first place? Where have they been? What have they been doing? How do they hook up with the Heller guys? Why? How do I tie it in with the love letters? Where does the story go? What are the conflicts? The resolutions? What happens?

Overload. Back up. Get out the tablet and the pen. Don't get ahead of yourself.

Okay. The Molner sisters. What's their story?

I think about sisters I know, what their relationship with each other is like. I think about loyalty, about that relationship being capable of overriding even big offenses one or the other of them might commit. About selflessness. Closeness. One of them taking the lead. One of them not as strong, more impulsive. The stronger one being more caretaker, making more sacrifices. But why? And over time, when do her own needs and desires override those sacrifices she's made...?

I begin to see the Molner sisters, and so I try naming them, trying on names until they seem to choose the right one themselves, one that fits.

I go through the same process with the Heller brothers. A story begins in bits and pieces. What can I use? What can't I use? How do the love letters fit in? Maybe it would be better if it's a journal rather than love letters. A journal might be more open and honest.

Easier for one of my heroines to relate to. To draw conclusions from. To see herself in.

I like that idea better than love letters. Seems more personal. So no love letters. A journal instead. And names—the main characters all have names now.

And I have writer's cramp and it's 4:30 p.m. and time to think about dinner. About cooking. About the laundry and those cookies I want to make because I'm wishing for them.

And there's that Heller hunk in my head again....

Cowboy.

Businessman, too?

Rich media mogul in cowboy boots?

More successful than his brother. More outgoing, too. Maybe there's some competition—or resentment—between them....

Yeah, that could be a good element.

Get out the Post-its and write it down before you forget....

Author Recipes
A Taste of Margie Wilson's Cooking

Margie Wilson's Café in Elk Creek isn't just an eating establishment, it's a meeting place where folks come in for coffee, a slice of pie and a chat with friends. Here are some recipes from Margie Wilson's Café.

MARGIE WILSON'S BREAKFAST SCRAMBLERS

2 eggs, beaten well
1 tsp water
¹/₄ cup cubed Canadian bacon
¹/₄ cup shredded sharp cheddar cheese
2 tbsp cubed fresh tomato
1 tbsp cubed fresh green pepper

Salt and pepper to taste
Splash of Tabasco sauce, to taste

Whisk all ingredients together. Place in frying pan with a little oil, cook stirring frequently to scramble.

MARGIE WILSON'S SECRET CHICKEN SALAD SANDWICH

1 cooked chicken breast or any leftover chicken
1 hard-boiled egg
1 tbsp chopped celery
1 tsp chopped red onion
1/8–1/4 cup mayonnaise
1/8–1/4 cup sour cream
(Mayo and sour cream may vary depending on size of
chicken breast—use enough to moisten well.)
1 tsp red wine vinegar
1 tsp soy sauce

Combine all ingredients. Add salt and pepper to
taste. Serve in croissant.

MARGIE WILSON'S ELK STEAK

1 16-oz jar hot or mild cherry peppers
2 lbs elk round steak (or beef round steak)
Canola oil
Fennel seeds
Crushed red pepper flakes

Drain cherry peppers, but reserve vinegar. Cut peppers in half.

Either have butcher tenderize meat or pound with meat mallet to tenderize. Cut meat into small pieces (2–3 inches).

Heat canola oil in an iron skillet. Carefully place meat in oil. Top with fennel seeds and pepper flakes.

When meat is browned, turn and season with more fennel seeds and pepper flakes, also adding cut cherry peppers. Continue cooking only till meat is browned on this side, too.

Transfer everything (oil, meat, seasonings, cherry peppers) to Crock-Pot or electric roaster oven. Deglaze the frying pan with the reserved vinegar from the cherry peppers. Pour over the meat. Add a little water—just enough to steam the meat for 1–1 1/2 hours until meat is tender.

Serve with all the drippings, peppers, flakes and fennel seeds.

This is great hot and great left over in a sandwich the next day.

MARGIE WILSON'S CHOCOLATE COCONUT CREAM PIE

1 pkg Oreo cookies

Food process (including cream filling). Press into 10" pie pan and freeze.

8 oz semisweet chocolate
1 1/3 cups heavy cream

Heat until chocolate is melted and mixture is smooth. Pour into crust. Press plastic wrap to surface. Refrigerate until firm.

2 cups coconut

Toast golden brown and let cool.

9 tbsp sugar
6 tbsp cornstarch

Mix.

6 egg yolks
3 cups milk
2 1/4 cups heavy cream

Beat together. Add sugar-cornstarch mixture and beat smooth. Microwave 6 minutes, stopping to beat after each minute or two until thick and smooth.

Then add:

6 tbsp butter
1 1/2 tbsp coconut flavor
1 1/2 tbsp vanilla

Beat custard well after these additions. Press plastic to surface and chill 1 hour. After 1 hour add toasted coconut, reserving a little to decorate top.

Pour coconut-custard over chocolate layer. Top with more whipped cream and sprinkle with reserved coconut. Chill.

THE HELLER FAMILY

A Family Tree

The Heller family and the Molner family have mile-deep roots in Elk Creek, Wyoming. Here's a genealogy of these two prominent families so you'll know who's who and how they're all related.

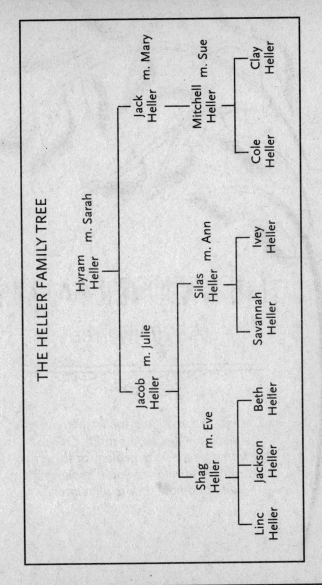

THE HELLER FAMILY TREE

Hyram Heller m. Sarah

Jack Heller m. Mary

Mitchell Heller m. Sue

Cole Heller

Clay Heller

Jacob Heller m. Julie

Silas Heller m. Ann

Savannah Heller

Ivey Heller

Shag Heller m. Eve

Linc Heller

Jackson Heller

Beth Heller

THE MOLNER FAMILY

A Family Tree

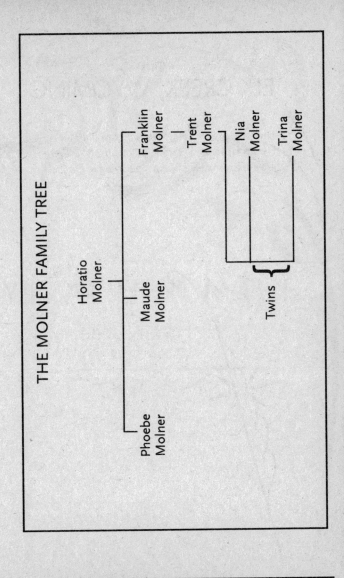

THE MOLNER FAMILY TREE

Horatio Molner

Phoebe Molner

Maude Molner

Franklin Molner

Trent Molner

Nia Molner

Trina Molner

Twins

A map of
ELK CREEK, WYOMING

The town of Elk Creek, Wyoming was founded by
Hyram Heller and Horatio Molner in 1905. There
are approximately 1,804 people living in Elk Creek.

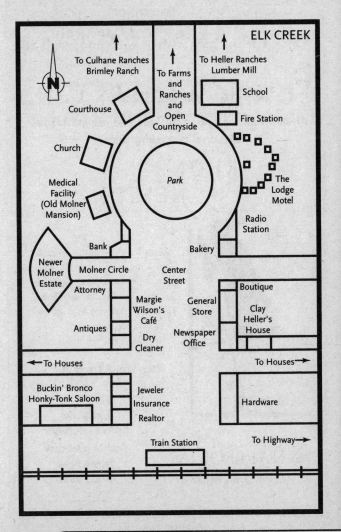

MAP OF ELK CREEK BONUS FEATURE

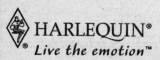

COLLECTION

You're invited to a Fortune family reunion!

Secret Admirer

USA TODAY
bestselling authors

ANN MAJOR

CHRISTINE RIMMER

KAREN ROSE SMITH

While Red Rock, Texas—beloved hometown of the celebrated Fortune family—prepares for its annual Spring Fling dance, three compelling couples discover the joy and passion of falling in love.

Join the party...in April 2005!

Where love comes alive™

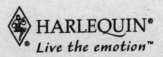

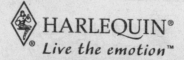

Logan's Legacy

Because birthright has its privileges and family ties run deep.

Follow her quest for love and his determination to avoid it... until fate intervenes.

Right by Her Side

A new Logan's Legacy story
by *USA TODAY* bestselling author

Christie Ridgway

The news that he was going to be a dad shocked the heck out of sexy executive Trent Crosby! But despite his doubts about Rebecca Holley— the accidental recipient of his sperm donation— Trent soon found himself yearning for marriage and family.

Silhouette®
Where love comes alive™

If you enjoyed what you just read,
then we've got an offer you can't resist!

Take 2 bestselling
love stories FREE!

Plus get a FREE surprise gift!

Clip this page and mail it to Silhouette Reader Service™

IN U.S.A.	IN CANADA
3010 Walden Ave.	P.O. Box 609
P.O. Box 1867	Fort Erie, Ontario
Buffalo, N.Y. 14240-1867	L2A 5X3

YES! Please send me 2 free Silhouette Special Edition® novels and my free surprise gift. After receiving them, if I don't wish to receive anymore, I can return the shipping statement marked cancel. If I don't cancel, I will receive 6 brand-new novels every month, before they're available in stores! In the U.S.A., bill me at the bargain price of $4.24 plus 25¢ shipping and handling per book and applicable sales tax, if any*. In Canada, bill me at the bargain price of $4.99 plus 25¢ shipping and handling per book and applicable taxes**. That's the complete price and a savings of at least 10% off the cover prices—what a great deal! I understand that accepting the 2 free books and gift places me under no obligation ever to buy any books. I can always return a shipment and cancel at any time. Even if I never buy another book from Silhouette, the 2 free books and gift are mine to keep forever.

235 SDN DZ9D
335 SDN DZ9E

Name	(PLEASE PRINT)	
Address	Apt.#	
City	State/Prov.	Zip/Postal Code

Not valid to current Silhouette Special Edition® subscribers.

Want to try two free books from another series?
Call 1-800-873-8635 or visit www.morefreebooks.com.

* Terms and prices subject to change without notice. Sales tax applicable in N.Y.
** Canadian residents will be charged applicable provincial taxes and GST.
  All orders subject to approval. Offer limited to one per household.
  ® are registered trademarks owned and used by the trademark owner and or its licensee.

SPED04R   ©2004 Harlequin Enterprises Limited